P9-CPY-369

SUSAN MALLERY

The *Seductive* *One*

POCKET STAR BOOKS
New York London Toronto Sydney

This book is a work of fiction. Names, characters, places and incidents are products of the author's imagination or are used fictitiously. Any resemblance to actual events or locales or persons, living or dead, is entirely coincidental.

An *Original* Publication of POCKET BOOKS

A Pocket Star Book published by
POCKET BOOKS, a division of Simon & Schuster, Inc.
1230 Avenue of the Americas, New York, NY 10020

Copyright © 2003 by Susan Macias Redmond

ISBN: 978-1-4165-3560-7
eBook: 978-0-7434-8043-7

This Pocket Star Books edition April 2010

10   9   8   7   6   5   4   3   2

POCKET STAR BOOKS and colophon are registered trademarks of Simon & Schuster, Inc.

Interior design by Melissa Isriprashad

Cover design by Lisa Litwack. Image © Jupiter Images.

For information regarding special discounts for bulk purchases, please contact Simon & Schuster Special Sales at 1-866-506-1949 or business@simonandschuster.com.

The Simon & Schuster Speakers Bureau can bring authors to your live event. For more information or to book an event contact the Simon & Schuster Speakers Bureau at 1-866-248-3049 or visit our website at www.simonspeakers.com.

Manufactured in the United States of America

To Maureen Child, an extraordinary writer who listened, encouraged, fumed on my behalf, and generally made me feel brilliant. May we always feel that glorious wind. Here's to wild success and friendship.

1

Borrowing a million dollars from the devil was one thing; picking a fight with him while doing it was something else.

Brenna Marcelli considered herself to be above average in intelligence. With her future on the line, there was absolutely *no* way she would be anything but perfectly pleasant during her conversation with Nicholas Giovanni. She would be confident, persuasive, even charming. She would not get crabby, beg, or think about sex. Especially not sex. No matter how good it had been.

But it *had* been great, she thought as she paced the length of the waiting area in the executive offices of Wild Sea Vineyards. Better than good. One time they'd done it on the beach, and that night on the news there'd been a report of an unexpectedly high tide. Brenna had always wondered if she and Nic were somehow to blame.

"History," she murmured as she clutched her portfolio more tightly to her chest. "Ancient history. This is a new decade—a new century even. I am empowered. I am impervious. I am really annoyed that he's keeping me waiting."

She turned and glared at the closed door leading to Nic's private office. When his assistant had asked her to wait and promised the man in charge would be with her shortly, Brenna had believed her. Now, nearly ten minutes later, the assistant had disappeared and there was still no sign of Nic.

"Just a power play," she told herself, then took a calming breath. "I'm not going to buy into it. He can keep me waiting as long as he wants."

Except her stomach was in knots, she had serious regrets about that fifth cup of coffee, and she had a bad feeling that if she stopped moving for too long, she would find that her knees were shaking. Not exactly the picture of professional confidence she wanted to portray. She really needed to—

The office door opened and the devil himself walked into the room.

Okay, maybe calling Nic the devil was a bit strong, but he was dark, dangerous, and at this point she would sell him her soul to get what she wanted. A rose by any other name and all that.

"Brenna." Nic spoke her name with a smile. As if they met on a regular basis. "Good to see you."

If only, she thought. She hadn't set foot on Giovanni land in ten years. And with good reason.

"Hi, Nic."

He motioned toward his office and she stepped into the inner sanctum. The room hadn't changed a whole lot since she'd last seen it. Still massive, still dominated by a desk built in the eighteenth century. The computer was new, as was the owner. Ten years ago Nic's grandfather had occupied the space. From here he'd run all of Wild Sea Vineyards. Now the old man was gone and Nic was in charge.

In charge and going places, she thought as she crossed to the map on the wall opposite the opulent desk. She studied the shaded area that detailed the Giovanni holdings, noting how much expansion there'd been in the past seven years. Nic had always wanted to be the biggest and best. He'd achieved that in spades.

Of course, focusing on the map allowed her not to think about that damn desk. Unfortunately, she was going to have to turn around and stare at it sometime. It wouldn't be so bad if she and Nic hadn't, well, done it on that desk.

It had been about three A.M. on a Saturday morning. The night had been still, cool, and incredibly romantic. Of course, when she'd been seventeen and in love, watching paint dry had been romantic.

"You're welcome to sit down," he said, a trace of amusement in his voice.

Sure, she thought as she squared her shoulders and turned to face her past. Nic worked here every day. He'd probably forgotten what had happened on that carved slab of wood. But not her.

She made her way to an oversize chair and sank onto the smooth leather surface. Nic walked around his desk and sat facing her.

"I was surprised to hear you'd made an appointment to see me," he said easily. "I hope everything is all right with your family."

"They're fine. Great, really. Francesca's engaged." More than engaged, but that conversation was for another time.

"That must make your grandfather happy."

She nodded and found her gaze settling on his face. Strong features, she thought, remembering the boy as she stared at the man. He'd always had strong features. Compelling eyes, a straight nose, a determined, maybe even stubborn chin, and a mouth that had once been able to kiss her into another time zone.

Despite the warm August temperatures, he wore a long-sleeved black shirt, dark slacks. Not exactly the jeans and T-shirts she was used to seeing.

"You're dressed for success," she said.

"In honor of our meeting."

He smiled, a slow, sexy smile that made her remember other smiles. Like the one he'd used to convince her it was really okay to make love late at night in the vineyard. It had been their first time and she'd lost her virginity to the sound of crickets and—

Let's stop this right now, she told herself. Trips down memory lane were only going to get her into trouble. She was here on a mission that had nothing to do with sexy smiles or the heat flaring to life low in her belly.

She forced herself to relax in the leather chair. She carefully crossed one leg over the other and tried for a faintly amused, possibly bored expression. Who knew if it really worked.

"All that trouble for me? I don't think so."

He chuckled. "All right. I have a meeting with several foreign distributors later this afternoon. I figured jeans would put them off."

Not if they were women, Brenna thought before she could stop herself.

"So you're expanding again," she said instead.

"Always. Be the biggest and the best."

"You're certainly going to win on volume."

"Don't they say size matters?"

"Only those who don't know how to use what they have." She remembered her vow not to argue with him about eighteen seconds too late.

"Sorry," she murmured.

He raised his eyebrows. "For disagreeing with me? There's a first. Now I'm even more intrigued." He grinned and leaned forward. "All right, Brenna. You're here, you're wearing a suit, and you're carrying what looks like a thick stack of papers. Why don't you tell me what's going on?"

So they were going to get right to it. She cleared her throat and set her portfolio on his desk. At that moment her brain hiccuped and every single intelligent, logical, financially sound sentence she'd practiced flew out of her head.

"I'm one of the best in the business," she began, then hesitated, wondering if that sounded too arrogant.

At least he didn't break into hysterical laughter. "I'll admit that I wouldn't want to go head to head with you in competition," he admitted.

The compliment boosted her confidence and made her want to wiggle in her seat. She satisfied herself with a slight smile. "As my grandfather says, aside from him, I'm the only one in the family with a passion for wine. I've lived it most of my life."

He started to say something, but she rushed on. There was no way she was going to let him remind her of the ten years she'd spent away from Marcelli Wines. Ten years she'd spent being an idiot.

"My grandfather has put me in charge of the winery. I know what's needed to take our success to the next level."

"So you're not here for a job."

"No." She flipped open the portfolio. "I'm here for a loan."

Nic straightened. "Why? You don't have a cash-flow problem."

"Marcelli Wines doesn't. Business has never been better. But I'm not them. I work for my grandfather. The company still belongs to him."

"You'll inherit."

If only. The truth shouldn't still hurt, but it did. It hurt a lot. "My sisters and I inheriting has become less of a sure thing." She paused, knowing that there was no point in holding back. He was going to hear about it eventually.

"It seems my parents had a child out of wedlock, as they say. A son. They were both still in high school. Due to family pressure, they gave up the baby for adoption."

Nic was cool as always. Instead of letting any emotion show on his face, he leaned back in his chair. "That would change things," he admitted. "When did you find out?"

"At our big Fourth of July party. It was our version of fireworks, to say the least. The point is, the long-lost baby is now a thirty-year-old man."

The Marcelli and Giovanni families might not have spoken in nearly three generations, but they had both grown up with the same traditional Italian values. Feminism had yet to arrive at the shores of their respective vineyards. Nic got it right away.

"Your grandfather is old-fashioned enough to be more comfortable leaving the family business to a male heir. I'm guessing the long-lost brother is interested?"

"It's a ton of money. Wouldn't you be?" she asked with a lightness she didn't feel. "All of which leaves me on the short end of the inheritance stick." Now came the tough part. "I've learned that the wine business is in my blood. I don't want to do anything else with my life."

"If you're right and your brother inherits, why wouldn't he keep you on to run things?"

"He might, but I'm not willing to wait around and see. Besides, I have my own ideas and plans. I want to start my own label."

He pointed at the portfolio in front of her. "Your proposal?"

She nodded. "I've detailed everything. What grapes I want to buy, the price of the inventory, barrels, storage. There's also some land I'm interested in."

"Starting a label doesn't come cheap."

"I know."

His dark gaze never left her face. "Where else did you go for financing?"

"Everywhere short of a loan shark."

He nodded. "Let me guess. They want to know why you can't get the money from your grandfather."

"That's some of it. They were also concerned that I don't have any collateral. I've explained that the wine is collateral, but that doesn't seem to impress them." She shrugged. "You're a man who likes to take risks, but only when they pay off. I'm the closest to a sure thing you're going to find."

He raised his eyebrows. "Really?"

Brenna could have cheerfully thrown herself in front of a moving delivery truck. She could feel the heat on her face, but with her olive coloring, the blush wouldn't show. It was a small consolation, but one she clung to like a life preserver.

"You know I can do this," she said, as if she hadn't caught the embarrassing wordplay.

"Maybe," he said. "But why would I want to add to my competition?"

For the first time since driving onto the property, Brenna relaxed. "Oh, please. If I'm lucky I'll be able to match ten percent of your production in five years. I don't think you're going to sweat me putting you out of business."

"Fair enough. Why did you come to me?"

"You're the only person I know with extra cash."

"Your parents would have helped you out."

"Possibly. But I didn't want to make them choose

between me and my grandfather. You're a neutral party."

"I'm a Giovanni. Doesn't that make me second cousin to the devil?"

Gee, just what she'd been thinking earlier, only in her eyes, the relationship had been a little closer.

Coming to Nic was her last hope, but also a calculated risk. The Marcelli and Giovanni families had been feuding for years. Her grandfather might find out about the loan if she'd secured it through traditional sources such as a bank, but he would never know if Nic funded her. Grandpa Lorenzo would cheerfully rip out his tongue rather than *speak* to a Giovanni.

Brenna and her sisters had never been all that interested in the feud. Nic hadn't been, either, which he'd proved the first time she'd met him. But to her grandparents— hostilities were alive and well.

"There's a certain irony to this conversation," she admitted. "I would think that appealed to you."

He studied her. Brenna would like to know what he saw, but on second thought—maybe not. She was still recovering from a disastrous, impulsive haircut. Several months at the family hacienda eating her grandmothers' cooking had added seven pounds to her already plentiful curves. She thought the suit she'd chosen looked pretty good on her, but was that enough? She'd come a long way from the seventeen-year-old who had promised to love Nic with her whole heart; but the question was, would he consider the changes good or bad?

"Rumor has it I'm a ruthless bastard," he said casually.

"I've heard. Should I be scared?"

"You tell me."

She could remember everything about being with Nic— the way he touched her, the way he kissed, the scent of his skin. She knew the boy he had been, but not the man. What was the same and what had changed? Or did it matter?

Ruthless bastard or not, she wanted the money.

"I don't scare easily these days." She pushed the proposal toward him. "Look it over and tell me what you think."

He rested his hand on the leather cover but didn't open it. "How much?"

The butterflies appeared in her stomach and began to fly in formation. She thought they might be practicing touch-and-go landings. Her mouth got dry, her palms got wet, and the room lurched once for good measure.

"A million dollars."

Nic didn't react in any way—at least not on the outside. He didn't blink, didn't shift in his seat; he didn't even smile. But on the inside, his mild amusement and intrigue turned to impressed amazement. Brenna had gone and got herself some balls.

He pulled his wallet from his back pocket and fingered the bills. "You want that in twenties?"

"I'm not in a position to be picky. Twenties are fine."

"I don't think I have that much with me today."

"Bummer."

She watched him, her big eyes betraying her nervousness. She was at the end of the line and they both knew it. If he turned her down, she wouldn't get her loan. Any dreams of starting her own label would be squashed. Oh, sure, she could buy a few tons of grapes on the open market, borrow equipment, and set up a few dozen cheap barrels in a garage somewhere. She might get a loyal following, a little notice, maybe a write-up in *Wine Spectator.* But without an infusion of cash, she would never have the chance to make it big.

Not that he gave a damn about that. What mattered to him were his goals. How did her request fit into the big picture?

He rose and circled the desk until he stood in front of her, then he leaned against the surface, his arms folded over his chest. It was a position designed to intimidate. To challenge.

Brenna reacted by uncrossing, then recrossing her legs. In the silence of the office the sound of her silk stockings brushing and shifting grated against his ears. He found himself watching the movement, staring at the hem of her skirt, picturing her thighs underneath. And above her thighs?

Paradise. At least that's what her body had been ten years ago. Dark, slick, secret—the road to redemption. Instead she'd steered him right to hell. Because of her, he'd been sent away from his home. He'd been exiled, abandoned, and written off for dead.

Unfortunately, the reminder didn't do a damn thing for the unexpected tension crawling through him. He tore his gaze away before he distracted himself with the wrong kind of memories.

"I'm not saying no," he told her.

"You're kidding!"

She sprang to her feet, which put her less than a foot in front of him. Close enough for him to see the various shades of gold and brown that made up her irises, and the tiny scar by the corner of her mouth. Close enough for her perfume to invade his personal space. The scent was different; his reaction to it was not. Long-forgotten heat awoke, stretched, and went searching for sustenance.

He ignored the temperature and the hunger. This was not the right time nor the place, and she was sure as hell not the right woman.

The thing was, he had a plan. Over the years he'd learned that a well-thought-out plan ensured that he always won. When the goal was revenge, it paid to be patient.

His instincts told him that Brenna's loan request was as unexpected as a home run off the first pitch. All he had to do was toss down his bat and circle the bases. But he wanted to be sure.

"It's a lot of money," he said.

She nodded as her mouth curved in a smile. "I know. I've detailed every penny. It's all going into the wine. I'm not taking a salary. Oh, Nic, the land I want to buy is just perfect for Pinot Noir. There's a sweet valley at the base of a hill that gets just the right amount of midday sun. That, combined with the fog and the salt from the ocean, creates perfect grapes. You'll see."

Her enthusiasm was as tangible as the hand she put on his arm. He acknowledged the contact—and his reaction to it—by sliding away and picking up her portfolio.

"I'll look this over in the next couple of days and get back to you." He raised his eyebrows. "How exactly do I do that?"

Brenna chuckled. "I suppose a phone call to the hacienda would cause problems for both of us. My cell number is on the proposal. If you don't get me, you can leave a message and I'll call you back."

"Fair enough."

She clutched her hands together. "Nic, I know it's a lot of money and that this is a risk for you, but I can do this. If you take a chance, you won't be sorry."

"I won't do it if there's a chance I will be."

Her excitement didn't flicker. "You're going to be impressed. I promise."

He had a feeling she was right. Besides, one of his rules in life was to take advantage of every unexpected opportunity. If he agreed, he would insist on keeping close tabs on what she was doing, which was the same as keeping close tabs on Brenna herself. Being close to her had only ever led to one thing.

So money wasn't the only risk. Was that good or bad?

He didn't have an answer, but he knew time spent with Brenna wouldn't be boring. Once again, they could be entering dangerous territory. The difference was this time he would be the one calling the shots.

Brenna drove back to the Marcelli winery, taking the long way around so she drove past the ocean. She rolled down the windows of her ancient Camry and let the warm salty air brush over her skin. Her suit jacket and high heels lay where she'd tossed them on the passenger seat. She had the radio cranked up and sang along with an old Beach Boys tune, delighting in the fact that although they'd been years and years before her time, she knew all the words.

At this moment she felt free and wild and happy and so excited, she probably could have taken flight, if not for the seat belt anchoring her. She leaned her head back and laughed out loud at the sheer pleasure pumping through her.

She'd done it. *She'd done it!*

Oh, sure, Nic hadn't said yes, not yet. But somehow down in her gut she just knew he was going to. He'd been willing to listen, something no one else had done, and listening was all she needed. Her carefully thought-out proposal was going to blow his socks off. Maybe even his pants.

"I hope I'm around when that happens," she murmured, then grinned at the thought of a bottomless Nicholas Giovanni.

Until this past spring she hadn't seen him in nearly ten years. He could have gotten wrinkled and paunchy, but instead he still had the power to make her entire body go up in flames. And maybe, just maybe, she'd seen a flicker of appreciation in his beautiful sex-god eyes.

After several years of a crappy marriage, abandonment by a creep of a husband, and nine months and seventeen days since her last sexual encounter, male admiration— especially that coming from Nic—was a balm to her battered and horny soul.

Not that anything would happen, she reminded herself. If Nic agreed, make that *when* Nic agreed, they were going to be business partners. There was no way she was going to be foolish enough to mix business and pleasure. Not with a million dollars and her future on the line. No one was *that* good in bed.

She turned into the entrance to the Marcelli Winery and sighed. Okay, from what she recalled, making love with Nic had been spectacular. Incredible. Life-altering. But not worth a million dollars.

She shifted uncomfortably. All this reminiscing about sex was getting to her. If she'd been a cat, she would have been rubbing herself against the nearest door frame. Not only was she going to have to avoid any sexual contact with Nic, she was going to have to stop thinking about him as anything but her loan officer. Nothing personal. Not again.

Fortunately her resolution coincided with her arrival at the family hacienda. Judging from the number of cars crowding around the rear entrance, the entire family was home.

The three-story Spanish-style home had been built in the late 1920s. Her great-grandfather had found plans for a house designed in the late eighteen hundreds by a Spanish nobleman with ten children, which made for lots of bedrooms. Good thing, she thought as she came to a stop in the shade of an old oak tree and turned off the engine. Currently the permanent residents of the hacienda included her paternal grandparents, her maternal grandmother, her parents, and herself.

"Humiliating but true," Brenna said as she slipped on her pumps and grabbed her suit jacket. "Twenty-seven years old and living at home."

Actually she'd moved back the previous spring when her jerk of a husband—a newly licensed cardiologist without a speck of gratitude or decency—had left her for a younger woman who happened to be a former cheerleader. He was poised to marry the bimbo the instant the computer print was dry on the divorce decree.

Brenna had no desire to have her soon-to-be ex back in her life, but she wouldn't mind a little justice. Her current favorite fantasy was some kind of genital infection that left him unable to enjoy the wedding night. Ever.

All revenge aside, one of these days she was going to take the time to find a place of her own. For now, it was nice to be where a houseful of people loved her.

She made her way up the rear steps and into the kitchen. As usual, the entire female contingent of the family collected there. Her two grandmothers held court over the food, with Grammy M stirring something on the stove and Grandma Tessa chopping vegetables. Her mother sat at the kitchen table, a box of wedding-invitation samples open in front of her. Katie, Brenna's older sister, and Francesca, Brenna's fraternal twin, stood in front of their mother.

Their defiant posture made them look like five-year-olds who had just been caught spray-painting the dog.

"What?" Brenna asked as she draped her suit jacket

over her arm. "I was gone two hours. What happened?"

"Nothin' terrible," Grammy M—aka Mary-Margaret O'Shea—said from her place at the stove. "Francesca has the most wonderful news."

Brenna's mother didn't look all that excited. "But we'd already picked a date and were about to order the invitations."

Wedding talk.

First baby sister Mia had come within weeks of marching down the aisle, only to call the whole thing off. Then Katie had gone and gotten herself engaged to Mia's ex-fiancé's father. Twisted, but so California. Francesca had fallen for the handsome CEO of a security company who found out within days of their meeting that he had a twelve-year-old daughter he'd never known about. A few weeks after that, Francesca had turned up pregnant.

Only Brenna had managed to escape love's sticky snare and the ongoing soap opera that was the Marcelli family. Her current plan was to avoid romance and focus on work. She might be open to a little meaningless sex, but a relationship? She didn't have the time *or* the energy.

She crossed to the kitchen table, grabbing an iced cookie on her way. After six months of her grandmothers' cooking, she didn't want to think about what her cholesterol level must be.

"Tell me everything," she said, stopping next to Francesca and eyeing her very beautiful, very *thin* twin.

Nearly two months pregnant and was Francesca showing? Not even close. Brenna knew that if *she* was ever to play host to a marauding sperm, she would plump up overnight and look as if she were giving birth to a watermelon by week nine.

Francesca shrugged. "I know we all talked about waiting,

what with the baby and all, but Sam and I have changed our minds. And Katie and I want to have a double wedding. It could be a triple one if you wanted to get married again."

Groans erupted from the grandmothers. Brenna's mother simply settled her elbows on the table and rested her head in her hands. "I'm getting too old for this," she murmured.

"A double wedding?" Brenna considered the possibility, while ignoring the comment about her getting married again. *That* was never going to happen. "It will be a cost savings," she reminded her mother as she draped her suit jacket over a chair. "You'll only have to feed the guests once instead of twice."

"What about the wedding gown?" Grandma Tessa looked up from her chopping. "We barely have time to make a dress for Katie and now this? Are you sure you want to go down the aisle in your condition? Not that we're not happy for you, Francesca. A pretty girl like you needs a husband."

"Yeah, ugly girls live to be single," Brenna whispered.

Katie's full mouth twitched as she tried not to laugh. "We're willing to put the wedding date back to give us all time to get everything done."

"You could have the weddings at Thanksgiving," Brenna said as she nibbled on her cookie. "We all know everyone in this family will be doing the happy dance to see two sisters married. For years everyone has despaired of ever getting us all hitched. Now we're halfway there. That gives us so much more to be thankful for."

Grandma Tessa muttered something Brenna couldn't hear. She half expected to see the older woman whip out her rosary for a quick trip around the beads. Fortunately Grandma Tessa contented herself with a couple of dark looks.

"Turkey-day weekend works for me," Katie said. "We could have the wedding that Saturday."

Francesca shrugged. "Sam doesn't care about the date. As for a dress, I'll pick something simple and flowing."

"Don't bother," Brenna told her. "You'll be nine months pregnant and still not showing."

Their mother raised her head. "I don't know. As it is, we'll be sewing day and night."

Family tradition dictated that any Marcelli bride have a wedding gown handmade by the women in the family. A great idea in theory, but beading lace took forever. Brenna wasn't worried about the additional sewing duties. She had a winery to run and therefore was excused from most of the needlework.

Their mother pulled out a pad of paper. "If we're going to have a double wedding, we need to start making lists."

The three sisters looked at one another and shook their heads. When Mom started making lists, an entire afternoon could fly by. Better to escape now.

"I'll get the drinks," Brenna said, heading for a rack on the far wall.

"I'll get chocolate," Francesca said.

Katie walked to the cupboard. "Cheese and crackers or cookies?"

"Cookies," Francesca and Brenna said together.

Their mother shook her head. "You girls aren't going anywhere. We have two weddings to plan."

Katie snaked a plate of cookies from the counter, kissed both Grammy M and Grandma Tessa, and hurried out of the room.

"Love you, Mom," she called over her shoulder.

Francesca quickly followed.

Brenna collected a bottle of wine, an opener, and two

wineglasses, then opened the refrigerator. As expected, there was a bottle of chocolate milk sitting on the top shelf. It was the Grands' contribution to Francesca's need to increase her calcium.

"You guys think of everything," she said as she shut the door.

Her mother glared at her. "We need to plan."

"We'll deal with it later," Brenna promised. "Don't worry. Everything will get done in time."

"I can't believe you girls are having wine. It's the middle of the day."

"We have things to celebrate," Brenna said.

Her mother's eyes narrowed slightly. "You seem exceptionally happy today. Why is that?"

Brenna wasn't about to spill the beans about her potential deal with Nic. Not to her parents. While she knew they would understand her need to stand on her own, the information would put them in an awkward position. Her paternal grandfather was still the head of the family and he wouldn't approve. Rather than make her parents take sides, she would keep her mouth shut.

She smiled and started backing out of the room. "Two of my sisters are marrying wonderful men. Isn't that enough to put a spring in my step?"

"Not by a long shot. What are you up to, Brenna?"

"Absolutely nothing. Cross my heart."

Grandma Tessa looked up. "You go to hell for lying, same as stealing, young lady. The good Lord knows all."

"Words to live by," Brenna said with a laugh as she turned and raced up the stairs.

2

*B*renna *followed* Katie and Francesca into the bedroom she and her twin had shared while they'd been growing up and where she'd returned to when she'd moved back into the hacienda. She set the wine and the glasses on the nightstand, then handed the chocolate milk to her sister. While Brenna went to work on the cork, Francesca flopped down on the bed opposite and Katie sat cross-legged on the foot of Brenna's bed.

"You know they're not going to leave us alone for very long," Katie said, accepting the glass of Cabernet Brenna handed her. "Mom's right. There's a lot to go into the wedding planning."

"So speaks Ms. Organized," Brenna said. She poured a glass for herself and raised it. "To my sisters getting married."

But neither of them responded to her toast. Katie stared watchfully, while Francesca looked concerned.

"What?" Brenna asked, kicking off her shoes and sinking onto the mattress. "You're looking at me funny and that always makes me nervous."

"Don't be nervous. It's just . . ." Francesca leaned toward her. "I'm worried about you." She glanced at Katie. "*We're* worried about you."

"Because I'm drinking wine in the middle of the day? I swear, it doesn't usually happen. Most of the time I'm too busy to stop for lunch, which isn't anything I ever thought I would say. Unfortunately with the Grands' cooking being as fattening as it is, skipping a meal once in a while doesn't work as a weight-loss plan." She patted her stomach. "I guess I'm going to have to seriously think about portion control."

Her two sisters exchanged a knowing glance. Brenna sighed in exasperation. "I hate it when you talk about me behind my back."

"We didn't," Katie said defensively, but as she spoke she tugged on a strand of her reddish-brown hair and bit her lower lip—sure signs that she was lying.

Francesca shrugged. "We're just a little concerned."

"Why?"

"Because we're getting married."

Brenna took a sip of the 1999 Cab; '98 had been a crappy year for California wines, but '99 had been better. She eyed the cookies and thought about grabbing one, but maybe she should wait until she got things settled with her sisters.

"Amazingly enough, your pending nuptials don't exactly impact my day," she said. "We'll be harvesting the Chardonnay grapes any day now, so I'm going to be too busy for the sewing marathon everyone is about to embark upon. But I'll be there in spirit."

"It's not about the dress," Katie said, then glanced at Francesca. "You tell her."

Francesca sipped her wine, then sighed. "We don't want your feelings to be hurt."

While she appreciated that they worried about her, she still had no idea what they were talking about. "Are you telling me you don't want me at your wedding?"

"Of course not," they said in unison.

"Then how could you hurt my feelings?"

"You're not seeing anyone."

They weren't making any sense. Brenna gave up on self-control and grabbed a cookie. "If the concern is I'll be depressed because I'm dateless, I swear I'll be fine." Right now a man was the last thing on her mind. Well, unless he had a million dollars to loan her. Then she was intensely interested.

Katie shook her head. "Francesca, this isn't the time for delicate psycho-speak. Just blurt it out." But rather than wait for her sister, Katie continued. "Francesca and I are worried that you'll be upset because we've finally found great guys and that bastard you were married to is getting married to someone else and you're all caught up in the winery and what if our long-lost brother really does claim it, and without the winery, you don't have a life and we're afraid our happiness is going to depress you." She paused to suck in a breath.

Brenna took a bite of her cookie and chewed. "Impressive lung control," she mumbled over the crumbs, then swallowed. "I'm fine."

Neither sister looked convinced. Brenna glanced between them. The Marcelli daughters were a perfect blend of their Italian-Irish heritage. Katie was mostly Irish with pale skin and reddish-brown hair. Francesca had the thick, dark hair from the Marcelli side of the family, but had also inherited hazel eyes and a tall, thin body from the O'Sheas. Brenna was pure Italian—dark hair, brown eyes, plenty of curves.

Which left Mia. Brenna smiled as she thought of her baby sister's bleached hair and high drama makeup. Mia had never met a tube of mascara she didn't like. But then, Mia had always been just herself.

Her sisters had been her best friends all their lives. No matter what else happened, she knew they would be there for her, as they always had been.

"This is your time," she told Katie and Francesca. "You don't need to worry about me. I swear, everything is great. More than great."

They didn't look convinced. Well, poop. She hadn't planned on telling anyone about her plans until things were settled, but maybe they would sleep better at night if they knew she wasn't about to drown her sorrows in a case of Marcelli sparkling wine.

Francesca's gaze narrowed. "What aren't you telling us?"

"A lot."

Brenna set her wineglass on the nightstand and stood up. She walked to her closet and pulled out a pair of jeans and a T-shirt and began to change her clothes.

As she reached for the button on the waistband of her skirt, she said, "I went to see Nic Giovanni about a loan. I think he's going to say yes."

After smoothing her shoulder-length hair, she turned back to find her two sisters staring at her. The combination of open mouths and wide eyes was pretty funny.

"No way," Francesca breathed. "You did *not* go to Nic for a loan, did you? You're really doing this? You're starting your own label?"

Katie clutched her wine in both hands. "How much did you ask for? Not the amount you said before because that was—"

"A million dollars," Brenna said cheerfully as she pulled on her jeans. "Or seven figures, as they say on the street."

"No way!"

Francesca sounded horrified. Katie mumbled something Brenna couldn't hear, which was probably for the best. Her business-minded sister would get caught up in payment schedules and the disaster of what would happen if Brenna failed. Something she wasn't going to let happen.

She hung up her suit, then plopped back on the bed. "I didn't decide to go to Nic on a whim. I've run out of options. I can't get a bank loan. Not without Grandpa Lorenzo giving his support. Everyone I talked to assumed that if he wasn't behind me, it must be because I'm a bad risk. Even as a good risk, I'd have a tough time. There isn't any collateral. I mean, I'm going to buy those four acres I want, so that would help, but I don't have a penny of my own to put down. It's not as if Jeff and I had any assets to split during the divorce."

Her sisters looked stunned and slightly panicked.

"What about the settlement money?" Francesca asked.

"Not even close to enough."

Brenna thought about the monthly payments her soon-to-be-ex husband would be sending. While the income would be nice, being reimbursed for putting his ungrateful ass through medical school didn't come close to the cost of starting a new label. If Nic came through—she crossed index and middle fingers on her left hand—Jeff's payments would barely cover the interest on her million-dollar loan.

"It's going to work out great," she promised.

"Nic Giovanni," Katie breathed. "You just went to him and asked for the loan? But you don't even know him. What makes you think he'll say yes?"

Brenna picked up her wine and cleared her throat. "He likes to take risks. He gave some other winery start-up money a few years ago. I read about it and remembered."

As for not knowing Nic . . . well, that wasn't exactly true. Ten years ago she'd known everything about Nic. Not that she'd ever told her sisters. Loving him had been her only secret. One she'd held close to her heart.

At first she hadn't told anyone because she'd assumed he wouldn't stay interested in her for very long. Then she hadn't told because keeping their relationship a secret had made it seem more special. And when it had ended, she'd been too ashamed by what she'd done to say anything.

"Start-up money is a world of difference from a million dollars," Francesca said. "What if it doesn't work? What if something bad happens?"

Brenna shrugged. "Then I fall on my butt."

"Owing a million dollars."

"I don't care. I have to try. You're right—I may fail, but I think it's unlikely. But if it does, I'll be okay. Even if Grandpa Lorenzo sells the winery, or leaves it to our long-lost brother, he'll still settle cash on each of us. It probably won't be a million dollars, but it will go a long way toward paying off my debt."

"So wait," Katie said. "Wait and use that money when you get it."

Brenna shook her head. "This is the right time. I can feel it. Besides, there are four acres I want to buy, and they won't stay on the market forever. There's a crop of Pinot Noir grapes with my name on them, some Chardonnay grapes. I have an idea for a fabulous cuvée. My life has been on hold for the past ten years. I'm not willing to wait any longer."

"What if Nic won't loan you the money?" Francesca asked.

Brenna didn't want to think about that, but she had to admit the possibility. "Then I don't have a choice except to wait. Look, I know I can do this. I have a well-thought-out plan, I know the industry, and I'm not afraid to bust my butt working twenty-four-seven. You both have to take a deep breath and trust me."

Francesca and Katie glanced at each other, then at her.

"You go, girl," Francesca said and raised her bottle of chocolate milk. "Let me know if there's anything I can do to help."

"I will."

Katie reached for a piece of chocolate. "So how did our neighborhood bad boy look? I haven't seen him in years, but the last time I did, I'll admit my heart did a little back flip."

Francesca chuckled. "I know what you mean. I saw him, oh, maybe a year and a half ago. He was coming out of the gourmet store in town. It was one of those perfect spring days. Cool, but sunny. He had on a black leather jacket and sunglasses. He smiled at me as he held open the door. I stood there and watched him ride off on his motor-cycle. It was really good for me."

Brenna rolled her eyes. "You two are pathetic."

"Come off it," Katie scolded. "Like you've never had a fantasy about Nic Giovanni. I don't think it's physically possible to be within a hundred feet of him and not think about sex. I refuse to believe you're immune."

Brenna was far from that. "He's good-looking," she admitted grudgingly.

Francesca hooted. "Yeah, right. There's an under-statement. He's dark, dangerous, and moves like a man who knows what he's doing in bed. Does it get any better than that?"

"I thought you were wildly in love with Sam."

"I am." Francesca didn't look the least bit embarrassed. "But along with every other female either twenty years older or younger than Nic, I've had a crush on him forever. So has Katie and Mia, and I'm guessing you, even though you haven't admitted it. Why is that?"

A crush? Did that describe it?

Katie rolled onto her stomach. "What gives, Brenna? Don't you have a Nic fantasy you want to share?"

"Sure. That he loans me the money I need."

"I want something juicier than that."

Brenna sipped her wine. Juicy? That she could provide.

"Nic is the first guy I ever slept with."

The room went utterly and completely still. Francesca froze, her drink halfway to her mouth. Katie paused in the act of reaching for another piece of chocolate. Brenna felt as if she'd found the freeze-frame button on a DVD.

Francesca recovered first. "Nic? Nic our neighbor? Nic Giovanni—the great-grandson of the hated Salvatore? The Romeo to our collective Juliet?"

"Uh-huh."

"Slept?" Katie asked. "As in *sex?*"

"Uh-huh."

"And you never said anything?" Katie sounded outraged. "I'm your sister!"

"Hey, I'm her twin and she didn't say squat to me!"

Brenna leaned back against her headboard. "There wasn't much to tell."

She ducked as Francesca threw a pillow at her.

"Talk," her twin demanded. "Start at the beginning and don't leave out any of the good parts."

"Especially not the sex," Katie added. "You slept with him? I can't believe it. We voted him the guy the three of us would most like to have had sex with back in high school. And you did it. And didn't tell us. How is that possible?"

"I'm not sure. It just happened."

Brenna set her glass on the nightstand and pulled her legs up to her chest, then wrapped her arms around her knees. After all this time she wasn't sure she could tell the story. Not because she'd forgotten or because it was a big deal, but because she'd gotten so used to keeping it all to herself.

Ten years after the fact, did it matter if the women she loved most in the world knew?

"It started when I was seventeen and Nic was twenty. I knew who he was and all, but we'd never had a real conversation. He caught me sneaking around the barrels over at Wild Sea. I knew they were tasting the wines before bottling. I'd heard so much about the hated Giovanni vineyards, and I wanted to see what all the fuss was about."

Francesca looked stunned. "You went over there?"

"Sure. Just snuck in the back. It was easy. I was tasting one of their Reserve Cabernets when Nic caught me."

That had happened ten years ago, and she could still recall the moment in detail. The sharpness of the wine on her tongue, the heat of the summer afternoon, the terror when someone grabbed her arm. She'd turned to see Nic. In that second before she tried to bluff her way out of the situation, she'd found herself drowning in his dark brown eyes.

She'd noticed everything about him. His height. The way he brushed his hair back and the single lock that flopped forward. The stubble on his jaw, the dust motes dancing in sunlight. Even the sound of birds outside and the distant rumble of voices.

"Did he get mad?" Francesca asked.

"I think he was more curious. I told him why I was there and that I wasn't doing anything wrong." She smiled as she remembered his failed attempts not to laugh at her audacity. "I'd just won two gold medals for wines I'd blended and I was pretty cocky. I told him they'd made a mistake in using new American oak barrels because it was putting too much vanilla into the wine. I mean that's great in a Chardonnay, but this was a Reserve Cab. You want berry and chocolate flavors. Some plum and—"

She broke off and glanced at her sisters. Katie had her head in her hands and Francesca slumped onto the bed.

"What?"

Katie looked up. "I know you'll find this hard to believe, but we don't care about the wine. Get back to meeting Nic."

"Philistines," Brenna muttered. To her, Nic and wine were two halves of the same equation. She couldn't have one without thinking of the other. But her sisters wouldn't understand that.

"Instead of throwing me out, he ended up having me taste several of the wines there. I gave him my opinion. Sometimes we agreed, sometimes we argued. I was always right, of course."

"Of course," Francesca said with a laugh.

Brenna grinned. "We spent the rest of the afternoon together. I remember being surprised by how much there was to talk about. I mean, I knew he was really cute and everything, but back then the wine was more important than any guy. I guess it still is."

Katie picked up her glass. "You are so in need of some serious therapy."

"Maybe Francesca will give me a discount."

Her twin shook her head. "No treating family members. There are strict rules about that. So then what? You hung out, it was great, and?"

"And a couple of days later I was out walking the vines and Nic found me. We talked for hours. I got sunburned, we were out for so long. This time we arranged to meet up again."

Brenna remembered how magical everything had become that summer. With Nic around, the sky was bluer, the ocean more salty. She'd laughed longer, slept harder, breathed more deeply than ever before.

"We became friends," she said slowly, feeling herself getting lost in the past and knowing that was dangerous territory. "We rode his motorcycle down to the beach for picnics, we—"

"You were on his motorcycle?" Francesca sounded outraged. "I can't believe it. I always wanted to go for a ride with him."

"Next time I see him I'll ask if he wants to take you."

Francesca rolled her eyes. "I don't want to go *now*. That's a teenage girl fantasy. Plus he probably didn't even keep his bike."

"It may not be the same one, but he still has a motorcycle," Brenna said. "I've seen him on it around here." She didn't say that watching him drive by made her blood race or her throat get dry. Nor would she admit that the sight of him in his black leather jacket had flooded her with memories. Having a crush on Nic at seventeen was acceptable. At twenty-seven it was just plain embarrassing.

"So you're hanging out together," Katie said. "Then what?"

"Then one day he kissed me. I was really surprised. I had a thing for him, but I figured he thought I was still a kid."

He'd frequently talked about how much younger she was than him and just as often she'd pointed out that while three years seemed like a big deal now, when they were older it wouldn't matter at all.

"He kisses great, huh?" Katie said.

"Not bad."

Francesca looked at Katie. "She is so lying. You know it was better than not bad. If nothing else, Nic has had plenty of practice."

"Are you telling this story or am I?"

Francesca shrugged. "Keep talking."

"So he kissed me and I was stunned and then he admitted that he liked me a lot and I admitted I felt the same about him. Things progressed as they do and one day we made love."

Francesca's humor fled. "You were only seventeen."

"I know. I was scared, but Nic was great and within a few days the sex was terrific."

"You never told us. You kept this from *me*," Francesca said, sounding hurt. "Of course it's all right, it's just . . ."

Brenna understood. She and Francesca were twins. "I couldn't say anything. I didn't want you two keeping my secrets and . . ." She smiled. "Somehow no one knowing made it even more special. I know that sounds silly and it probably was, but I liked having Nic all to myself."

"If you had Nic as your secret, would you have told us?" Katie asked Francesca. "Knowing how the three of us would talk about it, laugh about it, and study it from every angle?"

Brenna's twin grinned. "Hmm, tell you two all the details or keep Nic to myself. Not exactly a tough choice." She looked at Brenna. "Okay. I forgive you."

"Oh, good. Now I can sleep tonight."

Katie sat up and reached for the wine bottle. "I understand the *why* of keeping it quiet. What impresses me is that you could. There wasn't even a hint."

"I knew it would cause trouble. The families hadn't spoken in three generations. It's not as if Grandpa Lorenzo listened to me about anything anyway. Can you imagine the explosion if I told him I was in love with Nic?"

"Were you in love?" Francesca asked.

"Completely."

"So why did it end?"

"Nic went back to school. He was going to UC Davis, I was here. We didn't see each other."

She took the bottle from Katie and topped up her own glass, then took a drink.

She and Nic hadn't seen each other. But what she didn't tell her sisters was that they'd written. He'd sent his letters to one of her friend's. They'd agreed to see other people while he was gone. She still didn't know if Nic had gotten involved with another girl, but after falling in love with him, she'd been unable to get excited about any of the boys at her high school. She also didn't mention that when Nic returned, they had picked up where they'd left off. That this time when the relationship ended it wasn't over something as simple as Nic heading off to school. This time she'd been responsible.

"What did he say when you went to him for the loan?" Katie asked.

"He said he would think about it."

"That's a yes?"

"It's not a no. I should hear from him in the next couple of days."

Francesca shook her head. "Are you sure about this? You don't think it's the least bit dangerous borrowing money from the great-grandson of the family's sworn enemy?"

"Do any of us take the feud seriously?"

"No." Francesca picked up a cookie. "I hope everything goes well. Maybe he'll loan you the money for old times' sake."

"No teenage relationship is worth that much," Katie said.

Brenna couldn't help agreeing. What they didn't know and what she wouldn't tell them was there had been a time when Nic had hated her as much as he had once loved her. Not that she could blame him. If their situations had been reversed, she would never have forgiven *him.*

For the first time since going to him that afternoon, she felt a shiver of apprehension. If he wanted revenge, she was handing him the means.

No, she told herself. That wasn't possible. Nic wanting revenge would mean that she still mattered. It had been nearly ten years since their relationship had ended, and in that time he'd dated scads of beautiful women. She was just somebody he used to know and his interest in her project was about risk and opportunity, nothing more.

Francesca smiled. "Okay, Brenna. If you're determined to do this, then I want to wish you the best." She raised her drink. "To your new winery."

Katie raised her glass as well. "May you only rate ninety and above in *Wine Spectator.*"

Brenna picked up her glass. "To new beginnings. For all of us."

Nic called out greetings to the office staff as he walked to the executive offices of Wild Sea Vineyards. The door with the brass nameplate stating M. Moore, Chief Financial Officer, stood open. He knocked once and entered.

Maggie Moore, a tall, beautiful redhead with a brain like a computer, looked up and grinned. "I can always tell when you're around by the increase in the pitch of conversation among the office staff. You're a distraction."

"That's because they're all dancing around, trying to look at my butt."

She shook her head. "I should never have told you they did that."

"Why not? It's flattering."

"Yeah, and you strutted around here for weeks afterward."

"Can I help it if they find me irresistible? Besides, I've checked out my share of female body parts over the years. I consider it payback."

"Which you love. It's a curse, but you handle it with style and grace."

"Absolutely."

She laughed then and her green eyes crinkled at the corners.

Maggie had always enjoyed poking at his ego. For the past eight years she'd kept him from taking himself too seriously. When they'd transitioned from lovers to co-workers, that trait had kept things comfortable between them.

He nodded at the computer. "Are we making millions?"

"I'm doing my best to make that happen. When does harvest start?"

"Next week for the Chardonnay grapes."

"Am I supposed to be praying for rain or no rain?"

"No rain during harvest. While you're at it, mention that we'd like warm temperatures for the Cabernet and

Merlot grapes." He pulled out a chair in front of her desk and took a seat.

"I'll never remember all that."

"That's because you're not a wine drinker."

She touched her index finger to her lips. "You're not supposed to tell. It's my big secret."

"I know. I figure one day I'll use it for blackmail."

"Can I help it if I don't get the whole wine thing? Give me a milkshake kind of drink or something with an umbrella. I don't want to taste the alcohol if I don't have to."

He grimaced. "Strawberry daiquiris. Talk about a chick drink."

"I *am* a chick, thank you very much."

"I did my best to educate your palate, but you're beyond redemption."

Maggie didn't look the least bit chagrined. "I figure there are more people like me in the world than there are like you, so I don't care what you say." She glanced at her computer screen, hit the Save key, and logged out of the program.

"Okay," she said as she turned back to him. "Tell me everything. Are we going to be selling overseas?"

"I can honestly say we're going to have more orders than we can handle."

He brought her up to date on the meetings he'd held the previous afternoon. They'd gone late into the night, and by the time Nic had headed home, Wild Sea Vineyards had become the newest wine to be imported to the Far East.

"Dennis will be getting you specific numbers," Nic said, referring to their sales manager. "We're going to have to get up to speed on all the regulations and the hell of shipping the wine overseas. Once we get a start date, I'll want updated financials."

"No problem." Maggie made a few notes on a pad. "Dennis and I already have a meeting set up for later this morning. I'll add this to the agenda." She glanced at him. "So why aren't you thrilled about this?"

"I am."

"You don't seem excited. Isn't this a big deal? You've been working toward it for nearly a year. Why don't you look like a happy camper?"

He shrugged. "I got what I wanted. Now it's time to move on to the next goal."

"Maybe it's time to stop and enjoy all that you've already accomplished." She leaned forward and rested her elbows on her desk. "Nic, you're burying yourself in work. Have you ever thought about getting a life?"

"I have one."

Her mouth twisted. "You have the winery, which occupies about ninety percent of your time. The rest of your free hours are spent riding that damn motorcycle along the coast road and dating women you have no intention of ever settling down with. Don't you want something more significant than that?"

"You ruined me for other women," he told her.

"Not likely. You're the one who dumped me, remember?"

"No, I didn't. I'm too smart to let someone like you get away."

"Oh, sure. Say that now that I'm happily married with a toddler." Her humor faded. "When we first met you had so many plans and dreams. I never noticed they were all about business. In the past seven years you've made them all come true. Maybe it's time to focus on other areas of your life."

"Gee, thanks for the lecture, Mom."

"I'm being serious."

"I know. I appreciate the concern."

"But you're not going to listen to me." She sounded resigned.

"Not for a minute."

She sighed. "Why can't I get through to you?"

"Because you're a born rescuer and I don't need saving."

"You need something." She tapped her pen on the desk. "What about a dog?"

He laughed. Maggie always knew the right thing to say, even when he didn't want to hear it. She wanted him to be a well-rounded person. He wanted to win. As far as she was concerned, he'd achieved every goal he'd set for himself. Which he had. All but the one she didn't know about.

As for a woman in life, something permanent, it might be for other people, but not for him. He'd long ago learned that loving someone meant opening himself to being left behind and betrayed. Why bother?

"Maybe a dog," he said. "I'll think about it."

"You could get one of those sidecars for your motorcycle. Wouldn't that be great? You could buy doggie goggles and a little leather dog jacket."

He winced. "Not in this lifetime. I'd be getting a dog, not a dress-up doll. Does Jason know you're this twisted?"

"My husband adores me."

Nic was glad. When he'd come home after his eighteen months of exile in France, Maggie had just been hired to get the winery's books in order. She'd been five years older, new in town, and the softest touch around. The second she'd found out about his broken heart, she'd gone to work, healing him with everything from long conversations to nights of great sex.

Six months later he'd been back on his feet, and she'd been smart enough to end things before they got awkward. Over the years they'd stayed friends. She'd met Jason, had fallen in love, and gotten married. Nic had been happy for her. She'd always been the home-and-hearth kind.

"How's our cash flow?" he asked, changing the subject to something less personal.

"What do you want to buy? More land? Maybe a small island somewhere?"

"Very funny. Actually I was thinking of making a loan."

Maggie frowned. "To whom?"

"Someone I know wants to start a winery."

"And you just love training the competition?"

He shrugged. "How many new concerns make it?"

Maggie blinked. "You want to loan money for a winery start-up you expect to fail?"

"I don't expect it to fail." Not exactly. But Brenna had been out of the business a long time. Ten years ago he would have bet on her in a heartbeat, but now? He wasn't so sure.

"Are you making the loan yourself, or is this from the company?" Maggie asked.

"Which do you suggest?"

"It depends on terms. There are tax implications either way. How much money are we talking about?"

Nic settled back to watch the show. "A million dollars."

Maggie pushed to her feet and planted her hands on her hips. Her eyes widened and her cheeks turned as red as her hair. "Are you insane?"

"Is this how you talk to your boss?"

"I do when he's in serious need of therapy. You're considering loaning someone a million dollars and you think there's a chance they might *fail?"*

He shrugged. "It would be a good write-off."

"It would be really dumb. I mean it, Nic. I know this is your company and you can tell me to pound sand if you want, but this is a really, really bad idea."

"Have I ever told you to pound sand?"

"Not in so many words, but you frequently ignore my very sound financial advice."

"This may have to be another one of those times." He rose and faced her. "Work up a couple different ways to come up with the money. I don't know if I want to do it privately or through the company, so go at it from both angles."

"Why would you do this?"

He grinned. "Because I can."

3

Sweat prickled Brenna's back as the hot California sun burned through her T-shirt. She wore a wide-brimmed hat to protect her face and should have used gloves, but she didn't have the dexterity to feel what she was doing with them on. As a result, her fingers were bruised, her nails broken, and she'd been scratched from fingertips to wrist by dozens of grapevines.

As she crouched between the rows of lush plants, she inhaled the heady aroma of ripe Chardonnay grapes. She took the heavy bunches in her hand and carefully cut them free, imagining the pale green juice running free as the ripe, tender fruit was squeezed. Marcelli Wines Reserve Chardonnay was one of the best in the country, and this harvest was going to be one for the record books. As she worked, cutting grapes free and dropping them into the bin in front of her, she calculated tons per acre and bottles per ton.

When she'd first seen the potential success of the harvest, she'd wanted to hold some of the grapes back for blending. She had an idea for a cuvée she'd been wanting to try and this was the year. But her grandfather had refused to listen, instead telling her that they had always made Reserve Chardonnay from the best grapes, and he wasn't going to let any of them go to waste because she wanted to experiment.

"The man's a fool," she told herself as she shifted to the next plant and began cutting.

Around her the migrant workers who had shown up at the beginning of the week worked quickly, filling three bins of grapes for every one of hers. She didn't practice enough to be efficient and her heart wasn't in the task.

Yesterday they'd brought in the first grapes. She'd been there as they'd been carefully loaded on the conveyor belt that would carry them into the giant vat for crushing. She'd sorted and watched, then tasted the first juice of the harvest. One sip had told her it was going to be a good year.

The realization that it might be the last year for Marcelli Wines—if her grandfather went ahead and sold, or left everything to her newly found brother—had driven her from the winery and into the fields. She'd stayed there all day yesterday and had remained there today. She felt restless and tense. It had been three days. Why hadn't Nic called?

She'd been so sure he was going to loan her the money, but as time passed, she became less confident. Without him, there wasn't going to be a Four Sisters Winery. Without his money she was completely on her own. Her current checking-account balance hovered around twelve thousand dollars. Since she and Jeff had split, she'd been able to save most of her paycheck. Unfortunately combining that with the money her ex would soon be sending her wasn't close to enough.

The long row of plants stretched out in front of her.

Brenna continued to cut the clusters, ignoring those that weren't ripe enough, working methodically, wondering how much worse her shoulders were going to hurt by the end of the day when her cell phone rang.

Her youngest sister, Mia, was heading back from six weeks at a Japanese language school in Washington, D.C. Delayed at Dulles Airport by a canceled flight, Mia passed the morning by phoning her siblings and telling them about her adventures. She'd already called Brenna twice in two hours. Each time Brenna had been so sure it was Nic, that she'd barely been able to breathe. Now she knew better and didn't bother to glance at the caller ID.

"I'm busy," she said as she straightened slightly. "So stop calling me."

"Is this a bad time?"

The low male voice sounded nothing like eighteen-year-old Mia. Instead it sounded intimate, familiar, and too sexy for comfort.

"Nic?"

"I can call back."

She glanced around to make sure she wasn't likely to be overheard. The regular crew had long moved past her and was nearly halfway down the row. She shifted so she could plop down on her butt.

Her breathing hadn't stopped, but there was a tightness in her chest. Tension filled her. Was he going to tell her yes?

"This is fine. I'm helping with harvest and I could use a break."

"You're out in the fields?"

"Uh-huh. I'm hot and sweaty. I'm a real fashion statement."

"Why aren't you in the winery? Shouldn't you be worrying about the fermenting?"

"My grandfather and I had a disagreement, as usual. I'm in a snit, so I thought I'd come out here and sulk."

"His loss."

"That's my feeling." She wiped the sweat from her face. Her heart felt as if it were beating so hard it was going to jump into another dimension. "So, um, did you come to any decisions?"

"Yeah. I'm thinking about getting a dog."

Brenna glanced up at the bright sun. Had she been out for too long? Was her brain being poached?

"Okay," she said slowly. "Dogs are nice. Did you have a particular breed in mind?"

"A golden retriever. Not exactly an untraditional choice, but I want something big and friendly."

"They qualify."

"There's a breeder up in Ojai. I was thinking of heading out there this afternoon and taking a look. I already called and they have a litter of puppies that are just weaned. A couple are spoken for, but there are five or six available."

Okay—one of them was crazy. Why did Nic think she cared about him getting a dog? Was he telling her about the puppy so that she would think he was a swell guy even though he was going to turn her down?

"That sounds just peachy. I hope you have fun."

She'd blinked several times before she realized her eyes were burning. There was no way she was going to cry over this, she told herself even as her throat got all tight. Dammit, she'd been so *sure* he was going to say yes that she hadn't bothered with a fall-back plan . . . mostly because he *was* her fall-back plan.

The loss of her dream made her feel sick to her stomach. She wanted to curl up in a ball and die.

"Look Nic, I really need to get back to—"

"I thought you might like to come with me."

"I'm not in the market for a puppy."

"It would give us a chance to talk."

The sick feeling went away. Hope blossomed and grew until it pushed out every other emotion. "Do we have something to talk about?"

"I have a few questions. If I like the answers, then yes, I would say we do."

If Brenna hadn't been sitting she would have fallen down. "Are you going to loan me the money?"

"Like I said, I still need convincing, but I'm about seventy percent there. It's nearly eleven. Why don't you get cleaned up and head over to my place? Be here by noon and we'll go to Ojai. On the way to the breeder, we can talk about your proposal."

"Th-that sounds great. I'll be there."

"See ya."

She heard a click in her ear. She pushed the Off button on her cell phone, then flopped on her back on the dirt and burst out laughing.

"Holy shit!" she yelled to the heavens. "He's going to say yes!"

Thirty minutes later Brenna stood in front of her bathroom mirror and tried to manipulate the blow-dryer and a fat, round brush. Normally she simply let her hair air dry. Since the unfortunate incident of the haircut she'd impulsively indulged in after Jeff had dumped her, she hadn't bothered much with style. As her entire world had been reduced to the hacienda and the winery, there wasn't anyone to impress, so she'd let her morning routine slide to a quick shower followed by body lotion.

Right now she wanted to look dazzling. Not dressed up but attractive and confident. But what exactly did one wear when one wanted to be considered worthy of a million-dollar loan?

As she fumbled with the brush and tried to add a little volume and shine to her hair, she considered her options. Suit, dress, jeans, shorts. Nothing.

The latter made her both wince and smile. It had been ten years and fifteen pounds since Nic had seen her naked. She didn't think she should expose her more rounded self without some kind of warning. Besides, this wasn't about sex, it was about business. So a suit?

But it was August, damn hot, and they were going puppy shopping. Not exactly an itinerary for a skirt and pumps.

When her hair was somewhat styled and nearly dry, she tossed down the brush and blow-dryer, then lunged for her makeup case. At least she had decent skin with medium olive coloring that meant she didn't need much in the way of base or concealer. She smudged on a little eye shadow, applied mascara and lip gloss, then headed for her closet.

Three minutes later she'd settled on what she hoped was suitable puppy-shopping attire: khaki shorts, a teal polo shirt, and sandals. She slipped on a watch, simple hoop earrings, and ran the brush through her hair one last time before grabbing her purse and car keys and ducking out the door.

It was 11:58 when she pulled up in front of the Wild Sea Vineyards winery. The building facades hadn't changed in a generation, but a half dozen new structures had been added in the past few years. She could see the tasting building about a half mile away and all the tourists' cars parked in front. To her left and right were acres of grapes; behind her was the house.

She stepped out into the warm afternoon and pulled off her sunglasses. In the past hour she'd been too busy getting ready to think about being nervous, but suddenly the butterflies migrated to her stomach and began dive-bombing her pancreas. She felt hot, thirsty, tense, and apprehensive. If her emotions were a liquid, they would be thick, green, and bubbling.

The brew got worse when Nic stepped out of the winery. He wore jeans and a T-shirt. Dark sunglasses hid his eyes.

She'd seen him dressed like this hundreds of times, maybe more. So he was tall, muscular, and good-looking. She was only interested in his money. Nothing about the man appealed to her. Really.

Brenna shoved her car keys into her jeans pocket and sighed. She wasn't a very good liar, not even to herself. It might have been ten years and a lot of miles since she and Nic had been a whole lot more than friends, but some part of her remembered every detail of their time together. Especially the time they'd spent in bed.

She remembered the warmth of his skin. They'd mostly made love outdoors, so in her mind sun heat and Nic heat were almost the same. They'd discovered the sensual pleasures of making love in the cool June rain, by the beach in July, and under thick canopies of grapes on a sultry August night.

Their favorite indoor location had been the fermentation room, empty until harvest but still dark and quiet, smelling of yeast and magic. Sometimes, when she walked by the fermentation rooms at Marcelli and caught a whiff of that distinctive perfume, she flashed back to Nic's body against her, his hands everywhere, their need spiraling out of control.

Ten years, a lot of miles, and one failed marriage later, she still remembered . . . perhaps more than she should.

"You made it," he said, pulling off his sunglasses and offering a smile.

"I was motivated," she admitted, determined to act completely cool. "And curious. I never thought of you as the pet type."

"I've wanted a dog for a while. This seemed like a good time. You ready?"

She nodded and followed him to the multicar garage. Her thighs did some kind of weird shimmy thing, which made it hard to walk. She hadn't thought about getting there—to Ojai. This was Nic—the guy who rode motorcycles.

She had an instant vision of herself on the bike with him, riding behind, holding on, being really, really close. She would wrap her arms around him and feel each time he took a breath. Eventually their hearts would start to beat in unison, just as soon as hers stopped kicking into hyper-drive. It would be fun, intimate, exciting, and more than a little dangerous.

She couldn't wait.

He stepped into the garage and hit a button that activated an overhead door. Light spilled in from outside. As her eyes adjusted, she saw an expensive Jaguar convertible—the really sleek kind, a Land Rover, and three motorcycles. Which was two more than he'd had before.

As she glanced around for extra helmets, Nic walked to the Land Rover and held open the passenger door. "In case we come back with a puppy," he said. "I don't want it chewing up my good car."

Sensual heat drained out of her like water draining out

of a bathtub. Right. Nic was buying a dog. People didn't show up on a motorcycle if they were pet shopping. It wouldn't look responsible. It's not as if the puppy could wear a helmet and hang on from behind. What had she been thinking?

She hadn't, she realized as she slid into the passenger seat and waited while Nic closed the door. She'd been caught up in the past and feeling. Which was really stupid. What about her dreams? What about her mission? The drive to Ojai was her opportunity to convince Nic to loan her the money. She had to focus.

As Nic settled in next to her, she vowed to keep things strictly business. She was about to mention the loan when he spoke.

"Have you started harvesting the Reserve Chardonnay?" he asked.

"Yesterday."

He turned the key and started the engine, then glanced at her. "And?"

"The grapes are pretty spectacular," she admitted. "Exactly ripe, with just enough sweetness. You wouldn't have to have any talent to make this harvest a success. What about you? The Chardonnay grapes ready?"

"In most of the fields. I have crews out."

They backed out of the garage. He hit a remote to close the door, then turned the vehicle and headed down the main drive to the highway.

"And?" she asked, grinning. "Are you going to have a brilliant year?"

"It looks that way."

She wasn't surprised. She'd been hearing that it was turning into a good harvest for everyone. Which was a whole lot better than the years when everyone was scrambling. She still shuddered when she thought back to 1998 when California Cabernet had suffered from low yields due to uncooperative weather. The Cab grapes hadn't ripened correctly. It had been one of the few times she hadn't minded not being involved with Marcelli Wines.

"So what did you and your grandfather argue about?" he asked.

"I want to use some of the Reserve grapes for a cuvée. He thinks they should all be bottled as Reserve Chardonnay. They're our best-producing vines and I see his point, but I've had this idea for a great cuvée. He's a purist and old-fashioned."

Nic glanced at her. "Chardonnay is one of the most popular wines around. Why would you want to try something new?"

"Because I think blends are becoming more popular. Both Kendall-Jackson and Columbia Crest up in Washington State have done really well with Cabernet-Merlot blends. Qupe Winery has a cuvée that sells out about thirty seconds after it gets bottled."

"And because you like to experiment."

She shrugged. "I'll admit it. I want to create the perfect white wine. Light, slightly fruity. I want the finish to be crisp, with a hint of sweetness. Minimal oak. I want it to taste cold, even when it's not."

He glanced at her. "That's a tall order."

"It can be done. Assuming you cough up the money, I'm going to buy the Schulers' Chardonnay grapes. I have some Voignier on reserve up in Napa. I figure with the right blend and barrel fermenting I'll—"

"You're going to barrel ferment?"

She resisted the urge to roll her eyes. "You sound like my grandfather. Yes, I am. I know it's expensive and more time-consuming, but the blend will be smoother and the color lighter. Which is what I want."

"What about your Pinot Noir?"

She watched as they merged onto 101 south heading for the off ramp that led to Ojai.

"I went and saw the grapes last week. They need about another month."

"You know good Pinot's a bitch to make."

She turned to look at him. "I am more than up to the challenge."

He grinned. "Okay, so Chardonnay, a cuvée, and Pinot. Anything else on the Brenna Marcelli radar scope?"

She did ten minutes on her plans for the perfect Cabernet. As she wasn't able to grow her own grapes, not yet anyway, she'd lined up a list of potential purchases. Rather than buy in bulk from one seller, she would pick up small batches from several to get the exact blend she wanted.

"I'm going a hundred percent on this Cab," she concluded. "No Cab Franc or Merlot to smooth it out. I'm not looking for a wine that will cellar for twenty years, either. At least not at first. I want it good in three years and great in four."

"Don't we all?"

She allowed herself a smile. "The difference is I know how to do it."

"And I don't?"

"Did I say that? You do fine. Wild Sea is known all over the country."

"Volume not quality?"

The argument was familiar.

"I've kept track of Wild Sea wines," she said. "You know all this, Nic. You're too focused on getting the most number of cases per ton. You need to give up that last ten percent. It's not worth it. Oh, and there were a couple of poor barrel choices for the 2000 Reserve Merlot."

"This is how you convince me to loan you money? By insulting my wines?"

She shifted in her seat, adjusting the seat belt so she could face him. "If you didn't want my opinion, you wouldn't have asked."

"I don't recall asking."

"You phrased 'volume, not quality' in a tone of voice that implied a question. That's asking."

He glanced at her. "You're still stubborn."

"I'm also still right. You might outsell Marcelli Wines four to one, but we get nearly three times as many wins at competitions, and I'm sure I don't have to remind you about our ratings from the various magazines and critics."

"No, you don't. Want to compare gross profits?"

She wrinkled her nose. "Only if you want me to drool in your car."

"Let's save that for the puppy."

They left the freeway and turned onto the road to Ojai. August in California meant sunny days and little rain. In summer much of the state turned brown.

Brenna studied Nic's strong profile and the competent way he drove.

This was the longest they'd spent in each other's company in what felt like forever. She was nervous about a lot of things, but also oddly relaxed. Maybe because he'd always been so easy to be around. Because of their differing opinions on everything from wine to politics, they fought all the time. Yet their arguing was never hostile—instead it was more of a hobby they shared. They discussed with plenty of emotion, they called each other names, they even threatened bodily harm—in the best way possible, all without either of them ever really getting mad. At least they used to. Currently, they were only arguing.

She found herself wondering what he'd been doing for the past ten years. Oh, she knew the basics. He'd spent eighteen months in France, exiled by his grandfather, Emilio. Best not to think about that, she told herself. After all, Nic being driven away had pretty much been her fault.

In the end Nic had been vindicated when his grandfather begged him to return to run the family vineyard. Nic had agreed, taking over the day-to-day operations. When Emilio died, Nic inherited everything.

In the past seven or eight years Wild Sea had grown, mostly through acquisition. If a winery went out of business, or someone got tired of the ups and downs of the industry, Nic was there with the best offer to be had. He'd always said he wanted to be the biggest and best. By most standards, he already was.

"Why do you want to bother?" he asked, breaking into her thoughts. "You could fall on your butt and end up owing me a million dollars plus interest."

She'd done her best to forget why she was here. Suddenly it was show time. She considered the question.

"I was a fool to walk away from Marcelli Wines ten years ago. I didn't realize my heart and soul were buried in the land and that without them I was an empty shell."

"And here I thought you were happily married."

She tried to figure out if there was heat or sarcasm in his words, but couldn't hear either. Maybe it was just a statement.

"I thought I was, too. It was all an illusion. Now I'm back and I can't believe the difference. I never want to lose the land or the vines again. My grandfather has options he considers a lot more interesting than leaving me in charge, so I'm willing to take the chance. I don't consider failure possible."

"Some people would say that's arrogant."

"I don't care what some people say. I know what I'm doing. I have a plan. I'm not afraid to work hard."

"What *are* you afraid of?"

She straightened in her seat and stared out the front window. "Interesting question. I guess being stupid. Giving it all up for something that doesn't matter."

As soon as the words fell out of her mouth, she wanted to grab them and stuff them back. Of all the idiotic, insensitive, ill-timed things to say, that was it. If she wanted to make sure Nic didn't loan her the money, she'd just come up with the perfect strategy.

"So we have that in common," he said, his voice even.

She squeezed her eyes shut, then opened them. "Nic, I—"

"Don't sweat it," he said, cutting her off.

"But I really—"

"No, you don't. I'm not interested in the past. It's boring. I find the future far more intriguing. Assuming you make it through the first year, then what?"

She didn't know what to say. There were things she wanted to explain, despite the fact that he obviously didn't want to listen. Maybe she should just answer the question.

"Buy more grapes, make more wine. By year two I'll start selling. I know the distributors. I'm not worried about getting into restaurants and stores."

He was going to say no. She'd just blown the opportunity of a lifetime. Why couldn't she remember to think before she spoke? It wasn't hard. She had a functioning brain most of the time.

"I'd want a callable note," he said.

"What?"

"A callable note. There would be a payment schedule and a reasonable rate of interest. I'll even hold off two years until you have to start paying me back. But in return the note is callable at any time. You start to stumble, I'm not going to wait for the crash. I'll call in the note and take everything you have."

Her mind went blank. One second there were thoughts, the next, nothing. Her hands clenched tight, her legs felt icy cold, and her heart stood still. Then rational thought returned, as did her body temperature. She raised her arms and pressed her hands flat against the roof of the SUV.

"Did you just say you were loaning me the money?" she asked carefully.

"Uh-huh."

She glanced at him and saw he was smiling. "I can't believe it."

"Does that mean I shouldn't have the papers drawn up in the morning?"

"No. Please. Draw away."

Brenna started to laugh. She wanted to throw herself at Nic and kiss him. Good sense and a seat belt held her in check. Instead she rolled down the passenger's-side window and stuck her head out into the hot afternoon.

"I just got a loan for a million dollars!" she yelled to the trees. "I'm going to open a winery!"

Joy flooded her. She was going to get her chance. When she flopped back in her seat, she closed the window, then looked at Nic.

"For real?"

"You already announced it to the world. How could I say no?"

Happiness made her blood bubble like champagne. "I can't believe it. You actually have a million dollars."

"I have a whole lot more than that."

"Show-off."

"Hey, how about a little gratitude? I'm going out on a limb here."

She sighed. "I am grateful. You have no idea." She turned to him. "So why did you say yes?"

"I think you're a good bet."

After ten years of Jeff telling her that her life was uninteresting and second-rate when compared with him becoming a doctor and six months of fighting with her grandfather about everything from barrel time to labels, Nic's words made her glow.

"Yeah?"

"You know what you're doing. With a little luck and a lot of hard work, you can make your venture a success. I get good return on my investment. It's a win-win."

"The first bottle I produce is yours," she said. "As my way of saying thank you."

"A measly bottle? You owe me at least a case."

"All right. A case it is."

At this point she would have promised him a kidney. He'd given her the means to make her dream come true. Surely that was worth at least an organ or two.

4

The dog breeder lived in an old farmhouse on the edge of an orange grove. Nic pulled in behind a battered Jeep and turned off the engine.

"The woman I spoke with, Sara, said to follow the sound of barking down to the barn."

"Easy enough." Brenna glanced at him. "You do realize puppies don't come house-trained. They tend to piddle in the night and chew shoes."

He shifted to look at her. "I can handle it."

She grinned. "I wasn't saying you couldn't, O Great One."

"You're mocking me."

"I'm having fun. I'm still really happy about the loan."

As she spoke, she slipped off her sunglasses and he saw the humor in her dark eyes. The corners of her mouth curved up and she nearly quivered with excitement. While he had an ulterior motive for giving her the money, he decided to forget about that . . . at least for the afternoon.

"Let me guess," she said with a grin. "You want a male dog."

"Of course."

"That is so typically guy-like."

"What's wrong with that?"

"Nothing at all, although you could try to be a little more creative in your choices."

"There are girl dogs and boy dogs. How creative could I be?"

He climbed out of the car and was instantly assaulted by the sound of dozens of dogs barking. Brenna circled the Land Rover and stopped next to him.

"Okay," she said in a loud voice. "Now I know why your dog lady lives in the middle of nowhere. She wouldn't be a very popular neighbor."

"I guess not."

They headed down a stone path, which led them closer to the noise. Several large trees provided shade for about a dozen large kennel runs and a couple of barns.

Nic held the door open on the one marked "Guests" and followed Brenna into a brightly lit reception area. A teenage girl sat at a battered desk. She looked up and smiled.

"Hi. You're Nic, right? I'll let Sara know you're here."

She ducked out through a wooden door. Brenna crossed to the cinder-block wall and studied pictures.

"There seem to be some champions in the bloodline."

"Quality breeding is important."

"Are you going to be showing the dog?" she asked.

"No."

"I see."

He narrowed his gaze. "What does that mean?"

"Nothing." She continued to study the pictures.

"Brenna."

"Just that it's so you. You're buying a dog with a championship pedigree, but it's just a pet."

"It's *my* pet."

"I'm sure it will be very proud of that fact."

He did his best not to smile. "I just offered you an unsecured seven-figure loan. Shouldn't you be a little more humble?"

"I'm doing the best I can."

"Nic?"

He turned and saw a pleasant-looking woman in her fifties standing in the doorway.

"I'm Sara." The woman waved them in. "Come see the kids."

The puppies were kept in a large open pen partially in the shade. Eight fur balls in various shades of cream and pale gold tumbled together. The mother lay off to the side. Her weary expression explained that eight offspring were possibly seven too many.

"We try to let them out as much as possible when the weather is this nice," Sara was saying. "Now, I told you that two of the puppies are already spoken for. Let me show you which ones."

"Sure. What about their temperament?" Nic asked. "I run a winery and my dog will be free to roam a large area, but he'll have to interact with people. Is that a problem?"

"Not at all. Goldens are known for their friendly personalities. I breed family pets here, so I choose pairs that are good with children and not excitable."

Brenna tapped the gate. "Can I go in?"

"Help yourself."

She stepped into the pen and was instantly surrounded by eight excited puppies. Nic watched as she sank onto the grass and held out her arms. The fur balls climbed over her legs, scrambled up her chest, and stood on hind legs to nibble on her hair. She cuddled them close, laughing when they swiped at her mouth with doggy kisses.

"Tell me about their bloodlines," Nic said.

"Their great-grandfather was the first champion I raised," Sara told him. "He was a beautiful, gentle dog."

She continued to speak, but Nic only half listened. He found himself caught up in watching Brenna with the puppies.

Tiny paws messed up her sleek hairstyle. Mud prints stained her shirt and shorts. High-pitched yips of excitement mingled with her laughter.

"You are all too cute," she cooed and earned a doggy kiss.

A puppy ducked under her bent leg, drawing Nic's attention to the curve of her calf and the exposed length of thigh. She'd always been curvy in a way that he found sexy as hell. That hadn't changed. His gaze slipped from her thigh to her breasts.

He stiffened as he flashed back to the first time he'd seen her breasts. He'd nearly lost it when she pulled off her shirt for him and had unfastened her bra. He'd seen naked women before, but no one like her. For the first time in his life, he knew why the word *lush* had been invented.

At first he hadn't been able to touch. He'd been too caught up in looking. Then he'd been unable to resist what she'd offered. Full, sweet-tasting with dark nipples that tightened at his every touch. He'd filled his hands with her sensitive curves, exploring every inch of skin, licking and sucking until she'd writhed against him and they'd both been so hot that they'd—

Jesus. He jerked himself back to the present. Brenna still played with the puppies, Sara continued to talk about bloodlines, and he was as hard as a rock.

He shifted so that a fence post concealed his condition

and did his best to think about mundane things, like dog training and what kind of leash he was going to have to buy.

He forced himself to pay attention to Sara and started asking dog-care questions. Brenna looked up, a puppy in each arm.

"How on earth do you pick?" she asked. "They're all so adorable."

Sara unlocked the gate. "He'll have to go in and spend some time with them."

Brenna grinned. She set one of the puppies down and patted the ground. "Come on, Nic. The grass stains will wash out."

He stepped into the pen and sat next to her. Instantly several puppies clamored over her to get to him. They sniffed and barked and licked his palms and bit his fingers. When he picked one up, he felt its pudgy belly as it wiggled close and swiped at his face with a warm tongue.

"They like you," Brenna said.

"I'm a likable kind of guy."

"Maybe, but I doubt puppies are wildly discerning. They just want attention."

One puppy, a light beige-colored fur ball, dived for his boots and wrestled with the shoelace. The pup pulled the bow loose and tried to run with the lace in its mouth. It got up a good head of steam for maybe eight inches, then came to a sudden stop when the lace tightened.

Unprepared for the sudden change in momentum, the puppy tumbled onto its back and looked at Nic in surprise, as if asking what had just happened. Nic scooped him up in his arms.

"You think you can take me?" he asked the big-eyed fluff ball.

The dog woofed in agreement, wiggled to get closer, and tried to lick his face.

"Careful," Brenna warned. "You might find the puppy doing the picking rather than the other way around."

Even as she spoke, the pup cuddled close to Nic's chest, rested its head on his shoulder, and closed its eyes.

Nic knew he was a regular kind of guy. He was into sports, rode a motorcycle, and ran a successful corporation worth half a billion dollars. There was no way fifteen pounds of puppy was going to get to him.

But the warm weight felt surprisingly comfortable. Maybe Maggie had been right—maybe he did need something more in his life, even if it was just a dog.

"Tell me about this one, Sara," he said, indicating the puppy in his arms and avoiding Brenna's knowing smile.

"He's going to be a big guy. Just look at those paws. He's social and outgoing. A little stubborn."

"Aren't most males?" Brenna asked.

Sara held up her hands. "I don't have those kinds of conversations with clients," she said cheerfully. "You two can argue about that on the way home."

They probably would, Nic thought. Along with other things. Brenna had always been opinionated, and she wasn't afraid to stand up for what she believed. She also didn't mind admitting when she was wrong. Rather that was how she'd been ten years ago. He couldn't speak to who she was now.

He glanced at the puppy asleep in his arms. "I'll take him."

Thirty minutes later they were back in Nic's Land Rover with a large box of supplies in the back and a still-drowsy puppy on a blanket on Brenna's lap.

"We can put him in the carrier," Nic said as he started the engine.

She stroked the puppy's soft fur and shook her head. "I like holding him. As long as you don't mind."

Nic shrugged. She supposed the message was that simple homey things like dogs didn't get to him, but she'd seen the expression on his face when the puppy had fallen asleep on his chest. He'd felt a twinge of emotion.

She guessed he would rather eat glass than admit it, which was fine with her. She wasn't going to say anything. Well, not very much.

"Why a dog?" she asked.

"I've been thinking about getting one for a while, but my travel schedule made the idea impractical. I recently hired a new sales manager. He'll take over most of the accounts and do the bulk of the traveling."

"Must be nice," she said. "What will you do in your free time?"

"I have some new projects. They'll keep me busy. Not to mention training my new dog."

"Training, huh? Probably to attack strangers on sight. I'll warn my family members to stay clear of Giovanni land. I don't want my seventy-something grandfather coming home with a dog bite."

"Rufus won't be biting anyone."

She stared at him. "You've got to be kidding. Rufus? You'd name your poor dog Rufus?"

"Sure. What's wrong with it?"

"Everything. It's not a cute puppy name."

"He won't be a cute puppy for long."

She cupped the dog's face in her hand. "Look at those big eyes, that little black nose. Can you really call this sweetie Rufus? Think of the emotional pain from the other dogs in the neighborhood calling him Rufus the Dufus."

Nic shook his head. "You've been out in the sun too long, Brenna. The other dogs in the neighborhood won't be calling him anything because dogs can't talk."

"Not to us. But they can probably talk to each other. They'll tease him. He needs a more dignified name. Or at least something fun."

Nic made a noise in his throat that wasn't exactly a growl, but darned close. "What did you have in mind?"

"Anything but Rufus. How about Charlie, Marvin, Jack."

"Marvin?"

She rolled her eyes. "I'm brainstorming. You can't be critical and expect the creative process to work."

"I never thought that naming a dog would be considered creative."

"It's important. This is a name he'll carry for the rest of his life. It will say something about who he is. He'll either live up or down to his name."

He glanced at the sleeping puppy in her lap. "How about Max?"

She picked up a massive paw and held it in her hand. Hard to believe this little guy would grow into those feet, but he would. "Max works for me."

"Then that's what we'll call him."

As he spoke, Nic returned his attention to the road. Brenna stayed completely still, barely able to breathe. She knew that Nic hadn't meant the statement the way he'd said it. She was reading something into his words that didn't belong there. They had a business relationship now, nothing more. She'd learned her lesson about giving her heart and soul to a man and even if she was ever going to take that chance again, it wouldn't be with

Nic. Loving him had been a disaster . . . for both of them.

But the implied connection in "that's what we'll call him" unnerved her. She thought about the afternoon they'd just spent together and realized how easily they'd fallen into familiar patterns. As if they'd always been friends. As if the years apart hadn't happened. As if she hadn't betrayed him.

Old news, she told herself. For both of them. Nic had gotten over her, just like she'd gotten over him. They were business partners now. Nothing more. She couldn't afford for them to be anything more.

5

When they arrived back at Wild Sea Vineyards, Brenna figured she should leave, but Nic surprised her by asking if she could stick around for a little longer.

"I have a few questions about how you're going to make things work," he said.

She eyed him suspiciously. "You're not going to change your mind about the loan, are you?"

He grinned. "I already said yes. I don't go back on my word. You'll have the papers in the morning."

Being around Nic was hardly tough duty, and seeing as she already had a crush on Max and little to do back at the hacienda, with the exception of picking grapes or arguing with her grandfather, she agreed.

She helped him carry puppy supplies into the main house. The Marcelli hacienda was a huge Spanish-style structure, but the Giovanni home was more a one-story ranch style, with additions sprawling at both ends. Years ago, when Nic's grandfather had been out of town, she'd once spent the night. She still remembered what every room looked like and how many places they'd made love.

They walked through a utility room into a large remodeled kitchen.

"Where are you going to keep him?" she asked.

"There's an old storage room where he can sleep."

"A storage room? Is it heated? Does it have a window? Are you going to keep him locked up all the time?"

Nic shook his head. "You always assume I'm the bad guy. Maybe you'd like to check out Max's prison cell before complaining."

"He's just a baby. He's going to miss his mother and siblings. He'll probably cry all night. You should let him sleep with you."

"Not on a bet. He's little now, but soon enough he'll be full-grown. I'm not sharing my bed with an eighty-pound dog."

Brenna had the brief thought that she could offer to share Nic's bed, but she pushed the image of them together in a tangle of sheets from her mind and prepared herself to be appalled by Max's new home.

She should have known better, she thought, feeling more than a little foolish when she saw the "storage room." Maybe it had once been home to an assortment of boxes and pieces of furniture, but it was currently puppy paradise.

Indoor/outdoor carpeting covered the floor. Two big windows let in sunlight, while an alcove provided a quiet place for a big, cushy bed lined in what looked like sheepskin. Several chew toys and a bowl of water stood by the door. In the opposite corner was a large plastic container about six inches high and lined with newspaper. Sara had told them the puppies had been trained to use a "doggie litter box" in the night.

"I plan to feed him in the utility room. Or is that too much like torture? Maybe I should set a place for him at the table. But without a thumb, he's going to find using silverware a real bitch."

Brenna put the dog carrier in the closet and hung the leash and harness on a hook by the door. "Okay. It's a great room."

"Uh-huh." Nic put Max into the bed. The puppy stirred, then went back to sleep. "That would make me right and you . . ." He paused expectantly.

She rolled her eyes. "Wrong. Okay? You were right and I was wrong."

He walked over and draped an arm around her shoulders. "I love it when you say that."

The second his hand settled on her shoulder, heat exploded in her body. It was like being inside of a flare. One second there was nothing, then an audible rush, followed by a bright light and instant flames. She wanted to inch closer and have him touch her in more places. She wanted to run for cover.

Fortunately she picked a more rational response than either of those choices. She stepped to the window and looked out at the view.

"You have a nice grassy area back here. Max will like that."

"I have something you'll like more. Come see."

For half a second she thought he was talking about something, well, sexual. Her gaze involuntarily dropped to his crotch. The second she realized what she was doing, she jerked her head back and prayed that the heat of her face wouldn't manifest itself in a blush.

"Can you be more specific?" she asked from her place by the window.

"When are you going to learn to trust me?"

"When little wine bottles grow out of grapevines."

"It's not a bad thing, I swear."

"Uh-huh."

He stepped out of Max's room. "Come on. It will be worth it."

She hesitated, then slowly followed.

"Talk to me about barrels," he said when she'd caught up with him. They walked through the kitchen and back outside. "How are you going to get them?"

She needed a beat to make the conversational switch back to business. "I have some on order. I've also been calling around. A few people ordered too many and they're happy to sell the extra."

Good wine barrels cost several hundred dollars each. They had a limited lifespan and constantly needed to be replaced. Empty barrels invited mold and rot, so wine makers preferred to keep them full at all times. The trick was that production rates varied from year to year, so it was a constant guessing game to have the exact number around for any given vintage.

"Where will you be storing them?"

"Not at Marcelli Wines," she said. "I haven't rented space yet. I didn't want to make any commitments until I was sure I had the financial backing."

He'd led them to the winery. Several buildings created a small complex. The center building was the largest, and a recent addition. Brenna stared enviously at the new building, a state-of-the-art storage facility with several temperature-controlled rooms. Special shelves had been designed and installed to allow for easy access to any barrel. A computer kept track of what inventory was where. Everyone in the valley had heard about Nic's new facility. She'd even had a talk with the contractor and had gotten a bid on a smaller version for Marcelli

Wines. Her grandfather had said it was a waste of money.

"I don't suppose you have any extra room in there," she said wistfully.

"Sorry, no. But I do have this."

He crossed to one of the smaller buildings. She followed him inside and nearly fainted.

The structure was the size of a barn, with several walls dividing the space into open rooms and a loft overhead. Empty racks for stacking barrels stood lined up in rows. Large silver ducts cut across the ceiling and down the walls, providing rudimentary temperature control from the industrial-sized heater and air conditioner outside.

Brenna instantly began calculating capacity. If Nic would rent her this space, she would be able to keep all her wines in one location. Plus the Giovanni winery was within easy distance of her day job. She'd imagined having to drive across the valley to three or four different locations.

"How much?" she asked. "I'm willing to sign a two-year lease. That should lower the price."

"You're borrowing money from me only to turn around and pay me rent with it?" He shook his head. "We'll fold the cost into the loan."

Brenna swallowed hard. He was already delaying payments for two years. With the accumulation of interest and the deferred rent, she was racking up some serious charges. If she failed . . .

Don't think about it, she told herself. Success was the only option. When she'd turned Four Sisters into a viable label, Nic couldn't touch her. She only needed two years, three tops.

"Until then I owe my soul to the company store," she murmured.

"So tell me no."

She glanced at the open room. Plain old-fashioned lust overrode common sense. For once the feeling wasn't about Nic's body or what he could do to hers. Instead she wanted this for her wine.

"I don't suppose you've recently replaced your grape-processing equipment."

"As a matter of fact, I have."

Brenna tried not to make moany noises when she saw the collection of conveyor belts and pressing equipment. Yes it was old and would probably break down every fifteen minutes, but it wasn't being used by someone trying to get their own grapes pressed as soon as possible. She could work all night and not have to worry about being in the way.

"I don't know how to thank you," she said when Nic ushered her back outside. "You're doing so much more than I could have hoped for. I may have to give you two cases of wine."

"Maybe I'll have you create a blend for me instead."

"A Marcelli working on Giovanni wines? Wouldn't the heavens crack open?"

"Probably."

She squinted slightly into the sun and saw that it was much lower in the horizon than she would have thought.

"I should be heading back," she said. "I need to make an appearance so no one gets suspicious, and you have to feed Max."

Nic chuckled. "You're convinced I can't take care of him on my own, aren't you?"

"Puppies are a lot of responsibility."

"I think I can handle it."

At this point she figured he could handle anything. "I

had a good time," she told him. "And not just because you're loaning me a lot of money."

"It was fun," he agreed.

Too late she realized this was the wrong conversational tack. Suddenly things seemed really *personal*. She found herself wanting to step closer to him, or maybe have him step closer to her. She wanted to lose herself in his brown eyes, letting past and present blur. Her body was convinced it would be as good as it had been before, and she wasn't sure the rest of her didn't agree.

She wanted . . . a lot of things.

It seemed like a really good time to run.

"Okay, then," she said and stuck out her hand. "Thanks for everything."

He glanced at her hand. The corner of his mouth twitched—as if he knew he got to her. Maybe he did. Maybe he was doing it on purpose. If so, it was a small price to pay for the loan.

"I'm happy to help," he said solemnly as they shook hands.

She did her best to ignore the sensation of his skin brushing hers. For reasons that made absolutely no sense, she remembered a line from *Romeo and Juliet*, which she hadn't read since she was in ninth-grade English about a hundred years ago.

"Palm to palm, as those the palms kiss."

There would be no kissing, she told herself. Not palms or lips or any other body parts.

She pulled free of him and edged toward her car. "So I guess I'll be by tomorrow to pick up the loan papers."

"That would be fine."

"And, um, I'll just make myself at home with the pressing equipment."

"Not a problem. Let me know if you need anything else."

"Sure. I will."

She tripped as she reached her car, but caught herself before she fell. After giving Nic a quick wave, she slipped into the driver's seat and quickly started the engine. It was way past time to get to safety.

New rule number one, she thought as she drove away. Avoid Nic at all costs. The man was dangerous in more ways than she would have thought possible.

That night Nic stretched out on the sofa and picked up the old leather-bound diary he'd been trying to read for the past couple of weeks. It wasn't just the small cramped handwriting that defeated him, it was that the damn thing was written in Italian.

He'd studied the language at college, but his working knowledge was limited to asking the way to the library and a few good swear words. Which meant he spent more time thumbing through an Italian-English dictionary than making any progress in Sophia Giovanni's diary.

He'd come across the journal nearly two years before, when he'd been cleaning out his grandfather's study. The old man had been gone for nearly five years, but Nic hadn't been in any rush to get rid of his things. The house was plenty big, and for the most part Nic simply closed off rooms. But one winter afternoon he'd decided to rid the house of the remnants of what had been his last living relative.

Nic's parents had been killed in a car accident in Spain nearly fifteen years ago, although they'd abandoned their son ages before that. His parents hadn't been interested in much more than upscale travel and finding a really good party—preferably in Europe. Nic had been four when he'd awakened to find them gone and only his grandfather left to raise him.

He'd never seen his parents again. They'd sent occasional notes, had called from time to time. When they died, he'd barely felt a twinge. For him, family had meant him and the old man. His world was nothing like the Marcellis, where relatives lived in the old hacienda, loving and laughing and curing all ills with pasta.

A soft whine interrupted his musings. He glanced up and saw Max enter the living room. The puppy looked small and lost and scared. When he saw Nic, he whined a little louder.

Nic glanced at his watch. "It's getting late. Aren't you tired? I could take you back to your room."

Big brown eyes stared unblinkingly. A shiver rippled through the puppy. Max flopped onto his belly, put his head on his paws and began to whimper.

Nic swung around so his feet were on the hardwood floor and swore softly. "You're lonely," he said. "I bet you miss your mom."

Grumbling to himself, he crossed to Max and picked up the dog, then returned to the sofa. "How do you feel about baseball?" he asked as he settled back on the couch and propped his feet up on the coffee table.

Instead of answering, Max sprawled across his belly and sighed with contentment.

"Not a big fan, huh? We're going to have to change that. I like the Dodgers, myself."

Max swiped at his chin, then closed his eyes. Nic petted the soft fur on his back while he clicked on the TV and found the game already in progress. As he checked out the score, he closed the diary. He would get to translating it later. After all this time, what did the past, or family, matter?

Two days later Maggie cornered Nic when their meeting broke for lunch. He'd been watching her get more and more annoyed all morning and wasn't surprised when she grabbed his suit sleeve and tugged him out of the conference room and into her office.

Fire flashed in her green eyes and she looked furious enough to crack him over the head with a swivel chair.

"You object," he said mildly.

"On several levels. First of all, your consortium is made up entirely of men. There *are* intelligent women in the financial community. I would be happy to supply you with names."

He folded his arms over his chest and leaned against the door frame. "Low blow," he told her. "You know I don't care about anyone's gender. The takeover target is a traditional, old-fashioned man. Not the type to sell to a woman."

She crossed to her desk and sat on the edge. "That's another thing. Why all this sneaking around? Whenever you've wanted to buy another company, you've simply made an offer. This time you're creating a false front."

"My name can't come up in negotiations."

"Why?"

"He'd never sell to me."

"Then maybe you shouldn't be buying."

"Not an option."

Maggie couldn't know, but this had been his plan all along. He'd spent the last seven years of his life working toward this one goal. The Marcelli family had cost him everything. He would get his own back by taking away all that they'd ever worked for.

"It's a clean deal," Nic reminded her. "I've put together an impressive group of buyers. We'll make a fair offer. When it's accepted, they'll bow out and I'll take charge."

"I don't like it."

"I'm not doing anything illegal. Besides, it's going to work."

"I know. Who wouldn't be impressed by the CEO of a major bank, a senior partner in an investment firm, and the owner of the largest wine distributor on the West Coast all coming together? You do business with them, they like you, so they're doing you this one little favor. It stinks."

"Why?"

She straightened and glared at him. "Because you're not telling anyone the full truth. Not me, not them, certainly not Brenna Marcelli, who . . ."

He'd been waiting for Maggie to put the pieces together. From the look on her face, she just had.

"That's why you did it," she breathed, obviously shocked. "I couldn't figure out why you would loan someone that much money without at least taking a piece of the action. You made it a callable note, but even if you took everything back, you'd still come up short. The only way to make money on the deal is to have her succeed. But this isn't about her starting a winery at all, is it?"

He shook his head. "It's about leverage."

"Is she his daughter?"

"Granddaughter."

Maggie sucked in a breath. "You want to buy Marcelli Wines. But you're a Giovanni. You'd never be allowed to even take a walk on the property, let alone bid on it. To get around that, you put together a group of men that would make any prospective seller get down on his knees and give thanks. You have the cash and the credit to get more, so buying the company isn't going to be a money issue. What if the truth comes out and the deal goes south? What if there's a buyer more pleasing to Mr. Marcelli? Not for financial reasons but for personal ones. You can't risk that, right?"

Maggie had been with him long enough to know how his mind worked. She'd nailed it. "Right."

She stared at him. "You have to be the luckiest man alive. Because right in the middle of all this, fate hands you an ace. Lorenzo Marcelli's granddaughter comes to you for a loan, which you give her. Now you have in your possession a one-million-dollar callable note on someone who is very important to him. If he balks, you threaten to ruin his granddaughter. Because it's not about getting the money back, it's about reputation. You can make sure Brenna never works in this town again."

"That about sums it up."

"Why, Nic? What's so important about Marcelli Wines?"

A complex question. He would give her a simple answer that didn't begin to explain the situation. "I want it all. They're all that's left to buy."

"That's complete crap. There are dozens of other wineries in the valley. Why them?"

"We have a long history. Think of it as my way of ending the feud."

"It's personal, then."

"You know I don't let business get personal."

"Then how do you explain this?"

"Next to us, Marcelli is the biggest holding in the valley. They're everything we're not. Small, prestigious, almost a boutique winery. We'll modernize, expand, make a real profit. It's a smart move."

"What aren't you telling me?"

That ten years ago when he'd told his grandfather he was in love with Brenna Marcelli, Emilio had been furious. The old man—his only living relative—had forced him to choose. Brenna or his heritage. Nic had chosen Brenna and she'd chosen her family.

Always one to keep his word, Emilio had thrown Nic out and made sure no winery on the West Coast would hire him. Nic had gone to France, where he'd been forced to work as a day laborer in the vineyards.

After a time Emilio had come looking for him. There'd been no one else to inherit Wild Sea. So Nic and his grandfather shared real estate but they'd never reconciled. Emilio had never forgiven Nic for choosing a Marcelli over family, and Nic . . . he'd learned his lesson. All that mattered was winning.

Maggie walked past him and out into the hall. Once there, she paused and glanced at him over her shoulder. "I don't doubt that your plan will work perfectly. But let me ask you a question. What about Brenna's loan? Say you buy Marcelli Wines. Do you call it in?"

He hadn't thought that far ahead. "I don't know."

"I guess it depends on whether that would be an advantage to you or not."

"Probably."

She turned away. "You're a really smart guy. It's too bad you have to be such a bastard."

6

"*That's terrific*," Brenna said, going for a calm, yes-this-is-a-great-deal-for-both-of-us voice when what she really wanted to do was jump up and down, screaming like a teenage girl at a boy-band concert.

"I'll have a truck there as soon as you're ready. Absolutely." She grinned. "I'll put you down as getting a couple of bottles when the wine is ready. Talk to you soon. Bye."

She hung up the phone and slapped her hands on the kitchen table. "I love it when a plan comes together."

Still grinning and bursting with happiness, she recorded the information in the small Palm Pilot she'd bought the day after Nic had told her she was getting the loan. Three nights of cramming on the impossibly small device had brought her up to speed. She quickly entered the details on the Chardonnay grapes she'd just purchased, then cross-referenced them with the information on the Voignier already on order.

Using the calculator function, she estimated tons per acre, based on what she knew about the vineyards in question. Going against conventional wisdom, and her grandfather's opinion on the subject, she would be taking the first part of the pressing for her cuvée. She wanted her blend to be so spectacular that critics would weep and customers would buy by the case.

"In a perfect world," she murmured, entering the rest of the information, including how much she'd paid, and tapped in a note on the calendar reminding her to check the status of her grapes in a couple of days. She glanced at her watch and saw she needed to get back to the winery before anyone noticed she was gone.

She was just turning off her Palm Pilot when the back door opened and Katie walked into the kitchen.

"There you are," her oldest sister said. "Look what I found lurking by my doorstep this morning."

Brenna laughed when she saw Mia, her youngest sister, burst into the kitchen. As usual the eighteen-year-old was wearing too much makeup, belly-revealing clothes, and a navel ring.

Brenna stood and held open her arms. "Welcome home, Baby Sister."

"Brenna!"

Mia flew toward her. Brenna braced herself for impact, then staggered back anyway when Mia's hearty embrace turned into a collision.

"D.C. was so incredibly cool," Mia said, then kissed Brenna's cheek and sighed. "I met two cute White House aides, and when I told them about my broken engagement, they were thrilled to help heal my broken heart. Ah, summer love. But now I'm here and it's great to be home."

Brenna released her sister and laughed. "When did your heart get broken?"

Mia sniffed. "When I ended my engagement."

Brenna looked at Katie, who shook her head.

"I don't think your heart was even slightly cracked, let alone broken," Katie said.

Mia grinned. "The White House aides didn't have to know that. Besides, I liked all the sympathy."

"You would," Brenna said as she studied her sister's pretty face.

Like Francesca, Mia was a blend of the two sides of their family. Her eyes were light brown, and while her hair was darker than Katie's, it wasn't as dark as Brenna's, even without the blond streaks she painted in every couple of months.

Mia was the shortest of the sisters, as curved as Brenna, but without her tendency to gain in the hips.

"You look good," she told her. "Travel agrees with you."

Mia smiled her thanks, then her expression turned serious. "How are you? Getting over Dr. Dick?"

Katie winced. "Mia, you have the worst mouth."

"Oh, right. Because you never say anything bad. Jeff's a jerk. Screw him."

"Actually I don't believe that's my job anymore," Brenna said with a grin. "Not that it was ever that exciting."

Katie chuckled. Mia offered a high five, then headed for the refrigerator. "Where's Mom and the Grands?"

"In Santa Barbara. It's their monthly lunch-and-shopping day. They're going to be furious when they find out you showed up today."

"They'll get over it," Katie said dryly. "I could barely fit all her luggage in the car. I think she's moving back home."

"Am not." Mia pulled mozzarella and fresh basil from the refrigerator. "I'm staying until school starts. But I had to bring all my clothes."

"Of course," Brenna said. "You might be invited to a cotillion, and then what would you wear?"

Mia stuck out her tongue. "I'm starved. Where are the tomatoes?"

Katie glanced at her watch. "I really need to head back to L.A. I have meetings this afternoon."

Brenna pulled several tomatoes out of the pantry. "You think the brat is going to let you go?"

"She's right," Mia said. "Come on, Katie. You haven't seen me in weeks. Don't you want to hear all about my life in D.C.?"

"I heard plenty on the drive up."

"Okay, but now you can listen to me tell Brenna. The stories are even more interesting the second time around."

Katie slipped off her suit jacket and hung it over a chair. "Why did I even bother trying?" she asked, then picked up the kitchen phone and dialed.

While she explained that she wouldn't be returning to the office, Brenna removed fresh bread from a wooden box on the counter. She pulled several knives out of the drawer and passed one to Mia.

"So what did you learn?" she asked as she began slicing tomatoes.

"Tons. Japanese is a really interesting language. Verbally I do great. I can speak and understand, although my accent sucks. But the written language is so tough. All those characters. I passed and everything, but I felt like a moron the whole time."

Brenna put the tomatoes on a plate, alternating the thick slices with thin pieces of mozzarella Mia passed her way.

"She graduated top in her class," Katie said as she hung up the phone.

"Smart and beautiful," Mia said with a wink. "Kinda makes you want to hate me, huh?"

"I find your modesty to be your real defining characteristic," Brenna told her.

Katie opened the refrigerator and looked in several plastic containers. "Pasta salad, some kind of chicken dish." She sniffed the leftovers. "Chicken Marsala, I think."

"That's it," Brenna said. "We had it a couple of nights ago. I'd rather have pasta salad."

"Me, too," Mia said.

Mia finished with the cheese. After taking a bowl out of a cupboard, she collected olive oil, balsamic vinegar, and garlic to make a dressing. Brenna used kitchen scissors to cut up the basil.

"So what about this guy Francesca's engaged to?" Mia asked. "I was barely gone for what, two months, and she's getting married? And the whole pregnancy thing. I can't believe she got pregnant."

"I think Francesca is still getting used to that one, although she and Sam are both thrilled," Katie said with a laugh.

"So does the thought of a new generation being born take the heat off you or make it worse?" Mia asked.

Katie shook her head. "I've already announced no babies for at least a year."

Brenna laughed. "But they're not listening."

"Figures." Mia wrinkled her nose. "So what's Sam like?"

"I'd say the perfect man for our perfect sister. He also has a great daughter. Kelly. She's twelve." Brenna sprinkled the basil on the plate, then passed it to Mia.

"Since when did you have an interest in kids?" Mia asked.

"I always wanted them. Jeff was the one who said we had to wait. As much as I would like one now, I'm glad we didn't have any. It would have made the divorce a lot more complicated."

Mia poured the dressing over the cheese and tomatoes. While Brenna carried plates and flatware to the table, Katie set out a bowl of pasta salad, the bread, butter, and several kinds of sliced salami and ham. Mia slid the tomatoes and cheese plate into the center, then grabbed cans of soda for them.

"Looks good," she said as she sat down. "I loved the restaurants in D.C., but after so long away, I'm ready for the Grands' cooking."

Brenna sat across from Mia. Katie sat at the head of the table. Mia used a fork to spear tomato and cheese onto her plate, then reached for the bread. "So what else has been happening while I was gone?"

Katie shot Brenna a "let me" look. "Not much. Well, except that it turns out that Brenna slept with Nic Giovanni and got a million-dollar loan from him to start her own winery."

Mia froze in the act of biting into a piece of bread. Her eyes widened and the color fled her cheeks.

"Shut up!"

Katie made an X over her left breast. "Swear on Grandma Tessa's rosary."

Brenna spooned pasta salad onto her plate. "It was ten years ago." She looked up and grinned. "The sex. The loan is recent. As wonderful as I may think I am in bed, I have to admit I doubt I'm worth a million bucks."

"I don't know what to ask about first," Mia admitted when she'd chewed and swallowed her bread. "The sex or the winery. I can't believe you slept with him and didn't tell me. I hate being the youngest. I never find out anything good until years later."

Katie raised her eyebrows. "Obviously she decided the sex was more interesting than the money."

"Apparently," Brenna said. "Don't get your panties all in a bunch. I didn't tell anyone."

"I'll bet he was great," Mia said with a sigh. "Nic always looked like he knew his way around female anatomy."

"We're eating," Katie protested.

"Oh, right. Because you and Zach never pushed aside dinner to do it on the table," Mia grumbled.

Katie blushed slightly, but didn't respond.

"Just like I thought." Mia looked triumphant, then turned her attention back to Brenna. "You're starting your own winery? For real?"

"I don't have a choice," Brenna said. "Grandpa Lorenzo and I are arguing about everything. Working with him is a nightmare. Between how much he hates all my ideas and the recent discovery that we have a long-lost brother—the male heir our grandfather has always wanted—I figure my chances of inheriting are somewhere between 'unlikely' and 'it ain't gonna happen.' "

"But your own label?" Mia sounded both impressed and terrified. "A *million* dollars?"

"Absolutely. I came up with a great business plan, but I couldn't get any of the banks to listen. They wanted to know why Grandpa Lorenzo wasn't backing me himself. I didn't want to go to Mom and Dad for the money because they live here and it would have been awkward for everyone. So I went to Nic and he said yes."

She still had trouble believing it was all coming together for her. "He's loaning me crushing and pressing equipment. It's old—he's replaced his system with a state-of-the-art facility that is to die for. The crusher is—"

Mia held up her hands. "Spare us your ode to the grape crusher. The point is, that's a lot of money."

"I'm already spending it," Brenna admitted, feeling a

little terrified herself. Although it was a good kind of terror—sort of an "I can't believe my dreams are coming true" tension. "I'm buying four acres of perfect Pinot growing land down by the coast. I have barrels on order, grapes coming in. Two years from now, I'll have my first wine out in the world. In three I'll be making it."

Mia looked a little dazed. Still, she raised her soda can. "Wow. To Brenna and her new adventure. May you only ever sleep with men as sexy as Indiana Jones."

"And Nic," Katie added as she raised her glass. "After all, he's real."

"That's right." Mia picked up her fork. "So, Brenna. Ten years after the fact, does our dishy neighbor still get your motor humming?"

Brenna thought about her recent encounters with Nic and how after less than thirty seconds in his company she'd been ready to revisit the delights of the past in a very physical way.

"There seems to be some attraction," she said cautiously.

Mia hooted. "Some? You're lying. I can tell with my eyes closed."

Katie leaned forward. "So it's still there? The chemistry?"

Brenna nodded unhappily. "In a way I wish it weren't. I'm having some self-control issues. It doesn't matter, though. For one thing, I don't know if the feelings are mutual." Although she kind of thought they might be.

"For another," she said, making her voice more firm, "Nic and I now have business together. That changes everything. I can't sleep with the guy who loaned me a million dollars. It would be too weird."

"Good point," Katie said.

"What is wrong with you two?" Mia asked. "You don't

have to actually have sex with him to enjoy the experience. That's what fantasies are for."

Brenna grinned. "Sometimes, Mia, I like the way you think."

Just after sunset Brenna turned into the driveway leading to Wild Sea. Ahead of her, a truck pulled to a stop in front of the old building that housed the equipment Nic had loaned her. Brenna parked off to the side and climbed out into the cool evening.

Her heart beat fast and she was having trouble catching her breath, but for once her reactions weren't about being around Nic. She was really going to do this—she was about to take the first step on the road to making Four Sisters Winery a success.

She hurried toward the building and pulled open the wide double doors. The inside smelled musty, with the scent of previous harvests lingering along with the dust motes. The last rays of sun spilled in from high windows, bathing the ancient equipment in a patina of worn gold. Nic had told her he'd had all the machinery scrubbed out, and she'd already checked that everything functioned, so she could get right to work tonight.

Reverently she ran her hands over the crusher. Excitement flared inside of her. For the rest of her life she would remember this moment, she told herself. Years from now when someone asked where it had all begun, she would recall this night.

"Where do you want them?"

She looked up and saw two men carrying in baskets of grapes. She pointed to the open floor space and helped them arrange the baskets in rows. Twenty minutes later the truck was unloaded and the men left.

Brenna stood alone, surrounded by the best Chardon-nay grapes she'd been able to purchase. The scent of the fruit offered a hint of what could be. Possibilities, she thought, picking a grape and biting into it. Making wine was always about possibilities.

The grape was firm, tart, with a hint of sweetness. She let the juice linger on her tongue, absorbing the layers of flavors, imagining the taste in a year and a half when fermentation and oak and time combined to work magic.

"But first there's plenty of work," she murmured aloud, before loading the crusher.

She worked quickly, then flipped the switch. The machinery began to clink and grind, slowly crushing the grapes before they were moved into the presser. As the mixture traveled, she checked the temperature. If the grapes heated too much, they would begin fermenting as early as the pressing stage, which would be a disaster. But the weather was on her side. The day had been unseasonably cool, with a fog that never lifted. Her grapes were slightly chilled and a little damp.

She hurried to the far end of the presser and made sure the first vat was in place. After pressing, the grapes would settle, allowing sediment to sink to the bottom of the vats. That was as far as she would get tonight.

Tomorrow there would be more grapes. The process would continue through late September and harvesting of the Cabernet.

As the crushed mixture moved through to the presser, the smell of grapes grew stronger. Even with the doors open and a slight breeze drifting into the building, the sweet aroma became almost intoxicating.

She had just loaded another basket of grapes into the crusher when she heard footsteps on the cement floor.

Instantly her heartbeat quickened with anticipation. Brenna found herself smiling even before she turned to see who had joined her.

"How's it going?" Nic asked as he walked over to stand next to her. "I saw the truck pull in."

She motioned to the clanking equipment. "This is it. The beginning."

He grinned. "I thought about bringing champagne to celebrate, but that seemed like overkill."

"Probably, but I appreciate the thought."

"Nervous?" he asked.

"A little. I'm using this batch for my blend. They're premium grapes and I know I'm right to do this, but I can't help feeling apprehensive."

"Bucking convention is never easy."

"Not to mention the fact that I can hear my grandfather's voice in my head as he yells at me for wasting the best grapes."

"Need earplugs?"

She shook her head. "Just a little more time doing my own thing. I'll get over it."

He was standing close enough that she could see the stubble darkening his jaw. Nothing unusual there, she told herself. Many Italian men had heavy beards. Nic was simply one of those guys who had to shave in the evening before going out on a date. But this wasn't a date and he hadn't shaved and she found herself remembering how that stubble had felt against her skin when they'd kissed. The combination of rough beard and soft lips had been unbelievably erotic. Damn. It was hell to have peaked sexually at the age of seventeen.

Nic walked around to the presser. "How much are you doing tonight?"

"All of it. I want it settling before I leave."

He glanced at the baskets of grapes on the floor. "You're going to be here until dawn."

"Probably."

"Did you work today?"

She nodded.

"Are you working tomorrow?"

She smiled. "Sleep is highly overrated."

"I guess." He headed for the door. "I'll let you get to it."

"Sure. Thanks for stopping by."

Brenna watched him go, trying not to feel disappointed. This was her dream, not Nic's. He had his own winery to run—and he got to do it during the day, like a normal person.

She glanced around the big, open room, at the wooden walls, the staircase, and the cement floor. There wasn't a stick of extra furniture. She was going to have to dig up a desk and maybe even a radio, she thought. Otherwise the nights were going to get incredibly long.

Fifteen minutes later she checked the level in the presser. The crushed mixture filled the big container. As she watched the process, she imagined what it would be like eighteen months from now when she would see the finished wine filling bottles. Maybe she would invite her sisters to come by and they could have a party.

A clunking sound made her turn. Nic had returned with a couple of folding chairs and a box.

"You're not going to make it all night without coffee," he said, putting the box on the floor.

She saw a coffeemaker along with cups and a big bottle of water.

"I'll supply the grounds for tonight, but after that, you're on your own."

"Fair enough."

She tried not to read too much into his friendly gesture, or the fact that he'd brought two chairs. If Nic stayed, that would be nice. If he didn't, she would survive.

Nice, she thought as she picked up the coffeepot and carried it over to a wall plug. Nice? Right. Who was she kidding? Being around Nic wasn't nice, it was exciting and terrifying. It was like swimming with electric eels. She never knew where the shock was coming from. A sensible woman would stay out of the water. Funny, she'd been sensible once, when she'd married Jeff. And look where that had gotten her.

Nic cradled his coffee mug. It was sometime close to midnight and he knew he should head back to the house. Still, instead of standing, he stretched out his legs and watched as the first of the juice flowed from the presser into the waiting vat.

Brenna danced anxiously around the equipment as if she could make the process go smoothly by sheer force of will alone. Her brown eyes glowed with an intensity he envied. This mattered to her. She would be involved from the loading of the grapes into the crusher, through bottling the last drop of wine. If she had time, he would bet that she would be out hand cutting every single grape.

Wild Sea was important to him, but he no longer had the same intimate contact with his wine. The company was too big. While there were vineyards he controlled personally, the majority had managers who handled the day-to-day details. He checked on the process, but he didn't have a hand in every bottle they produced.

That's what comes from doubling the size of the company, he reminded himself. If all went according to plan, he would soon be adding Marcelli Wines to his holdings.

"Have you picked a name?" he asked.

Brenna looked up. "Four Sisters Winery."

He shouldn't have been surprised, but he was and wasn't able to stop himself from stiffening.

"What?" Brenna asked.

"Nothing. Great name." He shrugged. "Family was always important to you."

Now it was her turn to look uncomfortable. He waited to see if she would say anything, but she didn't.

"Did I ever tell you how Wild Sea got its name?" he asked.

"No." She shook her head. "No one has ever told me."

"The original plan had been to name the wineries after the family name. Your great-grandfather did that with Marcelli Wines, but Salvatore had a change of heart. In the 1920s there was only one way to come to America and that was by boat. It seems the crossing was very rough and my great-grandfather thought they were all going to die."

Brenna winced in sympathy. "I guess they didn't have great stabilizers back then."

"Probably not. According to my grandfather, Salvatore made a deal with the sea. He promised to name his winery after it if it didn't swallow them up."

Brenna smiled. "I never thought of your great-grandfather as the whimsical type."

"I don't think he was, but fear does strange things to people."

She sat next to him and sighed. "Sometimes I think it would have been very exciting to be alive back when Salvatore and Antonio started the wineries. All the promise of the future was in front of them."

He didn't point out that the first couple of years would have been filled with backbreaking work as the soil was prepared for the vines. No doubt there had been plenty of trips to church to pray for blessings and maybe even a miracle or two.

"I have my great-grandmother's diary," he said. "Sophia started it about five years before she married Salvatore and came here."

"You're kidding!"

He shook his head. "I've been reading it in bits and pieces. She talks about a lot of things, including Salvatore's particularly unromantic proposal. When he returned to Italy, he was considered successful. The match was arranged without anyone asking Sophia her thoughts on the matter. She didn't complain about that in her diary, but she did mention she was eager to see America. At least I think that's what she said. My Italian is lousy. She could have been talking about the laundry instead."

Brenna laughed. "I doubt that. Women usually don't discuss laundry in their diaries. Not that I could tell you for sure. My Italian is worse than awful. Why are you reading her diary?"

"I found it when I was going through my grandfather's things a couple of years ago. I pick it up from time to time and translate a page or two." He shrugged. "It's slow going. Plus I'm a present and future kind of guy, so the past isn't that interesting to me."

Brenna's humor faded. "I'm sorry about your grandfather. I wanted to come to the funeral, but I knew having a Marcelli there would cause a lot of talk and distract from the real purpose."

"Thanks, but it wasn't a big deal."

Brenna raised her eyebrows. "Of course it mattered. He was your family."

"Is that what it's called?"

She winced. "I know he was mad before, when you left,

but after you came back . . ." She swallowed. "Didn't things turn out all right between you? He left you the winery."

"I'm the only living Giovanni left. Who else would inherit?"

She looked away. Nic thought he read guilt in her body language. She was the reason he and his grandfather had become estranged in the first place. He considered pressing the point, but decided it had been too many years and too many miles. What did talking about all that now matter?

Silence filled the large room. Brenna shifted in her seat, then offered a shaky smile. "How's Max?"

Nic sipped his coffee. "Good. He's housebroken, as promised. I'm currently working on his need to chew everything he can find. I also want to get him into an obedience program."

"Because at least one living creature in your life should come when called?"

He grinned. "Exactly."

Brenna stood and checked the presser.

"When do you get more grapes?" he asked.

"Tomorrow."

"You're going to have to put your personal life on hold until harvest is over."

She laughed. "That would only be a problem if I had one, which I don't. I'm only interested in getting the winery up and running. Besides, I have my family around if I ever get lonely."

"You always did, but I was talking about something else. Haven't you bothered replacing your husband with a boy toy?"

"So not my style." She tilted her head. "Actually, I don't know that I have a style when it comes to men, but younger isn't it. If there were a man in my life, I'd want him to be older. Experienced. What about you? Any potential Mrs. Nic's around?"

"Not at the moment."

"So we're both at romantic loose ends."

She opened her mouth, closed it, then slapped her hand against her forehead. "Forget I said that."

He would like to, but it was too late. Tension sparked to life, filling the room and getting his attention. A smart man would change the subject, or leave. Funny how he only wanted to explore the possibilities. Playing with fire?

Not fire, he reminded himself. Fire would imply a need and he didn't have that. Anything he felt was simply mild interest. Blood heated and stirred. Okay, mild sexual interest, but nothing more. He'd learned that lesson a long time ago.

Brenna turned and moved to check the vat. Somehow Nic found himself on his feet, walking toward her. The smell of the grapes surrounded them, reminding him of all those times they'd made love in the Wild Sea Winery. They'd done it in this very room. Did she remember?

She turned and found him standing next to her. Brenna didn't jump, but she looked uneasy. He studied her eyes, searching for an awareness that matched his own. He found caution and desire.

"It's, um, really late," she said. "You don't have to stay and keep me company."

"I know."

He found himself wanting to push her. Or was he pushing them both? Was he testing to see how much attraction still flared between them? Was he trying to punish her?

"Nic."

His name lingered on her lips, forcing his attention to her mouth. He reached for her and lowered his head at the same time. She could have backed away, but she didn't.

Instead she stood still as he kissed her, softly, gently.

It was an innocent kiss. Their mouths remained closed and, except for his hand on her arm, there wasn't any body contact.

He waited for some hint of what had existed before. A flare of heat, a spark of some uncontrolled need. But there wasn't any of that. Kissing Brenna felt—

Hot, thick, and heavy desire slammed into him. He nearly staggered from the impact of the blow. A hunger so deep it gnawed down to his soul grew exponentially until it threatened his ability to maintain control. Aching need exploded, blocking out every thought, rational or not. He wanted with a fury that left him barely standing.

He parted his lips and deepened the kiss. For a nanosecond he thought she wouldn't respond, that he would be forced to take what he needed more than his next breath. But then she moved against him and her mouth opened. His tongue brushed against the sweetness of her lower lip before slipping inside.

She welcomed him with a hot, aggressive kiss that told him she felt it, too. The taste, the fiery wanting building inside of him, the pressure of her body against him, were all familiar. Passion spiraled between them, as it always had— frantic, desperate, amazing. She clung to him, straining to get closer. He rested his hands on her back and explored her from shoulders to hips, relearning her body. At the second he dropped his hands to the curve of her rear, she flexed forward, bringing her belly in contact with his erection.

His first thought was that they could do it on one of the chairs. He would sit down and she would straddle him. They'd done it that way before, and if his memory was anything to go by, it had worked like a charm. His second thought was that if she kept rubbing against him, he was going to lose it right there—something he hadn't done since he was about fourteen. His third thought was what the hell was he thinking?

Brenna pulled back at the exact second he released her. They were both breathing hard. He didn't doubt that the fire flaring in her eyes matched the heat in his own. Her gaze dropped from his mouth to his hard-on, then made a quick return trip. She half turned away and cleared her throat.

Nic found himself both aroused and furious. Not the safest combination. He knew why he wanted her, but he didn't want to think about why he was pissed off. The anger surprised him. He didn't want to know what it meant, so he ignored it.

"I should go," he said abruptly.

Brenna nodded without looking at him.

Nic headed for the door, then hesitated. He wanted to say something, but right now there weren't any words. He swore under his breath and walked into the night.

The hours after midnight had turned cold. He waited for the decrease in temperature to do something to ease his arousal, but blood continued to pulse painfully in time with his rapid heartbeat.

Okay, the passion shouldn't have come as such a surprise. It had always been there between them. As long as he was aware it was a possibility, he could control it. *Would* control it. Tonight he'd been caught off guard, but that wouldn't happen again. The anger was something else, though. He should be over the past. He wouldn't let it control him. Not ever.

As he walked to the house, he reminded himself that he had a plan. That's all this was. Playing with Brenna was a side benefit. He wouldn't let it be more. He wouldn't let her matter. Not again.

7

Why had Nic kissed her?

As the question passed through her brain for the four thousandth time that day, Brenna found herself no closer to an answer. She didn't know why he'd kissed her, and she sure didn't know why she'd let him. It had been stupid. He was her . . . She hesitated. Not business partner, but something. The man had loaned her a lot of money. She shouldn't go around kissing him. Their relationship had to be strictly business. Actually, in the best of all worlds they wouldn't have a relationship at all. They would nod as they passed each other at the grocery store, nothing more.

But last night she'd done a lot more than nod. If she hadn't come to her senses when she did, she probably would have been ripping off her clothes and begging him to take her.

She crossed to the large fermenting vat in the main building of the Marcelli Winery and checked the temperature of the pale liquid inside. After noting the number on her clipboard, she walked to the next vat.

It didn't mean anything, she told herself. It couldn't. She

and Nic were old news. Last night had been . . . a warning, she decided. That was it. He'd kissed her, she kissed him back, and that was certainly something they couldn't do. Not if she was going to stay sane, not to mention safe. As far as she was concerned, Nic Giovanni was still dangerous. Pathetic, but true. She would avoid him and thereby avoid the problem. And should she find herself in his company— because she was spending a lot of time at his place—she would treat him like a co-worker. There would be no intimate conversations, no lip locking of any kind, and certainly no naked body parts pressing and slipping together in a way designed to make both people feel as if their entire—

"Snap out of it," she muttered as she walked to the next vat. "Work. Concentrate on work."

Easier said than done when the yeasty smell filling the room reminded her of making love with Nic. She sighed. Why couldn't he have been a car mechanic? Then they could have made love in an auto shop instead of a winery. She could easily go the rest of her life without smelling motor oil. Wine and wine-making scents, on the other hand, were impossible to avoid.

So why had he kissed her?

Brenna nearly screamed out loud when she realized she'd mentally circled around to the damn kiss again.

"Brenna? Are you in here?"

"Yes, Grandpa."

A distraction, she thought. That was something.

She wove her way through the massive vats toward the door. Grandpa Lorenzo stood just inside the fermentation room. He held several sheets of paper in his hand. She recognized the brightly colored logo in the top corner and felt her need to scream increase. Judging from the look on the elder Marcelli's face, this wasn't going to go well.

"I have the new label designs," he said when she stopped in front of him. "For the Reserve Chardonnay."

She clutched her clipboard to her chest and vowed she would not react, no matter what he said.

Despite his seventy-plus years, her grandfather stood straight and tall, several inches taller than she. He might have gray in his hair, but his dark eyes were still young and expressive. They could flash with anger and disapproval. Gee, they were doing it right now. She braced herself for the complaint.

"What is this?" he asked, holding up the first design. "A horse? A goat? We now have animals on our labels?"

Abstract designs in cool colors swirled together in the center of the label, before bleeding out into the mossy green of the border.

"It's not a goat," she said. "It's not anything. Just colors and shapes together."

He turned the paper around so he could squint at it, then shook his head. "No goats."

He flipped through the six remaining designs. "Too flashy. Too new. Why do we have to change the labels on the Reserve Chardonnay? The old labels work fine. People know what they look like. Simple. Marcelli Wines in big letters. Not this."

He flung the sheet with the picture of the arch over the entrance to the winery at her. Brenna caught it and set the paper on her clipboard.

"We've been using the same label for five years, Grandpa. It's time for a change." She willed herself to be patient. "We discussed this. You agreed."

He dismissed her with a flick of his hand. "I wouldn't agree to such nonsense. I hate them all. Who did you hire to come up with these?"

Brenna's teeth ached from grinding them together. "A firm in Los Angeles. I picked them because they were innovative and excited by the project." She took the rest of the pages from him. "I happen to like what they've done."

He frowned. "Not the goat."

"It wasn't my favorite, but I thought the others were great. Obviously you didn't. I'll phone them and have them send us out some more ideas."

"Tell them to make the new labels like the old ones."

"If you want them exactly the same, what's the point in bothering with a new design?" She sucked in a breath. "I know our loyal customers recognize our label, but they would still find us with a new one, and we might attract new buyers."

"So now you know what our buyers think, eh?"

"I've been reading up on marketing. I've given you several articles. Didn't you look at them?"

He shrugged. "I'm busy. Besides, what do they know? My father started Marcelli Wines from nothing. He took this earth and he created all that you see around us. When they respect that, we'll talk."

Brenna wasn't even sure who "they" were. Before she could ask, her grandfather sighed heavily and tossed the labels on the floor.

"You need to respect the old ways."

Hardly a news flash, she thought as she gauged the distance to the door and wondered if running screaming into the afternoon would make her feel better. It wasn't quite as good as running screaming into the night, but a woman had to make the best of what was available.

"I respect the old ways," she said, striving for calm. "I'm also interested in what the new ways have to offer."

He shook his head in obvious disgust. "Your brother, he would listen."

Brenna was so stunned, she nearly dropped the clipboard. "What? My brother? The guy you've never even *met?* How on earth do you know what he would do or not do? That is such an unfair thing to say to me. If Joe has any interest at all in this winery, it's only for the money."

She would know. When she and Francesca had gone to meet Joe Larson, their long-lost brother, he'd shown little or no interest in the Marcelli family until he'd heard there was a winery worth about forty million dollars.

Lorenzo drew his thick eyebrows together. "The wine is in his blood."

"I don't think so. You can't be serious about leaving everything to him."

Her grandfather shrugged. "I do what I have to do."

He turned and left.

Brenna sank onto the floor and rested her head on her knees. "This is *not* happening," she murmured. Her eyes burned, her chest hurt. There was no way her grandfather could really leave the winery to someone he'd never met. Blood or no blood. And doing it just because Joe was a *guy?*

"This sucks," she whispered.

It more than sucked. It hurt down to her bones. Of course she'd known that having a brother changed things, but she'd hoped she'd been wrong.

The designs for the labels lay where Grandpa Lorenzo had tossed them. Apparently her disagreements with him over the labels were the least of her problems. Things had gotten so difficult that she and her grandfather couldn't go a day without arguing about something. Half the time she expected him to fire her. Except she was family and he couldn't.

But he didn't have to keep her in charge. If he hated everything she was trying to do, why not hire someone who would hang on his every word and do things exactly as he wanted? He could also change his will, if he hadn't already.

"Just a reminder of why starting my own label was the right thing to do," she told herself as she scrambled to her feet. "It doesn't matter what he does. I'll have my own winery to worry about."

But the words didn't offer as much comfort as she would have liked. Nothing in her world was the way she thought it would be. Not her past and certainly not her future.

"Final figures," Nic said when he entered Maggie's office and slapped the folder on her desk. "Read them in awe."

She raised her eyebrows, then flipped through the pages. "As long as you're not letting success go to your head."

"Would I do that?"

"Answering that the way I want to would be unprofessional." She closed the folder. "I'll work up a projection based on these numbers. You'll have it in the morning."

"Great." He sat down in the chair in front of her desk. "What about the numbers for Marcelli Wines?"

She flipped through a stack of papers by her computer and handed him several sheets. He read the estimations for gross sales, broken down by region.

"That's as good as we can do without looking at their books," Maggie told him. "I had the sales guys nosing around, but they can only find out so much."

"This is good," he said.

The sales projections were even better than he'd thought. There was plenty of profit to be had. Once he'd modernized everything and streamlined operations he would—

He glanced up and saw Maggie watching him. "What?"
She shrugged.

"You still disapprove of what I'm doing," he said.

"That's too strong a word. I don't like it, but liking it isn't part of my job. I keep thinking about that loan to Brenna Marcelli. What are you going to do with her? Destroy her?"

"That's a little melodramatic, don't you think?"

Maggie shook her head. "Gee, Nic, you've loaned her a million dollars and given her the chance to start her own winery. She's moving ahead with the belief that all her dreams are about to come true. Yet at any moment you could call the loan and pull the rug out from under her. I'm guessing when that happens she's going to be a little broken up. What would you call it, if not destroyed?"

"Interesting question."

"Do you have an answer?"

"Not yet."

The callable note gave him options. Now that he'd seen Brenna in action, he knew that given time, she could make a go of Four Sisters Winery. Maybe he would sit back and collect interest like one of the good guys. Maybe not. The only thing he knew for sure was that seducing her hadn't been part of his plan, but since that damn kiss he hadn't been able to think of anything else. Maybe it was time for a different plan.

"You're looking very predatory," Maggie said. "I don't want to know what you're thinking."

He grinned. "You're right."

Her gaze narrowed. "Maybe I'll go meet Brenna Marcelli and see for myself what she's like. If I hate her, I won't feel so guilty about being a part of all this."

"You haven't done anything but your job. You have no guilt in this."

"Easy for you to say."

He knew he couldn't talk Maggie out of her feelings. She'd always been a soft touch. "Suit yourself."

"Aren't you going to warn me not to say anything about the secret plot to purchase her family's winery?"

Nic stood. "No. You work for me. You'd never be indiscreet. That would mean breaking the rules. Something you don't do."

"You do it all the time."

"I know. That's why I always win."

"In the past you've won without breaking the rules. Something tells me that this time is different. Be careful, Nic."

"Always," he promised as they walked to the door.

They both knew he was lying, but Maggie wouldn't say anything. Had Brenna been privy to the conversation, she would have called him on it in a heartbeat. Of course if she knew about his plans for Marcelli Wines, she would have his head mounted on the fence dividing their property.

Not something he wanted to think about. He would be fine just as long as Brenna didn't find out the truth until it was too late to stop him.

It had been a good night's work, Brenna thought sometime after midnight as she watched the last of the grapes move from the crusher to the presser. Her second load of Chardonnay grapes had arrived on time. The quality had been everything she'd hoped for—each bunch had been ripe and bursting with flavor and juice. She'd managed to put her latest fight with her grandfather behind her. She refused to think about him or her brother showing up and claiming everything. Even better, she was only thinking of

Nic every forty-eight seconds, a marked improvement from earlier in the week. In a day or two she might work up to ten whole Nic-free minutes at a time.

It was that damn kiss, she acknowledged. He was too sexy by half. If that hadn't happened, she might have been able to convince herself that whatever she remembered from the past was simply time rewriting history. She could have convinced herself that no one was that good. Unfortunately reality had been better than her memories. She'd gone from zero to take-me-now in less than five seconds. Just her luck—she was hotter than a Ferrari.

"So I'll get over it," she told herself, stepping back from the presser.

She would have to. She and Nic were all about the past and that was a place neither of them was likely to want to go. Her life was here in the present.

She crossed to the open doors and breathed in the cool air. She could hear crickets and other night creatures. The sky was clear and it seemed as if she could almost reach up and grab a star or two. Would it grant her a wish if she promised to set it free? What would she wish for?

Brenna returned to her equipment. Not success, that was too easy. Not love. She might be alone right now, but she wasn't lonely. Peace, she thought. Or maybe contentment.

Before she could decide, she heard a fast, clicking sound, followed by a yip and a slide. She glanced at the open door and saw Max slipping around the corner before loping into the big room. He looked around, saw her, and barked with delight.

Brenna barely had time to brace herself for the fact that where Max was, Nic was soon to follow, when the puppy plowed into her. She laughed and bent down to gather him into her arms. He wiggled and licked at her face, his whole body vibrating as his tail wagged so hard it went in circles.

"Hey, good-looking," she said, holding the puppy close. "How are you?"

"Not bad."

She had to swallow before looking up to watch Nic enter. She hadn't seen him in a few days, and she hated that she'd actually missed him. He wore his usual uniform of jeans and T-shirt, which managed to emphasize his broad shoulders and long legs. Every cell in her body went on alert, while a small biplane flew through her brain, dragging a banner behind that read "I want some more of that."

Honest to Pete, she really had to get a grip.

"Actually I wasn't talking to you," she said. "Max and I were having a moment."

"That dog has quite the life."

She set the puppy on the ground. When Max went off to investigate exciting smells, Brenna tried to keep her attention off of Nic's mouth. Was it her imagination or could she actually see the sparks arcing between them?

"So how's it going?" he asked, moving closer to the presser.

"Good." She couldn't help grinning. "Okay, it's going great."

"Modest as ever."

She nodded.

"This is the fourth night you've worked late. Have you been getting any sleep at all?"

He'd noticed how many nights she'd been here? She told herself not to read anything into the comment. Nor would she allow herself to think about how he'd circled around the equipment to stand fairly close to her. The sparks continued to arc, but she was determined to ignore them, too. If Nic was going to pretend nothing had happened, she could pretend five times better.

"I'm getting by on an hour or two. This is my last batch of Chardonnay. Then I get a break until the Pinot comes in, then the Cabernet."

Max trotted by, heading for a dark and puppy-appealing corner. "He's up late," she said.

"I was doing some paperwork. I like to walk him before I head up to bed."

Ah, the *b* word. It took her a second to clear her brain of the erotic images that had instantly popped up. She and Nic had mostly made love in nontraditional places, but they'd done it in bed just enough for her memory to provide the appropriate erotic slide show.

"You thought I'd be a lousy dog owner," he said. "You were wrong."

"I never thought that."

"Liar."

She couldn't help chuckling. "Okay, maybe I was a little concerned that you weren't ready for the responsibility."

"Is this where I remind you I run Wild Sea?"

"Business and puppies are very different."

"Tell me about it. The business has never chewed my shoes."

He was smiling at her. Despite the attraction and the yet-to-be-discussed kiss, she felt some of her tension ease. Why was it that being around Nic always felt so right?

On second thought, she didn't want an answer to that.

He jerked his head toward the vat. The first of the juice spilled into the big stainless-steel container. "May I?"

She nodded. He collected a plastic cup from the bag she'd left on the floor and held it under the stream. To the untrained palate, the liquid would be little more than intense grape juice, but Nic would taste the subtleties and the possibilities.

He sipped, frowned, and sipped again. Then he looked at her and swore. "What did you do?"

"The grapes are from three different vineyards. Instead of getting one delivery from each location, I arranged for five smaller deliveries. I've coordinated so I get grapes from all three locations on the same day. It cost a little more, but I've been able to blend from the crushing stage instead of later in the process. The different grapes are already working on each other. Isn't it the best?"

He took another sip. "How did you pick the grapes?"

She explained how she'd spent a lot of the past couple of months driving around the valley, figuring out what vineyards got what kind of sun.

"I might have snuck on and tasted a grape or two over the past month," she admitted. "Then I placed my order. My quantities were small enough that even people who don't usually sell were willing to give me a ton or two. Including one of your foremen."

His dark eyes narrowed. "You're using Wild Sea grapes?"

"Just a few of your best."

"Well, hell."

She tried not to feel smug, but it was difficult. "You have all the raw material, Nic. You need to use it better."

"Thanks. Want a job?"

"I already have one, but if things change, I'll let you know."

She knew he wasn't seriously offering her employment, but it was nice to know she'd impressed him.

"You think you're hot shit," he complained. "This is like the time you lectured me on the quality of the oak we were using for our wines. You were what, sixteen?"

"Probably. You can't go cheap if you're going to ferment in wood. It would be better to go straight to stainless."

He finished the juice and tossed the cup in the trash. "You'll be happy to know I listened. Thanks to you I made a lot of changes here at Wild Sea."

She appreciated knowing that. "If only I could say the same thing about my grandfather."

Nic crossed to one of the chairs and pulled it out. Brenna sat down and he settled across from her.

"Is Lorenzo still making things difficult?"

"Difficult being an understatement. We're arguing about everything. First he complains that the labels are too old-fashioned. We need something new. I happen to agree with him—in fact, I've been bugging him about it for a while. So I get new labels designed. Suddenly he says there's nothing wrong with the old labels, we shouldn't change anything, yada, yada."

"Did he forget? Is this an age thing?"

"No. It's a make-Brenna-crazy thing. He's always been a curmudgeon, but it's worse than it's ever been. He's on my case about everything. Now he's talking about my brother. 'Joe would listen to me about the old ways,' " she said, lowering her voice to sound more like Lorenzo's. "I always knew having a brother show up didn't help my case, but I guess . . ."

She swallowed and looked at him. "Joe inheriting is more real to me now. I don't like it."

Nic's expression tightened. "At least if he inherits, it will stay in the family. It beats Lorenzo selling."

"Not by much. I can't believe he would leave everything to a virtual stranger. That would kill me. I would almost rather he sold." She tried to smile. "I guess you would, too.

That way I would inherit cash instead of a piece of the winery and I could pay you off."

"I'm not worried about that."

Must be nice not to worry about a million dollars, she thought wistfully. She suddenly had a thought.

"You could afford to buy Marcelli."

Nic raised his eyebrows. "Was that an invitation?"

"No. My grandfather would never sell to you." She shook her head. "Crazy. I know you wouldn't try to buy Marcelli, but who else would? Never mind. I don't want to think about it. Everything is so complicated."

"Hang tough," Nic told her. "It will get better. You've always been important to your grandfather. He'll come around."

Brenna stiffened and leaned back in her chair, instantly wary. Her family wasn't exactly a safe topic of conversation.

Nic held up his hands in a gesture of surrender. "I meant that in a good way. You two used to argue, but in a lot of ways you're the granddaughter closest to him."

She nodded. "I guess I still am. I know some of the problem is that I moved away." She hesitated, not wanting to start down that path, either. For people who hadn't seen each other in years, she and Nic sure had a lot of things they couldn't talk about.

"Was your grandfather angry about the divorce?"

Brenna didn't know what to say. Talking about her marriage to Jeff—even the dissolution of the marriage—felt very twisted.

Nic shrugged. "You don't have to answer that if you don't want to."

"I don't mind." She didn't. Not exactly. "My grandfather was pretty cool about the whole thing. The whole family was. Everyone claimed to adore Jeff right up until he asked for a divorce, then suddenly they all claimed to have hated him from the beginning. I know they were rewriting history to make me feel better, but I didn't care. Besides, it worked."

"A good Italian family like yours. I'm surprised no one offered to take him out."

She laughed. "I never thought of that. You're right. They should have."

The night seemed very quiet now. Brenna wasn't sure why Nic had shown up tonight or why they were talking about her divorce, but she didn't want to break the spell by asking. Sitting here like this felt really good. Awareness kept her blood zipping through her body in a way that made her feel alive and breathless. While a foolish part of her wanted a repeat of the kiss they'd shared before, the sensible side was grateful for something as uncomplicated as conversation.

"How do you do feel about your ex now?" he asked.

She shifted in her chair, slightly less grateful for uncomplicated conversation. He wanted to talk about Jeff? What did that mean?

"I'm not sure how to answer the question," she admitted.

"Are you still mad?"

"No. I was angry and bitter for a while, but that got old. I still resent that I worked my butt off at jobs I hated to put him through medical school. I paid the bills for him to become a doctor and then he left. It's never fun being a cliché."

Nic stared at her. Something flickered in his dark eyes, but she didn't know what he was thinking.

"He's not rich?"

The question hit her like a slap. Logically she knew she

shouldn't have been surprised, but she was. After all this time did he really think she'd done what she'd done for money?

"Jeff was dirt poor. I never married him for his fortune."

She waited for Nic to ask why she had married him, but he didn't.

"Was there someone else?" he asked instead.

"For him, yes. In fact he's marrying her as soon as our divorce is final."

"Are you okay with that?'

"I'm no longer fantasizing about him contracting a disease that makes his privates fall off, which I think makes me a broad-minded and mature individual. It's not exactly the same as wishing him well. Most of the time I don't think about him. I regret marrying him, but I can't change the past."

"Divorce can be a bitch."

Not the reaction she'd been hoping for. She'd thought maybe Nic would express his feelings about the past . . . namely theirs. Eventually they were going to have to talk about what happened. Just not tonight. She was dealing with too much already.

"You never married," she said, then realized how he could take the question and hoped he wouldn't.

Nic raised his eyebrows. "You're right. I didn't."

She wanted to explain that she hadn't meant to imply anything by her question. It wasn't as if his decision not to marry had anything to do with her. Although now that they were talking about the subject, she really wanted to know why he hadn't picked up a wife somewhere along the way. It couldn't have been due to lack of female interest.

But she wasn't brave enough to ask and he didn't offer. Instead he sat there looking both relaxed and dangerous, which was quite the trick.

The tension returned. She fought against the urge to throw herself at him, and he . . . well, she didn't know what he was thinking.

Obviously not about their kiss, she realized when he looked at his watch and said he had to be getting back.

"Max needs his beauty sleep," he told her as he stood.

She rose and looked around for the puppy. Max had curled up on her jacket in the corner. Nic walked over and scooped him up. Max barely stirred.

"Good luck with that," Nic said, jerking his head toward the vat. "Don't forget you promised me a couple of cases."

"I believe it was just one case, but I'll see what I can do."

"Night."

She watched as he headed for the door.

Nic was that irresistible combination of dangerous and sexy. The sleeping puppy in his arms only added to his charms. Sexual predator and nice guy. Women had sold their souls for a whole lot less.

Brenna liked to think that she was smart enough to have learned from her past mistakes. Falling for Nic all those years ago had only complicated her life. Falling for him now would mean she hadn't learned anything. The problems they'd had before still existed, along with a couple dozen more. Nope, the best course of action was a business-only relationship. Nothing personal, nothing intimate. Nothing stupid.

Unfortunately, where Nic was concerned, she'd never once done the right thing.

8

Brenna was so tired, her eyelashes hurt. But it had been worth it, she reminded herself as she opened the back door and stepped into the hacienda.

Three days ago she'd been offered some premium Chardonnay grapes that were normally never available for sale. It had meant working the better part of a week from dusk until dawn, which also meant little or no sleep for her. But now that the work was done, she could walk into the fermenting room and see all the gallons of wine she was going to produce. Four Sisters Winery would open with a bang.

The downside was she only had a couple of days until the Pinot grapes were ready, so if she wanted to sleep, this was her day. She'd managed to duck out of the Marcelli Wines office early. Now all that lay between her and fifteen blissful hours in her bed was the distance of the house.

She crossed the kitchen, then came to a stop when she heard voices in the living room. She recognized the Grands, her mother, and her sisters. There was also a less familiar voice belonging to Francesca's soon-to-be stepdaughter.

Brenna hesitated. While she adored Kelly, she really, really needed to get some sleep.

There was a low murmur of voices followed by loud laughter.

"Hell," Brenna muttered, walking toward the sounds. She was a sucker for her family.

"Hi, all," she said as she entered the living room.

Everyone looked up and called out a greeting.

The women were sewing, beading lace for Katie's and Francesca's wedding gowns. It was slow, meticulous work that made Brenna's hands cramp.

"I know you want to help," Katie said holding up a lace rose.

"I would love to except I'm really busy right now. You know, with extra work."

She emphasized the last two words, hoping her sister would get it. Katie wasn't slow-witted, so she must have chosen to ignore the hint. Instead of giving Brenna a break, she simply batted her eyes and said, "Come bond. You know you want to."

"Yes, stay, Brenna," twelve-year-old Kelly said.

Brenna could have blown off her sister, but she had a harder time refusing Kelly. Grumbling under her breath that this was her own fault for not slipping up the stairs when she had the chance, she sighed heavily and crossed to the large coffee table. She chose a piece of lace from the pile there, and collected a bag of beads. Katie passed over needles, and Kelly shifted to make room for her on the sofa.

"What are we talking about?" Brenna asked the girl.

"Your mom and the Grands are discussing menus, but Katie and Francesca aren't saying what they want, which is making everybody else crazy. Not me. I don't care, but I think Grandma Tessa is getting a twitch."

Brenna glanced at her grandmother, who was deep in conversation with Francesca. "Why is the menu changing?"

Kelly grinned and her green eyes sparkled with humor. "I don't know. I mean, it's just, like, food, right?"

Brenna pulled one of her curls. "You are so not, like, Italian."

Kelly giggled.

"So are you excited about school starting in a few weeks?"

Kelly rolled her eyes. "I'm so totally not. Although my dad said I can have a lot of new clothes because I finally convinced him that styles are completely different here on the West Coast. Francesca helped. She told him it wouldn't be good for my self-esteem to look like a geek."

Brenna laughed. "Do we still use the word *geek?*"

"You guys do, because you're, well, old."

"Gee, thanks, brat."

Kelly grinned. "I didn't mean that in a bad way."

"Of course not."

"Really, Brenna. It's just you guys haven't been in school for a while. You can't know what's cool."

"That I'll accept. You're going to have to be the one to keep us informed of the coolness factor."

Kelly nodded. "I can do that. Francesca's wedding dress is really beautiful. Have you seen the picture?"

"No." She held out her hand. "Give it up, Sis."

Francesca passed over a photo torn out of a bride's magazine. Brenna studied the elegant gown and knew that her twin would look stunning.

"I tried to get her to wear my dress," Mia said. She shifted and tucked her legs under her. "But she said it was too fitted at the waist."

"I said we could take it out," Katie added. "But I'm afraid that would mess up the lines."

Francesca shook her head. "Even if we could do it, I don't want to wear Mia's dress. It's not me."

Mia raised her eyebrows. "Is that a statement about my taste? Because if it is, I'm going to remind you that I'm only eighteen and I'm still in college, so by Kelly's standards, I'm the queen of cool."

"The only thing you're the queen of is annoying," Brenna said mildly.

Mia stuck out her tongue.

"Oh, that's mature," Katie said, rolling her eyes.

Francesca smiled. "Mia, your dress is beautiful, but it wouldn't look nearly as nice on me as it did on you."

Kelly bounced on the sofa. "Mia, I never saw your dress. Do you still have it?"

"Sure."

Mia started to put down her lace, but Katie, Brenna, and Francesca all glared at her.

"Don't even think about it," Francesca warned.

Mia grinned at Kelly. "We'll sneak upstairs later, when the wardens are sleeping."

Kelly nodded happily.

"What about the menu?" Grandma Tessa asked. "We have to decide on what we're eating."

"What about burgers?" Brenna offered.

Even her mother frowned at her for that one.

Brenna held up one hand. "Don't hurt me. I was just kidding. Are you serious about changing the menu just because it's going to be a double wedding?"

Her mother frowned. "This isn't for the wedding, dear. This is for the engagement party."

Brenna glanced at her two engaged sisters. "You're

having an engagement party? When was this decided?"

"A couple of nights ago," Katie said. "You were otherwise occupied."

"Do people still do that kind of thing?"

"We do," Grandma Tessa said firmly.

"It was Katie's idea," Francesca said.

Katie sighed. "You are so lying. It was your idea."

"They were both wantin' a special celebration," Grammy M said. "I think it's a fine idea."

"Will you be bringing Grandpa Gabriel?" Kelly asked.

Grammy M shrugged as if it didn't much matter, but there was a smile tugging at the corners of her mouth. "Maybe."

Brenna laughed. Her seventy-something grandmother had found romance with Francesca's fiancé's grandfather. The two seniors were forever sneaking out to dinner together and had even planned a cruise in the fall. Grandma Tessa claimed to be appalled that they would share a room without the benefit of a priest blessing the union, but Grammy M simply said that she was too old for sex outside of marriage to be considered a sin. Brenna was thrilled to know that she came from a gene pool that was still interested in the wild thing far into the December years.

"We want something fairly casual," Katie said. "Maybe a buffet outside with white lights strung all over. Just family and good friends."

"Sounds nice," Brenna said.

She looked at her sister as she spoke and saw Katie was watching her carefully. She turned her attention to Francesca. Her twin's expression matched Katie's. She could tell they were once again caught up in "poor Brenna not having a relationship."

"I'm fine," she said.

"Of course you are," Grammy M said fondly. "Why would you be otherwise?"

Brenna shook her head. How could she convince her sisters that she was completely happy for them? She couldn't be more happy. As for wanting a relationship for herself . . . right now her schedule didn't allow for a lot of boy-girl time. She was too busy trying to make her dreams come true. Besides, as long as Nic showed up every couple of days and made her toes curls, she didn't actually need the real thing. Fantasizing about him was about twenty times better than any reality with a guy she was likely to meet.

Nope, right now single felt exactly right. Well, except for missing sex.

Three days later Brenna parked in her usual spot at Wild Sea and headed in to check on her wines. Amazingly enough, it was still daylight. Her nonnocturnal visit was due to yet another argument with her grandfather, this one about what wines they were serving at a tasting dinner for the Marcelli distributors in town for a promotional weekend. After asking her opinion, her grandfather had detailed what he thought was wrong with every one of her choices. Rather than throw a temper tantrum—which had been her first choice—she'd made a graceful exit and ended up here.

She crossed to what she'd begun to think of as "her building" and stepped inside.

Instantly the scent of fermentation assaulted her. Brenna inhaled deeply, savoring the changes from yesterday, knowing tomorrow would be different, too. The subtle alterations told her things were going well.

"Knock, knock. Brenna?"

Brenna turned and saw a woman entering the building. Her guest was tall, with thick auburn hair and a model-perfect face. Brenna didn't know if she should be more bitter about that or the woman's slender body. Just being in the same room with her made her feel short and lumpy.

She tried reminding herself that while she couldn't be considered tall, except by the vertically challenged like Mia, she was of average height. If she wanted to be less lumpy, she would have to stop eating the Grands' cooking.

"Have we met?" Brenna asked as the woman approached.

The woman smiled and held out her hand. "We haven't been introduced, but I know who you are. I'm Maggie Moore, the chief financial officer for Wild Sea. I work for Nic."

"Ah," Brenna said, fighting a sudden blast of jealousy. How like Nic to hire a beautiful woman in a job traditionally held by men.

"If you're looking for him, he's not here," she said.

Maggie smiled. "Actually I was looking for you. I wanted to meet the infamous Brenna Marcelli."

"I'm infamous?" Brenna asked. "Gee, no one sent me a memo."

"I'm not sure the title extends past my office. I handle the finances for Wild Sea."

"I sort of guessed that by your job description."

"I know about the loan."

Now Brenna was really confused. "That was a private loan. I didn't borrow the money from the corporation."

"Oh, I know. But even Nic doesn't happen to have a million dollars in his checking account. Once he decided how he wanted to structure the deal, he had me draw up the paperwork."

Brenna wasn't sure why she needed to know this. "Is there a problem?"

"Not at all." Maggie's smile was friendly. "Like I said, I just wanted to get to know you."

Brenna wondered what Nic might have told this woman about her. Somehow she couldn't see him spilling his guts about the past, but then, she'd been wrong before. Was Maggie more than just an employee?

As soon as she asked the question, she realized it wasn't likely. For one thing, Nic wouldn't have kissed her the way he had if he'd been involved with someone else. For another, a quick glance at Maggie's left hand told her that the woman was married.

"How long have you worked at Wild Sea?" Brenna asked.

"Almost nine years." Maggie grinned. "It's kind of sad because even though I'm around all this wonderful wine, I don't really drink it."

Brenna chuckled. "Does Nic know?"

"Yes, and it really bugs him. He tried to teach me about different wines once, but I kept nodding off during his explanations." She pointed at one of the vats. "Which explains why I have to ask what you're doing in there."

"Making Chardonnay," Brenna said. "I'm fermenting a portion in oak and the rest in stainless steel. The stainless allows for easier temperature control. Barrel fermenting is more expensive, but it allows me to—"

She broke off and shrugged. "Sorry. I get a little carried away."

"Don't apologize. I'm impressed by your enthusiasm."

"This is important to me. I've wanted the chance to run things my way, and now I finally have it. I plan to take all the credit, but I'm also putting myself on the line to take all of the blame if things go wrong."

"Could they?" Maggie asked.

"Sure. Wine making is as much art as it is science. I pay attention to both."

"Doesn't everyone?" Maggie asked.

"Most do. But once a winery gets big, it's difficult to be intimately involved in every step. That isn't going to happen here."

Brenna stopped again and sighed. "I did it again."

Maggie shook her head. "I can see your determination in your eyes. The only thing I've ever felt so passionately about is my daughter." She laughed. "That sounds horrible. I love my husband completely. He's wonderful, but it's not the same as loving my child. Does that make sense?"

"Sure."

Maggie glanced at her watch. "Speaking of Annie, I have to head home so I can spend the evening with her. Daddy has to work late, so it's girls' night at home." She held out her hand. "It was great to meet you, Brenna."

"Likewise," Brenna said, shaking hands.

She watched Maggie leave. What on earth had that been about? If she didn't know better, she would say that Nic's CFO had been checking her out. But why? He'd already given her the loan. Maggie couldn't stop what had already happened.

"Not that it matters," she told herself. But it was curious.

Was it wrong to love a grape? Brenna hoped not, because she had a serious case of hero worship for her Pinots.

She stood just off a gravel road, on the edge of her perfectly wonderful four acres. To the west stretched the Pacific Ocean for as far as the eye could see. To the east were the foothills, and tucked in between was paradise.

She knew there were those who thought that land this

incredible would be wasted on something like grapes when dozens of million-dollar homes could have been built here, but Brenna considered those kind of people not only short-sighted but lacking a soul.

She crouched down by a mature vine and studied the well-shaped clusters.

Did it get any better than this? The grapes had ripened evenly. They were plump and rich in color. She could smell the promise of their flavor, and when she picked a single grape and bit into it, she actually moaned. Another day, maybe two, and then they would be ready to pick. She was going to kick butt with this harvest.

As she stood, she heard something in the distance. She recognized the rumble of a motorcycle, but even as her body went on alert and her thighs heated, she told herself that hundreds of people rode motorcycles on this narrow coastal road and that she was a fool if she allowed herself to think it might be Nic. It was the middle of harvest, for heaven's sake. The man had better things to do than ride up like some leather-clad sex god just to jump-start her motor.

Unfortunately the thought of him got her heart pounding the way it did those rare afternoons she dragged her ample backside to aerobics class. Did that mean being around him constituted an actual workout? Could she start the next exercise craze? The Nic Giovanni workout plan? Think about sex with Nic for twenty minutes a day and lose ten pounds a month? If only. All she got from thinking about Nic was unbearably horny.

She told herself to stop staring at the road and pay attention to the grapes she'd come to admire, but she couldn't make herself turn away until she'd actually watched the non-Nic person ride by. Maybe she would even wave.

The motorcycle rounded the bend and she was able to

see the driver. The helmet did nothing to disguise the rider's familiar features. Okay, so it was Nic. That didn't mean he was going to stop . . . did it?

Before she could decide, he pulled up behind her car and turned off the engine. The sound of the waves was audible again, along with the call of the seagulls. Brenna told herself that she should take this opportunity to be one with nature. Instead she watched as he took off his helmet. Sunlight brought out the brown highlights in his dark hair and emphasized his tanned arms. He looked as if he'd walked out of a movie poster for a 1950s bad-boy movie. White T-shirt, black jeans, motorcycle boots. Where was a poodle skirt when you needed one?

"I had a feeling you'd be here," he said as he set his helmet on the seat and started toward her. "Escrow closed today and I knew you couldn't resist gloating over your purchase."

He'd come looking for her? Wow.

"I'll admit to having a moment or two with my grapes," she said.

"How are they?"

She waved out a hand. "Take a look. You'll kick yourself for thinking the lot was too small to bother with."

He raised his eyebrows, then turned his attention to the tidy rows of grapevines. He walked in a couple of paces, then crouched to examine the grapes.

It was close to sunset. Rather than stare at Nic, or his spectacular behind, she turned her attention to the western horizon, where the sun sank toward the edge of the sea. Already the heat of the day had faded from this patch of land.

"Not bad," Nic admitted when he walked over to stand next to her. "They're nearly ripe."

"You forgot perfect. Did you see the color? How plump they are?"

"You got lucky. I don't understand why they sold this land to you for pennies when they could have gotten millions from a developer."

Brenna hadn't paid pennies; buying these four acres had taken a chunk of her loan, but she also knew that she'd gotten an amazing deal.

"It's about the wine. They didn't want this land to become another exclusive development community. I had to promise to only grow grapes on this land for at least ten years."

He stared at her. "You're kidding. You had to promise?"

She nodded.

"Is it in writing."

"No, and it doesn't have to be. I'll keep my word. They understood what I was trying to do."

"They're idiots."

"No, they're committed."

"If they're not, they should be."

Brenna tried not to smile, but she couldn't help grinning. "You're such a businessman. Pragmatic, unfeeling, only interested in the bottom line."

"Yeah, right. And you're the wine-making genius."

"Thank you."

"I was being sarcastic."

"I prefer to pretend you were serious and offering me a compliment."

"Figures."

Nic watched the breeze tug at Brenna's hair. The shoulder-length style was different from the waist-length hair she'd had as a teenager. While he liked them both, the longer hair was more erotic. There had been plenty of times when he'd felt the silky ends trailing down his belly as she'd—

He consciously slammed the door to that particular memory. Instead he searched for a distraction. When he found it, he had a hard time keeping his face straight as he anticipated the explosion.

"Too bad the rows are so close together," he said casually. "If they were farther apart, you wouldn't have to pick the grapes by hand."

As he expected, Brenna turned on him with all the intensity of a mama bear protecting her only cub.

"There is absolutely no way in hell I would let a machine on this land. I know you're in favor of anything that saves money, but I'm more interested in getting it right than getting it cheap."

Her eyes flashed fire as she spoke. She planted her hands on her hips, glaring at him as if he'd just spit on her shoes. She was insulted, ill-tempered, and more than ready to take him on. Damn if she didn't look sexy as hell.

The more she glared, the more his blood heated. He thought about pulling her close and kissing her, but the last time he'd done that, he hadn't been able to sleep for two days. The wanting had been relentless. Worse, it had been specific. He hadn't been interested in finding someone else to scratch his itch. For reasons he didn't understand, the need had only been about Brenna, not just about getting laid.

"How are you going to get them picked in time?" he asked. "You haven't had time to line up a crew."

"I'm calling in a few favors. I'll do some of the work myself. It will get done."

He didn't doubt that. Brenna was nothing if not determined.

Some of the annoyance faded from her expression. She

dropped her hands to her sides and tilted her head. "Guess who I met the other day?"

He shrugged. "I have no idea."

"Your CFO."

"How'd you run into Maggie?"

"She ran into me. She said she wanted to put a face to the name."

So Maggie had kept her word about meeting Brenna. Had she gotten her questions answered? "Maggie was impressed by the amount of money I loaned you. I'm not usually such a soft touch."

"Is that what it's called?" she asked.

"Do you have any complaints?"

She considered the question. "Can I get back to you on that?"

"Sure."

He glanced at the setting sun and knew that he should be heading back home. He had books to go over and a meeting with one of his managers. But he found himself reluctant to leave.

"I'm still working on my great-grandmother's diary," he said.

"How's that going?"

"I spend more time looking up words in the dictionary than translating, but I'm making progress." He glanced at her. "I could have it all wrong, but from what I can figure out, Sophia was in love with Antonio Marcelli."

Brenna stared at him. "No way."

He nodded. "That's what I thought, too, but it's all there in the diary. There's some mention of Antonio leaving for America and how much she missed him. He told her he would be back for her and asked her to wait."

"Did she agree?"

"I think so."

Brenna frowned. "Then how did she end up married to Salvatore, and why didn't she marry Antonio and come here with him?"

"He didn't get back in time. The Marcelli family wasn't as respected as the Giovanni family, which is why her father was reluctant to let her marry Antonio and go off with him."

"You're making that up."

"Would I lie to you?"

"If you thought it would bug me."

He chuckled. "All right, but this time I'm not. She waited for Antonio to return for her, but he didn't. When Salvatore came back, talking about his success and asking for Sophia's hand in marriage, her father agreed."

"She wasn't consulted?"

He shook his head.

Brenna rolled her eyes. "That is just so typical. Let me guess. They got married and Antonio showed up the next day."

"Just about. She tried to put off the wedding, but her parents wouldn't let her. The night before her wedding, she vowed to put her love for Antonio behind her and swore she would be a good wife."

Brenna shook her head. "I never heard about any of this. Do you think Sophia is the reason for the feud? Did the two friends fight about loving her or something?"

"It can't be that. Sophia and Salvatore married in the late 1920s. Salvatore and Antonio went to Europe during the Second World War to collect the European cuttings. They grew fine for a couple of years before the Marcelli vines died out and Antonio accused Salvatore of destroying them. Who would wait over fifteen years for revenge?

From what I've heard about my great-grandfather, Salvatore wasn't the patient type. If he'd suspected something, he would have taken care of business a whole lot earlier."

"Good point. Still, it's very strange." Brenna looked at him. "I wonder what would have happened if Antonio had married Sophia."

"Neither of us would have existed."

She sighed. "Families are so complicated. My grandfather is getting completely weird on me. Your parents walked out when you were still a kid and—" She pressed her lips together. "Sorry. I know you don't like to talk about your folks."

He swore. Once, years ago, he'd made the mistake of telling what had happened with his parents. He'd admitted his ambivalence. How he'd refused to miss them, yet couldn't help wondering what would have been different if they'd stuck around. Brenna had understood. She'd held him and somehow being in her arms had eased the confusion. He'd trusted her. Not a smart move, considering what had happened later.

Silence stretched between them. Nic glanced at his watch. He was going to be late for his meeting. He should—

"Did I tell you Francesca and Katie are having a double wedding?" Brenna asked in what he guessed was an attempt to change the subject. "It's going to be over Thanksgiving. Things should be interesting, what with Francesca being pregnant and all. At least we know she and Sam are a fertile couple. Anyway, because that's not enough work, they're having a double engagement party, too. It's gotten to the point where I'm afraid to walk into the house. If everyone isn't knee-deep in beading lace, there are tastings for various menu selections and arguments about invitations. I think they should just elope."

"Unlikely."

"Tell me about it. I work all day for my grandfather and then all night on my new business. I'm exhausted, which means when I bead lace for the wedding gowns everyone is making, I end up sticking myself. It's not fun."

"You'll enjoy the party."

"If I'm awake for it."

She shoved her hands into her back pockets, which made her chest stick out. He tried not to notice.

"It's the family stuff," she said. "Sometimes I think it's really twisted, but it's a part of who I am. I can't seem to escape it."

"I remember."

She winced. "Sorry."

"No problem. I can see that very little has changed."

Her gaze narrowed. "That's not fair."

"Why not? It's true."

It had always been true. Family was the most important thing in Brenna's life. He would bet that wasn't different. In fact, to prove it, if only to himself, he would conduct an experiment to see exactly how far he could push her before she snapped.

"Are you taking anyone?" he asked.

"As in a date?" She laughed. "That would require a social life, which I don't have. Not that I'm complaining. I would rather have the beginnings of a winery than a man."

"On behalf of my gender, thanks for the compliment."

"You know what I mean."

He did, but that wasn't important. "If you're not seeing anyone, then you could invite me."

9

*I*nvite Nic? Brenna blinked several times. Invite Nic? Sure. Of course. She didn't have a date and he was available. It was the perfect solution.

Not.

Take Nic? A Giovanni? Great-grandson of the hated Salvatore Giovanni? She stared at him, unable to think of a single thing to say. He couldn't be serious. He had to know that it was impossible. He had to remember—

She sucked in a breath. Of course he remembered and maybe that was the point. All those years ago she had been so worried about what her family would think if they knew she was involved with Nic. He'd wanted her to tell them, to declare her feelings for him. She'd wanted that, too—sort of. But she'd been afraid of what they would say. Of what would happen. The reality had terrified her.

It might have been ten years, but she could still feel that cold fear swirling in her stomach.

The humor faded from Nic's face. "Don't sweat it. I was kidding."

Was he? She still didn't know what to say. "It's not going to be a really big party," she blurted out. "Just family and friends."

Oh, right. That had certainly made things all better. What? If there were going to be a lot of strangers there, she would be more comfortable inviting him?

She reached out to touch his arm. "Nic, I'm—"

"I know. Whatever." He glanced at his watch. "I'm late for a meeting." He jerked his head toward the grapes. "Congratulations. You picked a winner."

He walked to his motorcycle and pulled on his helmet. Before she could think of a single rational, intelligent explanation for how she was acting, he was gone.

"That went well," she muttered and kicked at the dirt.

What was going on here? Was Nic actually serious about going to the party with her? They weren't seeing each other—not in the dating sense. She wasn't sure she would even categorize their relationship as "friendship." They had business dealings and more sexual chemistry than should be legal, but little else. She sighed. Okay, they had a past that would make a soap-opera writer jealous, but no one was talking about that.

She turned toward the road and stared at the bend where Nic had disappeared. Telling herself to forget the whole thing wasn't going to work, mostly because she found herself wanting to take him to the party.

How strange was that? Did she think that one family social event would make up for all she'd done—or not done—in the past?

"I didn't do anything wrong," she said firmly.

She crossed to her car and pulled open the door. If she didn't know better she would have sworn he'd been playing with her when he'd first mentioned going to the party, but something had changed. It was almost as if her inability to say yes had hurt him.

No way. Nic hurt by her? Now? Right.

Except he'd almost looked . . . wounded.

She slid into her car and pulled the door shut. What was going on? Were they both experiencing flashbacks? Were the blasts from the past confusing an already complicated situation?

Until she and Nic had met up again, she had believed with every fiber of her being that she was long over him. That what they'd once had didn't matter. After close contact of the Nic kind, she knew better. There were some things that simply didn't go away, regardless of the passage of time. Those life-altering moments lingered, and Lord knew that every second with Nic had changed *her* life.

Talk about a complication. If only she could forget the past, things would be a lot easier between them. Forgetting Nic would be—

Impossible, she thought. Even if it was smart, she didn't want to. She liked that they'd been young and in love. She liked that he had been her first time. She liked remembering how his hands had trembled when he'd undressed her and how his dark eyes had promised to make everything perfect between them.

And he had. He'd been tender and caring. She could still see the expression on his face as he'd entered her. He'd been much more experienced, but he'd lost it in about thirty seconds after declaring it had never been like that for him before.

She remembered the first time he'd told her he loved her. They'd been sitting out in the vineyards on a warm summer night. The stars had bathed them with a soft, sparkly light as they'd made love on an old blanket. Afterward, Nic had pulled her to her feet. They'd both still been naked and she'd shivered a little. He'd touched her face, her shoulders, her breasts, and had kissed each of her palms. Then he'd placed her hand on his chest, right over his heart.

"I love you, Brenna," he said, his expression intense, his voice thick with emotion. "I've wanted to tell you for a long time, but I wanted to wait until the perfect moment. I'll love you forever. With my heart, my mind, and my body."

She'd started to cry and he'd held her. Finally she'd managed to whisper that she loved him, too. For always. At seventeen, eternity had seemed possible.

Brenna turned off the coastal road and headed back for the hacienda. She had to blink against the burning in her eyes as she recalled Nic leaving to go back to college. She'd done her best to be brave. He'd been so sensible, promising that he would love her but saying he wasn't going to tie her down. He wanted her to enjoy her senior year of high school.

She'd known what he'd meant. She'd been free to date other guys, none of whom had interested her. How could they? She was in love with Nic.

The year had crawled by. They'd managed to steal a few hours together over Christmas, but nothing after that. He'd been working and unable to get away more. Brenna had been so afraid he wouldn't still love her come the summer. They'd met out in the vineyards, at a prearranged time. She'd practiced acting casual in case he told her he didn't love her anymore.

They'd taken one look at each other and they'd known. It was as if the time apart had been seconds instead of months. Looking at Nic was like falling into the sun. Their reunion had been one of her life's perfect moments.

There had been so many. Nights and mornings. Conversations, quiet times, laughter, and even tears. There had never been anyone like him for her. Jeff had never come close.

Brenna pulled under the arch at the entrance to the Marcelli lands. Her grip tightened on the steering wheel. She could still see the diamond ring he'd slid onto her finger.

Marriage and children. She could have had that with Nic. She could have had it all. Brenna thought about Kelly, Francesca's soon-to-be stepdaughter. If she'd accepted Nic's proposal, she would have children of her own now. They would be a family. Instead she'd married Jeff.

She parked her car and slowly climbed out. Her body ached, as if she'd just fallen down a mountain. It was always that way when she allowed herself to revisit the past for too long. Regrets, *what-ifs*, *could-have-been*s. They flung sharp weapons that cut her heart and burned her soul.

Ten years ago she'd made the safe and easy choice, and she'd been paying for it ever since. She'd walked away from her heart's desire because she'd been afraid of what it would cost. Never again. That was why she'd wanted to start the winery—to prove to herself that she'd learned her lesson. Nothing was ever going to stand in the way of her dreams again.

A nice sentiment, but it had little to do with the problem at hand. Had Nic been serious about accompanying her to the party? And if so, was she going to invite him?

Maggie tore off the crust from the sandwich she hadn't finished and tossed it to Max. The puppy caught it in midair and swallowed without chewing.

"You're going to make him fat," Nic warned.

"I know, but I can't resist his big brown eyes. He's so sweet."

"He needs to learn table manners."

Maggie wrinkled her nose at him. "You're too strict. You need to lighten up."

"What happens when Max is ninety pounds of begging dog?"

She laughed. "I guess we eat indoors and keep him out."

Nic sipped his iced tea. "I can see I don't want you around when he starts his obedience classes. You would never insist he behave."

"You're right. I wouldn't. I guess it's something of a surprise that my daughter is somewhat civilized, huh?"

"I think we have your husband to thank for that."

She picked up another bread crust, but this one she tossed at Nic. "You're insulting me."

"Only a little."

Maggie sighed, then picked up her pen. "Okay. Back to business. We've been over the expansion, the new equipment on order, and the Far East deal. Oh, Jeremy wanted to talk about the bottling equipment. I told him to make an appointment with you."

"Not a problem."

While Maggie made more notes, Nic let his attention wander to the vineyards in the distance and the clusters of grapes ripening in the bright sun.

Today was a good day. Rather than have their meeting inside, Maggie had suggested lunch on the lawn. A table had been set up in the shade, and the lunch-room catering staff had provided the food.

The sun was warm, the sky clear. It was the kind of

afternoon that made him want to take off on one of his bikes. Except he'd done that yesterday and he'd ended up somewhere he never should have been.

At the time driving by Brenna's newly acquired acres had seemed like a good idea, but later . . . he'd regretted the impulse.

Or maybe he just regretted mentioning the party.

He'd offered to be her date as a joke. At least, that's how it had started. But as soon as he spoke the words, something had shifted inside of him. He could rationalize the slight tightening in his chest and stiffness in his legs by saying he remembered being that twenty-year-old kid who'd been desperately in love with a girl whose family hated him. But he had a feeling his reaction was about more than that.

"Earth to Nic," Maggie said, waving a hand in front of his face. "Where did you go?"

"Back about ten years."

She studied him. "About the time your grandfather sent you away?"

He nodded.

"I always felt bad about that."

He chuckled. "You weren't here when it happened and you didn't have anything to do with it. How could you feel bad?"

"I just did. When you came back from France, I could tell you'd been hurt even though you never talked about what had happened between you two." She sighed. "You were *family*. Emilio had no right to send you away."

"According to him he had every right."

"He was wrong."

"Maybe."

His grandfather had asked him to choose and Nic had.

Unfortunately he'd chosen Brenna instead of Wild Sea, and the old man had never forgiven him for that. Nic had been equally furious about being kicked off the property. The fact that his grandfather had come back eighteen months later, begging him to return hadn't been enough.

He thought about that difficult first year when he'd finally come home. Maggie had been there for him. "You got me through some tough times. You were good to me."

She shrugged. "I wasn't doing anything I didn't want to do."

"Was I good for you?"

Her smile turned tender. "More than you'll ever know. You made me feel special. For the first time in my life I wasn't a tall, gawky carrot-top with freckles. You thought I was beautiful and I could almost see myself that way. You gave me confidence."

"To go out and marry someone else."

She laughed. "Come on, Nic, you weren't really hurt when I broke up with you. Admit it."

He shrugged, not willing to concede the point, even if she was right. "If I was so great, why did you end things?"

She hesitated, as if not willing to tell him the truth.

He leaned toward her. "I'd like to know."

"It's embarrassing." She smiled wryly. "But if you insist. The reason I ended things was I knew you'd never fall in love with me, and I didn't want to fall in love with you. I'd already had enough heartache in my life. So I broke it off while I still could."

Love? Nic had never known, never guessed things were that serious for her. He studied her green eyes and wondered if he'd inadvertently hurt her all those years ago.

"So I got you all primed, and then your husband came along and plucked you like a ripe peach."

"Absolutely." She grinned and whatever shadows had drifted into her eyes faded away. "Besides, I wanted to get married and you weren't interested in anything permanent. You still aren't." She pointed a finger at him. "At some point you have to be willing to give your heart and take a chance. Do you really want to die old and alone?"

"Are those my only options? I took your advice and got a dog. That should count for something."

"Not enough. What about letting people in your life?"

Nic understood the theory, but didn't get the point. Everyone he'd ever cared about had walked away from him. As far as he could tell, the love thing wasn't working in his world.

"I have people in my life," he told her.

"You have friends, but no romantic interest. When was the last time you were serious about someone? And before you ask, no, a three-week sexual relationship doesn't count."

"What about a four-week one?"

She glared at him. "You know what I mean."

He did, and he wasn't answering the question. What was the point? He avoided serious relationships. The last one he'd had had been with Maggie. Before that, Brenna. While he hadn't minded when Maggie ended things, Brenna's betrayal had destroyed him.

"Stick to your numbers," he said, tapping the papers on the table. "They're what you know best."

"You're dismissing my concerns."

"I know."

"Fine. Be lonely. I don't care."

They both knew that she was lying. While Nic would never admit it, he liked that Maggie cared. She was a good friend.

"I appreciate the advice," he told her. "But I'm okay."

"Maybe." She eyed him. "Speaking of women . . ."

"Were we?"

"I was. I met Brenna Marcelli the other day."

"So I heard. What was that about?"

"I told you I wanted to check her out and see if I had to feel guilty." Her gaze narrowed. "She's very nice and she's working hard to make her winery a success. I can't believe you're going to take advantage of her."

Nic had lots of plans to take advantage of Brenna, but not in the way Maggie meant. "She'll be fine."

"Will she? Are you really going to give her the time she needs to get her business up and running?"

"I don't know."

"Dammit, Nic, why not? Why did you offer her the loan if you're just going to screw her over?"

He didn't like the question. "I told you. I haven't decided what I'm going to do."

"Is all this because she's Lorenzo Marcelli's grand-daughter, or is there something else I don't know about?"

"My life is an open book."

"Right. One that's written in invisible ink." She collected her papers. "Until recently I've always admired how you did business. You've always been completely straight-forward. Because of that, you've always been able to look yourself in the mirror. I would hate to see that change."

She stood and walked away. Nic watched her go. He told himself that Maggie didn't understand what he was trying to do. She saw things as black and white, but life was more complicated than that. Sometimes winning was expensive, but he'd always been willing to pay the price.

Besides, he'd yet to find a deal he couldn't afford. There was no reason to think this one was different.

• • •

Francesca stepped into the basted gown and pulled it up over her hips. Brenna waited until the bodice was in place, then carefully pinned the back closed.

"How does it feel?" she asked her twin. Grammy M had just finished the initial assembly of a thin cotton dress they would use as a pattern for the actual wedding gown. Once it was fitted, the garment would be taken apart. When there was eighty-dollar-a-yard silk involved, it was best to experiment on cheap fabric first.

"Good. It's a little loose in the waist. I wish I could know how big I'm going to get between now and the wedding. Should we let it out more?"

Brenna fingered the cotton and found she could pinch about two inches of fabric. "I'll ask one of the Grands. They have more experience with that sort of thing." She bent down to see where the hem should be. "Are these the shoes you're wearing?"

"Uh-huh."

She slipped several pins into the fabric, then straightened. "So the party is this Saturday. You must be excited."

"I think it will be fun."

Not exactly the word Brenna would have used. She cleared her throat. "So here's the thing. I was thinking of maybe, you know, bringing someone."

Francesca spun around to face her. "You're kidding. Like a guy?"

"Yes, a guy."

"But I didn't think you were seeing anyone."

"I'm not." She and Nic weren't "seeing" each other. They were . . . She sighed. She had no idea what they were doing. "The problem is I don't want to make trouble. It's your party, it's your special day."

"What trouble? The Grands will be thrilled that you're dating. They want you to get married again."

"Not to Nic Giovanni."

Francesca's perfect mouth dropped open. "Nic? You want to bring Nic?"

Brenna nodded. She'd been mulling over the concept for three days, and she'd come to the conclusion that, kidding or not, Nic's feelings had been hurt when she hadn't instantly agreed to take him. While that wasn't exactly her responsibility, she still felt bad. Maybe it had something to do with the chemistry bubbling between them or maybe she was still feeling guilty about the past or maybe she'd slipped into madness. Whatever the reason, she wanted to ask him. But only if her sister agreed.

"We were talking the other day and I mentioned the engagement party and he said he would like to go and I thought maybe I'd bring him." She looked at Francesca. "But I know it will be really uncomfortable, so I didn't want to do that and ruin the party."

Her sister grinned. "I think it's a terrific idea."

"Oh, please. Talk about the fur flying."

"But that's perfect. We haven't actually booked any entertainment."

"Very funny. It could get ugly."

"No way." Francesca returned her attention to the mirror. "Grandpa Lorenzo will grumble, but I don't think anyone else will care. You should bring him. A nice, romantic night under the stars. Anything could happen."

"That's what I'm afraid of," Brenna mumbled. She sighed. "I talked to Katie and she pretty much said the same thing."

Francesca met her gaze in the mirror. "So you're going to do it?"

"I'll call him and see if he wants to come with me."

Francesca's gaze narrowed. "Are you sure there isn't anything between the two of you?"

"There's nothing," Brenna said. But when she turned away to busy herself with the box of pins, she crossed her fingers. There was something; she just couldn't figure out what it was.

"You're offering a lot of cash," Bill Freeman said. "Are you sure about that?"

"Lorenzo Marcelli is an old-fashioned businessman." Nic glanced down at the final draft of the offer. "Cash will appeal to him. I want to keep things clean."

Bill grinned. "Any cleaner than this and I'd sell to you."

"You don't own Marcelli Wines."

"You make me wish I did."

Roger White flipped to the second page. "You're promising to keep all the employees for at least two years. I heard that he's got his granddaughter running things these days. Will that apply to her as well?"

Nic understood Roger's concern. An angry family member who had just lost an inheritance could be a liability. "The clause stands." He held up his hand before Roger could interrupt. "Brenna Marcelli will quit the second she finds out I'm the actual buyer."

"You're sure?"

Nic thought about Brenna's temper and how she was going to feel about the deal. They'd even discussed him buying Marcelli, however briefly, before she'd dismissed the idea. As much as she would hate him buying out her inheritance, she was going to be even more furious at being played for a fool.

"I'm positive," he said.

She would want to skin him alive. Not that he would blame her. If someone was doing to him what he planned to do to her, he would be out for blood. Brenna's need for revenge would be hampered by the million-dollar callable note he held. No matter what, he was going to win.

They discussed a few more points, then adjourned the meeting.

"You're a hell of an opponent," Roger said, shaking hands with Nic. "Remind me not to piss you off."

Nic grinned. "You want that in an e-mail?"

"Sure."

He opened the conference room door for the men. Bill paused. "You're going to make a lot of enemies with this one, Nic."

"I can live with that."

The older man studied him for a second, then shrugged. "If you're sure."

"I am. I've wanted Marcelli for a long time."

"You're about to get them."

Nic watched them leave, then returned to the table to pick up his copy of the offer. One more pass and it would be ready. Bill and Roger would present it, and then the real game began.

Lorenzo Marcelli would be a fool to dismiss the deal, but Nic knew his acquisition wasn't a sure thing. Marcelli Wines was a family business. There was more than just money at stake. But he was confident.

He crossed to the window and stared out at the winery. To the left was the building where Brenna's wines were fermenting. She showed up every night and worked until dawn. Despite her years away from the business, she still had the magic touch. He didn't doubt that every one of her wines was going to be a medal winner and sell out in days.

If he gave her the time she needed.

He felt a twinge right between his shoulder blades. Guilt? Not possible. He hadn't done anything wrong. This was business.

The phone on the conference table buzzed. He walked over and hit the speaker button.

"Yes?"

"Nic, you have a call on line seven. A Brenna Marcelli."

"Thanks." He hesitated before pushing the flashing button. Why would she be calling him?

"Let me guess," he said by way of greeting. "You sold your four acres of Pinot to a theme-park developer for a cool five million."

She laughed. "Not even on a bet. Your assistant said you were just getting out of a meeting. Are you planning to produce wine coolers?"

"Yeah, we're going to blend them with tropical fruits."

She made a gagging sound. "That's disgusting. Not even you would do that."

"I would if the profit margin was right."

"Oh, please. What about family pride? Anyway, I didn't call to lecture you about your shady business practices."

Ouch. "Good to know. Why did you call?"

"Well, that's an interesting question." She cleared her throat. "I, ah, I told you before about the engagement party. For my sisters. Anyway, if you're not busy Saturday, I thought maybe you'd like to go with me. Not as a date or anything. Just as, well, I guess I don't know. Friends. Or something."

He sat and stared at the phone. Brenna inviting him to the family homestead? For a party? Unbelievable. He would never have guessed she would change her mind.

"Nic?"

"I'm here. I'm surprised."

"I know. It's just . . ." She sighed. "I can't explain it. Just tell me if you want to go."

"Sure." Why not? This was a chance to see operations up close. Brenna would be happy to give him a tour. They would spend the evening together, which wasn't much of a hardship. "I'd like to go with you."

"Great."

He couldn't tell if she sounded relieved or horrified.

"What time?" he asked.

"Say six-thirty. But I'll pick you up. It might be dangerous for you to drive onto Marcelli property by yourself."

He chuckled. "Will I be shot on sight?"

"Instant death would be the least of your problems. So I'll see you Saturday."

"I'm looking forward to it."

Funny. When he hung up the phone, he found he really was.

10

Brenna was so nervous, her knees were knocking. Since she was trying to drive her car, this wasn't a good thing. Fortunately it was an automatic, and she didn't have to worry about using a clutch.

"What on earth was I thinking?" she muttered as she turned onto the main highway. "I wasn't thinking. Okay, I was, but with the wrong part of my brain."

Actually, there was no excuse for what she'd done. She wasn't even a guy, so she didn't have the "little head" to blame for her poor decision. The night was going to be a disaster and she had no one to blame but herself.

She'd invited Nic to the party in part because she felt guilty, in part because her grandfather was driving her crazy and she wanted to act out against him, and in part because she wanted to spend some time in Nic's company. Were those good reasons or bad reasons? Did it matter at this point?

And what about her family? Should she have warned her parents? Her sisters all knew and had been supportive, if Mia teasing her about still having the hots for Nic counted as support. She pressed a hand to her stomach to try to calm the uneasy rumbling that was the result of her nerves.

At least she looked good, she thought, trying to find a bright spot in the one-act spoof that was her life. Over the past couple of weeks she'd actually been too busy to eat, and, miracle of miracles, she'd lost a couple of pounds. So the sleeveless black sheath she'd wanted to wear had slid over her hips without a single whimper of protest. She'd chosen fashion over comfort and had borrowed a pair of impossibly high black strappy sandals from her mother's department-store-sized collection. Mia had fussed with her hair, using a combination of mousse, gel, and hairspray that gave her normally uncooperative hair lift and shape. A touch of makeup, a spray of perfume, and she was ready to go.

Except for the chorus line warming up in her midsection.

She turned from the road onto Wild Sea property. If only this didn't feel so much like a date. Was it a date? It couldn't be. She and Nic didn't date. Some days they barely spoke. But she'd asked him to a party and she was picking him up in her car, so it looked like a date. Sort of.

She arrived at the house far more quickly than she'd wanted to. Once there, she didn't have an excuse to linger in the car, so she forced herself to get out and walk to the door. She was shaking and hyperventilating. What the hell had she been thinking?

After knocking on the front door, she tried to calm herself. She was a mature adult who could handle any situation. She was—

Nic opened the door and smiled at her. Just like that, one smile and her brain went from al dente to mush. She couldn't think, couldn't speak, probably couldn't breathe, although who cared about that? The man looked amazing.

Dark slacks, dark shirt, dress shoes, gleaming hair,

freshly shaved cheeks, and a delicious glint in his brown eyes. Italian sex appeal at its very best.

While she was still trying to collect her synapses and force them into functioning, Nic leaned forward and kissed her cheek. "You look great."

She swallowed and managed a smile. "Thanks. You, too."

He held open the door and she stepped inside.

"I know I'm early," she said as she clasped her hands together. "I was ready and I couldn't stand the waiting. Plus I had to get away while I could. The place is complete chaos. Between the Grands trying to get the food ready at the last minute—because God forbid we should hire a caterer instead of just serving staff—my mom rearranging the flowers, and Grandpa Lorenzo changing his mind about the wine, I thought a timely escape the best course of action." She glanced around the living room. "This hasn't changed much, has it?"

"Not really."

She tried to tell herself that the two of them being alone in Nic's house after dark didn't mean anything. She'd been here before when they'd needed lamps. Of course, that had been many years before, in the dead of night, and for the sole purpose of finally making love in a bed.

Best not to think about that, she told herself. Best to just study the furniture and pretend she was completely fine with her plans for the evening.

Nic watched Brenna's gaze dart around the room. She looked nervous enough to jump out of her skin.

"You didn't tell them about me coming to the party, did you?" he asked.

She sucked in a breath. "My sisters know. They're all really excited about meeting you." She smiled. "Between the motorcycle and black leather jacket, not to mention your reputation for being a troublemaker as a kid and a ruthless businessman now, you're something of a legend in these parts."

"I'm flattered."

He led her to the sofa. While she sat, he crossed to the table by the window and poured them each a glass of Cabernet.

"Wine?" Brenna asked as she took the drink. She stood up and clutched it in both hands. "I guess it won't hurt."

"Are you going to be like this all evening?"

"What? Insanely tense? Maybe. Is that a problem?"

He studied her large eyes, the fullness of her mouth, then looked lower at the simple black dress that skimmed over her lush curves. He didn't even get as far as her bare legs before he felt interest stir.

"Not a problem at all." He touched his glass to hers. "To your sisters' happy engagements."

"To not throwing up on any of the guests."

"Is that a real possibility?"

"I sure hope not."

She held the glass up to the light and studied the color, then inhaled the fragrance. After swirling it around several times, she inhaled again.

"Brenna, just drink the damn thing."

"What?" She glanced from the glass to him. "Oh, sorry." She took a sip. "It's lovely."

"Now I know you're really nervous. You never compliment my wines."

"I know. I guess I should. Some of them are very nice."

He winced. "Nice, huh? Maybe you'd like to be our spokesperson."

She set her glass on the coffee table. "I'm sorry, Nic. I know tonight is going to be fine. I'm really glad I'm taking you."

He waited for the "but" part of the sentence.

She sighed. "But I'm terrified. Silly, huh?"

"Understandable."

"Do you mind if I pace?"

He waved his arm. "Feel free."

"Thanks."

She kicked off her sandals, then, barefoot, walked the length of the living room. "I'm a grown-up. I'm a capable person. My parents are going to be fine with this. We're going to have a good time."

"Who are you trying to convince?"

She looked at him. "You don't look the least bit worried, so I guess just myself."

He watched her resume her pacing. She crossed and uncrossed her arms, then paused by a window and stared out at the night. Her apprehension didn't surprise him, but his reaction to it did. He would have thought he would be pleased by her discomfort, that this night would be a victory for him. Instead he felt badly for putting her in this position and he wanted to do something to make her feel better.

"Brenna, I don't have to go," he said before he could stop himself.

She turned to face him. "Oh, yes, you do. I'm prepared to bring you onto Marcelli land and have it out with my grandfather. I have no idea what's going to happen with my parents, but my sisters are all waiting to watch the show. I have a bunch of crap in my hair just so I can look nice, and I'm wearing shoes that are going to cripple me. I didn't do all that just so you can back out at the last minute. You're going to the party if I have to drag you there by your ears."

He chuckled. "All right, then. A gracious invitation like that is difficult to refuse."

Her gaze narrowed. "You think this is all pretty funny."

"I don't think it ranks up there with war and pestilence." He set down his wineglass. "You need to relax."

"I can't." She held up a hand and watched as it trembled. "I'm shaking."

He crossed to stand next to her and took her hand in his. After rubbing her fingers, he bent down and kissed the inside of her wrist. He could feel her rapid pulse fluttering against his lips.

"Maybe we should give you something else to think about," he said.

Her eyes widened. "Nic, I—"

He waited, but she didn't continue.

Truthfully, he hadn't planned this. He'd been more focused on the party and seeing the Marcelli family close up than on spending the evening with Brenna. Now that she was here, he found himself mesmerized by the sweet scent of her body and the way her breasts rose and fell with each breath. She'd always been attractive, but tonight she was beautiful. Soft, vulnerable, all woman, and sexy as hell.

He could hate her, he could ignore her, he could even do his best to forget about her, but he'd been unable to stop wanting her. Just being close was enough to get him hard. As blood pooled in his groin, he moved in closer. She didn't back away, not even when he lowered his head and kissed her.

Nic tasted of wine and temptation, Brenna thought when his mouth brushed against hers. It was a heady combination, one she didn't think she could resist.

As their lips pressed together, she pulled her hand free of his and wrapped her arms around his neck. Okay, this probably wasn't the smartest thing she could be doing right now, but leaning against him, kissing him, *wanting* him just felt too good.

She parted her lips and he swept into her mouth. The second his tongue brushed against hers, she felt her good sense sizzle into smoke and drift away. She lost herself in the heat that exploded between them. He'd always had the ability to make her body respond on the most primal level, and tonight was no exception.

She clung to him, wanting their bodies to touch as much as possible. At the same time she needed to explore, to remember, to feel all those magical things that had only happened with Nic. As he deepened the kiss, she moved her hands down his shoulders to his back. His was broader than she remembered. Stronger. Yet his muscles still clenched and released as she touched him. She traced his narrow waist and hips, then circled back to cup his rear. When she squeezed, he thrust his hips forward and she felt his erection.

He was hard and thick and the things he'd been able to do to her filled her mind. Her memory flashed pictures of them making love while her body remembered the pleasure. Every part of her ached as liquid desire pooled low in her belly. Her panties were already wet, her breasts swollen, and both she and Nic were wearing way too many clothes.

He cupped her face and broke their kiss. Before she could complain, he pressed his lips to her cheeks, her eyelids, then her jaw. After nibbling his way to her neck, he licked the sensitive skin behind her ear. Shivers danced across her skin.

He kissed his way down to her throat, where he paid homage to the hollow before kissing her chest, just above the neckline of her dress.

When she felt the slow slide of her zipper being eased down, she reached for the buttons on his shirt. She got three of them undone before she had to drop her arms to her sides so he could pull her dress off her arms and let it settle at her waist. The silky fabric barely paused before slipping to the floor, leaving her wearing nothing but panties and a bra.

Nic returned his attention to her mouth. He kissed her thoroughly, exploring her with a devastatingly erotic dance that left her boneless. Had she been in the mood to protest her undressed state, she was too occupied to speak a word. Not that she wanted to complain. Not when she felt his warm hands move from her waist to her breasts. Not when he cupped her curves through the lace of her black bra and brushed his thumbs against her already tight nipples.

Need spiraled through her. Her breath caught as she waited for the next sweep of his fingers, then the next. Had anything ever felt this good? Even as his touch eased the pressure in her breasts, need continued to build between her legs. She reached for the bra clasp and fumbled with the hooks. When she managed to unfasten them, she pulled off her bra, then grabbed Nic's hands and placed them back on her body.

The flesh on flesh made her moan. He held her breasts in his palms and squeezed them gently. Long fingers explored her sensitive skin, then teased her nipples. He seemed to know exactly how she liked to be touched, how fast, how hard, how . . . everything.

This time when he broke the kiss, she caught her breath in anticipation. He bent his head and pressed his open mouth to her breast.

Wet heat surrounded her. He circled her with his tongue, then sucked her deeply into his mouth. Brenna held on to his head, holding him close, barely breathing as she concentrated on the pleasure spiraling through her body. He moved to her other breast and continued the dance. She felt him tug off his shirt.

When he pulled back and straightened, she opened her eyes. He was bare to the waist. His hair was mussed, his eyes were heavy-lidded with passion. As his hands reached for his belt buckle, she slipped off her panties. He unfastened his slacks, then took her hand and pulled her to the couch.

When he was seated, he shoved down his trousers and briefs, allowing his erection to spring free. Brenna sucked in a breath as she stared at him. At one time she'd known his body as intimately as she'd known her own. She knew what he liked to do, what he fantasized about, and how to make him come in less than fifteen seconds. Of course he knew the same things about her.

She liked being on top, she liked him playing with her breasts while he was inside of her, and most of the time she liked it slightly less than civilized. Had he remembered or was this just dumb luck on her part?

He reached for her hand and drew it to his mouth. But instead of kissing her fingers or her wrist, he bit down on the thick pad by her thumb. A silly thing that had always driven her wild. Shivers rippled through her. Damn him. He remembered everything.

Still watching her, he released her hand and grabbed her by the waist. She knelt on the sofa, straddling him. With their eyes locked and a part of her unable to believe this was really happening, she lowered herself onto him.

She was hot, slick, and more than ready. He was hard as a rock. He filled her completely, making her stretch to accommodate him, and before they'd even begun to move, she felt the first quivering promise of her release. So much for self-control. The only saving grace was the way his eyes dilated and his mouth stretched into a straight line. She wasn't the only one barely hanging on.

Still watching him watch her, she shifted so that she could raise and lower herself. He cupped her breasts and rubbed her nipples. The combination was pure paradise.

Tension built from the inside out. She rested her hands on muscled shoulders that were as hard as the rest of him. As she moved up and down, she found herself falling into a rhythm that felt familiar and incredible. He pulsed his hips in time with her movements. When the pitch of her need increased, she tried to look away but couldn't. Not even when the first deep contractions pulled at her.

She told herself to hold on, to make it last, to—

The shudder of her release made her cry out. She moved faster as her body convulsed around him, pulling him in deeper. More. There was so much more. He dropped his hands to her hips and urged her to keep moving, his body matching her pace, taking her through every ounce of her release.

It was only when the last muscle relaxed that he tightened his hold on her and groaned. She felt him push in as far as he could. He shook violently and closed his eyes, then was still.

Brenna tried to catch her breath. Aftershocks rippled through her as she lost herself in the sense of well-being that flooded her. Strong arms pulled her close. She nestled against Nic's bare chest. His heat and familiar scent surrounded her. He stroked her back, slowly moving along the length of her spine. She smiled. Talk about amazing. Talk about—

Oh. My. God.

She sat up and stared at him. He had the contented expression of a well-pleasured man. One corner of his mouth turned up.

"Unexpected, but very nice," he said.

Nice? Nice! What on earth had she been thinking? She and Nic had just had sex. Sex!

She closed her eyes and shifted so she could slide off him. When she was free, she curled up on the sofa, her bare butt against his hip and covered her face with her hands.

"Just shoot me now," she muttered, wondering how things had gotten so out of hand so fast.

Nic placed his hand on her hip. "Look at the bright side," he told her. "At least you're not still worried about what your family is going to think when you show up with me."

He had a point. Great. Not sure if she should cry or burst into hysterical laughter, Brenna stayed where she was. Maybe she could disappear into the fabric and never be heard from again. She didn't plan to ever move again . . . right up until Nic leaned close and whispered, "It's ten to seven. Want to get dressed and go to the engagement party, or stay here and do it again?"

For reasons that still didn't make sense, she'd chosen the party. Brenna sat in the passenger seat of Nic's Jag, smoothing her hands over her dress and trying not to think about how mussed she must look.

Five minutes in the downstairs bathroom had allowed her to repair her makeup and smooth her hair. Her dress wasn't even wrinkled. She should have looked exactly as she had when she'd left the hacienda an hour before, but something was different. Maybe it was the sated, slightly stunned expression in her eyes, or the shape of her mouth—now swollen from Nic's kisses. Or maybe it was the aura of guilt and stupidity surrounding her.

If the dashboard hadn't been covered in such a lovely,

soft leather, she would have banged her head against it in an attempt to knock some sense into herself. Sex with Nic? Could she have been more impulsive? She was no longer a starry-eyed teenager who still believed in happily ever after. She was a mature woman with a plan for her life. A plan that didn't include screwing up an important business relationship.

She drew in a slow, steady breath. Time to be calm. Time to be one with the universe. Time to ignore the fact that her panties were soaked and that the trembling in her body no longer had anything to do with nerves.

Was anyone going to be able to figure out what they'd just done?

"You okay?" Nic asked.

"Fine."

"Really?"

"No."

She glanced at him. He looked calm and in control. How like a man.

"Want to talk about it?" he asked.

She shook her head. What was there to say? That she was sorry she'd lost control and given into the desire that seemed to always be on the fringes of their up close and personal encounters? Of course she was sorry . . . almost.

Just then he turned from the road onto the long driveway that led to the hacienda. Brenna stiffened. Sex or no sex, she'd just brought the enemy onto Marcelli land.

Nic pulled in behind a silver BMW. There were several dozen cars parked along the wide road. White lights hung from trees and illuminated the walkway up to the three-story hacienda.

He'd grown up only a few miles from this house, but his world couldn't have been more different. How many times had he crept out in the early evening and made his way to the Marcelli home? How many nights had he hidden in the bushes and watched through the brightly lit windows, hungry for the family he'd seen living inside? They'd belonged to each other, and to a boy who had belonged to no one, their lives had been perfect.

When he and Brenna had met and fallen in love, he'd actually thought he might one day be a part of this. A part of them. Welcomed into the family as one of their own. He'd wanted that nearly as much as he'd wanted her. In the end he'd lost both.

He shook off the memories. He wasn't that kid anymore. He was a successful adult who had a shot at owning all this. Not the house—he no longer cared about that—but the land and the name.

"For the first time in my life, I'm wishing for a few minutes with Grandma Tessa's rosary," Brenna murmured. She turned to him. "Ready?"

He nodded and stepped out of the car.

From where he stood, he could see the large tent filling the backyard. The sides had been rolled up, allowing the evening breeze to drift across the set tables. More lights crisscrossed through the trees. People stood in groups, talking, laughing, holding wineglasses, no doubt toasting the happy couples with the best Lorenzo Marcelli had to offer.

"This is all going to be okay," Brenna said when he moved next to her. She glanced at him and gave a faint smile. "I'll give you a tour later, if you'd like."

"Will it include your bedroom?"

"Very funny." She drew in a deep breath. "Let's do this."

He followed her toward the party-goers. The sound of

music drifted to them, and as they neared the house, he spotted a dance floor set up in a garden. Two couples stood out in the swaying crowd. He recognized Brenna's sisters— Katie and Francesca.

A uniformed young woman approached with a tray of drinks. Brenna took a glass of champagne, handed it to Nic, then snatched another for herself.

"If this is a small get-together for family and friends," he said, "what does a big party look like?"

She gulped half her glass of wine. "I know. My mother doesn't do things by halves, so that's a problem. This time it was compounded by the fact that Katie is a professional organizer who specializes in giving parties for the rich and famous. It's not a good combination if you're going for small and intimate. I should warn you that dinner has about seventy-five courses."

"Then I won't fill up on hors d'oeuvres."

She finished her champagne and set the empty glass on the edge of a garden planter. Nic took his first sip. Rather than admit he might be a little nervous at the prospect of meeting the Marcelli clan, he concentrated on the light scent and blend of bubbles and flavors in the sparkling wine. It was good. He tasted it again and decided that when he was in charge, he would expand production.

Brenna scanned the crowd. "Over there," she said and linked her arm with his. "We'll start easy and work our way up from there."

He followed her gaze and saw her mother talking with an older couple he didn't recognize. As they approached, Colleen Marcelli glanced over at her daughter, smiled, looked at him, and froze.

Her eyes widened, her mouth dropped open, and she nearly spilled her glass of wine. But as quickly as it had come, the shock faded. Colleen excused herself from the older couple and approached them.

"Oh, God, oh, God," Brenna muttered. Her fingers tightened around his arm. "Stay calm. Just stay calm."

He wasn't sure if the instruction was for her or for himself. Either way it was good advice.

"Brenna," Colleen said as she approached. "You look lovely."

Brenna cleared her throat. "Thanks. Um, Mom, this is—"

"I believe I already know your friend."

Nic braced himself for the attack. Colleen handed her glass to her daughter, took his free hand in hers, and studied his face. "I see a lot of your grandfather in you," she said. "And your father. Do you go by Nicholas or Nic?"

He hadn't expected the question. "Nic."

"Well, Nic, this night has been far too long in coming." She smiled. "We're delighted to have you here."

Then she leaned forward and raised herself on tiptoes and kissed his cheek. "Welcome."

Her graciousness surprised him. "Thank you, Mrs. Marcelli. I want you to know I'm here as Brenna's guest. Not to make trouble."

"Colleen," she said. "Trouble was the furthest thing from my mind." Her expression turned wry. "I've always thought the feud between our families was pretty silly, although my father-in-law would disagree. Now that you're here, I can't help thinking this meeting is years too late. I'm sorry about that."

"Not a problem."

He spoke the words easily. She sounded sincere. As if she *were* sorry. Brenna had always said her mother was a warm and caring person. Until now, Nic had never believed her.

Colleen glanced through the crowd. "Now, where is my husband?"

As she turned to look at the people standing by the tent, Brenna finished her mother's champagne.

"One down, the rest of the clan left to go," she whispered. "Of course she's going to want an explanation later. Any ideas on what I should tell her?"

"That you're hot for my body and think nothing of seducing me at a moment's notice?"

"Bite me."

He grinned. "When and where?"

Brenna's gaze narrowed, but before she could snap at him, Colleen reached for his hand again. "There's Marco. Come along. I'll introduce you." She smiled at her daughter. "I won't keep him long."

Brenna waved her hand. "Keep him for as long as you want. I won't mind a bit."

He glanced back and mouthed "liar" as Colleen led him away to introduce him to their guests.

Marco Marcelli concealed his surprise better than his wife had, but he was just as gracious. Family friends from the area were obviously shocked to see him on Marcelli land, but they smiled politely. Nic figured there would be more than one midnight call about the party.

The grandmothers were reserved, Tessa Marcelli more so than Mary-Margaret O'Shea. Still, they welcomed him. Nic wondered if they would be so friendly if they knew that he and Brenna had once planned to run away together.

He knew what their reaction would be if they figured out he was going to use every means at his disposal to buy Marcelli Wines. But he understood that. If the situation were reversed, he would be just as furious.

Nic found himself an observer rather than a participant

in the evening. He'd known about the Marcellis all his life. His grandfather had talked about the family, he'd run into them at local events, passed them in the post office. But except for Brenna, he'd never spoken to them. Now they were accepting him as one of their own.

He'd always seen them as the enemy. Funny how they were turning out to be just regular people.

"I'm Mia," a young woman said, slipping between Nic and Colleen. "The youngest, the smartest, the most fun. And you're Nic Giovanni."

"I know."

Mia grinned. Streaks of blond lightened her dark hair. She wore a strapless dress that barely came to mid-thigh and high heels that looked expensive and dangerous. Heavy makeup emphasized her big eyes and full lips. She was Lolita at eighteen.

Mia took his hand in hers and brought his arm around behind her so he rested his palm on her hip. "Everyone is talking, but then you expected that."

"It's not a big surprise."

"You like making trouble."

He thought about the trouble he and Brenna had made early that evening. "Sometimes."

Mia placed her fingers on his chest. "All my sisters had wild crushes on you when they were growing up, even me. Of course, I'm the only one who will admit it."

"I'm flattered."

Her brown eyes crinkled at the corners. "But not shocked."

"No."

"Do you have the hots for my sister?"

Before he could decide on a politically correct answer to a charged question, he heard a low murmur of voices behind him. He disentangled himself from Mia and turned to find Lorenzo Marcelli stalking toward him.

"Who let you in?" Lorenzo demanded. Anger and insult pulsed in every word.

Suddenly Marco was at Nic's side. "Nic is a guest."

Lorenzo moved closer. "He wasn't invited. No Giovanni would ever be invited."

"He's with Brenna."

A muscle twitched in the old man's cheek. He muttered something in Italian, something Nic couldn't catch or translate, then turned and moved away.

Marco put a hand on Nic's shoulder. "You'll have to excuse my father. He's an old man. Very stubborn. For him the feud between our families lives on."

Nic glanced at Lorenzo as he disappeared into the crowd, then turned back to Marco. "I'm glad you don't agree with him."

Marco smiled. "It was sixty years ago. I have trouble remembering last week." He dropped his hand and held open his arm. "Here comes your date."

Nic saw Brenna approaching.

"I heard the thunder of disapproval clear across the lawn," she said. "Did he say anything awful?"

"Nothing unexpected," Nic said. "I'm an intruder."

"Termites are an intruder. You're a welcome guest," Marco told him. "We will have dinner soon. You'll eat, you'll talk, you'll enjoy."

Brenna smiled at her father. "You sound like Grandma Tessa."

Marco winced. "Don't tell me I sound like an old woman."

He kissed her cheek and stepped away. Brenna pulled Nic to the edge of the crowd. "How's it going? Is it too awful?"

"Everyone is being very gracious."

"Except my grandfather."

"I didn't expect anything different."

"Me, either. I wonder if he'll fire me."

Nic raised his eyebrows. "Are you serious?"

"No." She sank into a chair. "He'll be crabby for a few days, but nothing more. I saw my mom introducing you to people."

"She's been very nice." He took the seat next to hers. "Mia said all your sisters had crushes on me."

Brenna rolled her eyes. "Great. Like you need an ego boost. I gotta tell you, Nic, you're not as hot as all that."

He leaned close. "Yes, I am. Do I need to remind you what we were doing—"

She cut him off with a frantic shake of her head. "Don't say anything. My grandmothers could hear. Do you know how completely creepy that would be?"

"Okay, I don't want the old ladies knowing, either."

She looked at him. "Is this too weird? Being here like this? I mean I never invited you before."

Before. When they'd been desperately in love. When belonging had mattered as much as loving her.

"It's not what I expected," he admitted. "I didn't think I'd like your family."

"But you do?"

"Most of them."

Not that his feelings would make him change his mind about buying. Liking or not liking didn't affect business decisions.

Katie and her fiancé joined them. Nic listened to the conversation more than he participated. Most of his attention was captured by the lands around the hacienda. The sun had fully set and most of the view was in shadows, but he could make out rows of vines stretching into the distance.

Behind them were the winery buildings, and the tasting room beyond that. Marcelli Wines was smaller than Wild Sea. Smaller, but more prestigious. Once they were a part of his holdings, he would have achieved everything he wanted. He would be the best. It was all here, within his grasp.

Dinner was the blur of courses that Brenna had promised. Colleen had rearranged the seating, putting Nic on her right and Brenna next to him. Lorenzo was at a different table, with his back to them.

"Save room for dessert," Brenna said, leaning close to speak in his ear. "The Grands outdid themselves with this amazing cake they make. The cream filling is probably illegal, it's so good." She sighed. "I've been living here since March. I don't dare get my cholesterol checked. As for dieting, forget it."

His gaze dropped to her breasts, and he instantly remembered them bare and filling his hands. The memory expanded to include the sight of her, naked, flushed with need and riding him with an abandon that had left him so hard, he practically winced with pain. As far as he was concerned, there wasn't a damn thing wrong with her body, except that it was too clothed and they weren't alone.

He reached for his wine. The full-bodied Cabernet did nothing to stop the flow of blood south. In three seconds he was shifting uncomfortably in his seat.

He still hadn't figured out how making love with Brenna fit in with his plan. His first thought had been that while it had been great, they probably shouldn't do it again. But on second thought . . .

He reached for her hand and slid it across his thigh

until her fingers encountered his erection. She looked at him, her eyes wide, her mouth slightly parted.

"What's that all about?" she asked in a whisper.

He pressed his lips to her ear. "You naked, riding me to hell and back."

She swallowed and pulled her hand free. "We can't talk about this. My mother is right next to you."

"I know. That makes it more exciting."

She reached for her water glass. "You're nothing but trouble."

He leaned close again. "Tell me you're not wet and I'll shut up."

She took a drink of water, deliberately turned her back, and started speaking with the man on her other side. Nic chuckled. While Brenna was pretending to ignore him, he ran his finger down her spine. He was rewarded by a slight shiver and goose bumps breaking out on her arm.

Nearly an hour later, as the plates were being cleared, Marco stood up. The crowd quieted. He picked up a microphone from a stand by the table and walked to the front of the tent.

"I would like to thank all of you for coming to help our family celebrate. Engagements and weddings are always special, but Italian weddings"—he grinned—"they're events."

Everyone laughed.

"The Marcelli family has a long, proud history."

Marco outlined the founding of the winery, omitting any reference to the connection with the Giovanni family or the feud that had occurred. As Nic listened, he glanced at those in attendance. Lorenzo had turned his chair to face his son, but never glanced in Nic's direction. Mia winked when he caught her eye and Katie smiled. Even Grandma Tessa raised a glass of wine in his direction.

His plan to buy Marcelli Wines had been born nearly ten years ago. Except for Brenna, the Marcellis had been faceless enemies. He'd never connected them with people he might come to know.

He told himself nothing had changed. So what if he'd met them? Was he going to walk away from years of hard work just because he'd been treated well at a party? He was a man who went after what he wanted, and he wanted Marcelli Wines. End of story.

But he had the uneasy feeling that despite his conviction, something had changed. Something he couldn't define or even explain.

He shook off the thought and returned his attention to Marco.

"My daughters, Katie and Francesca. I would ask that you raise your glasses to toast them and the fine men they will marry. To my—"

A loud gasp from Colleen silenced him. Beside him, Brenna turned to see what had shocked her mother.

"I can't believe it," she said with delight and got to her feet. "He's here."

Nic frowned. He saw a man walking toward the gathering. He was tall and casually dressed, with a duffel bag slung over one shoulder.

Brenna walked toward him, which got Nic on his feet and moving toward her. The man stopped in the light of a hanging lantern. Nic knew he'd never seen the guy before, but his features were oddly familiar.

"Seems like my timing is off," the stranger said to Brenna as she approached.

"Only if you weren't planning on making an entrance."

She was smiling and happy. Nic glared. So who the hell was this asshole and how did he know Brenna?

11

*B*renna had figured the day's roller-coaster events had peaked when she'd brought Nic to the party. But she'd been wrong. The fun just kept on coming, this time in the unexpected arrival of her long-lost brother.

She couldn't remember the last time she'd been this confused about one person. Joe Larson could destroy her hopes and dreams with a single sentence. She should hate him. Yet she didn't. She was actually happy to see him, in a twisted, ambivalent, why-was-this-happening sort of way.

"Have any trouble finding the place?" she asked.

"Nope."

"Are you here for the money?"

Joe grinned. "You cut right to the chase, don't you? Maybe I'm interested in meeting my family more than collecting an inheritance."

"Are you?"

He glanced at the watching crowd. "It's more of a reception than I expected."

"An engagement party for two of my . . . our sisters. Francesca, the one you met with me, and Katie."

"How many of those folks are actual relatives?"

"More than you'd think. At least you can meet them all at once."

Joe Larson, all six feet plus of Navy SEAL–honed muscle and brawn, actually took a step back. "Great."

"And a hundred of their closest friends."

"You know how to make a guy feel welcome."

"This can't be worse than night ops in enemy territory."

His dark gaze settled on her face. His expression was unreadable, but she thought she might have seen wariness in his eyes. One corner of his mouth turned up. "Want to bet?"

"Not really." She turned toward the tables. "It's Joe."

A whispered buzz swept through the crowd. Most of the guests wouldn't know who Joe was, but her parents did, as did her sisters. Mia spilled the beans by popping to her feet and clapping her hands together.

"That's my brother?" she asked in obvious delight. "This is so cool."

"Mia," Brenna murmured for Joe's benefit. "She's the baby of the family. Too smart for her own good and we all adore her. You met Francesca already, and the guy beside her is Sam, her fiancé. Katie is standing over there. Next to her is Zach, *her* fiancé. Grandpa Lorenzo is the fierce-looking old guy. His wife, Grandma Tessa, is next to him, and Grammy M is sitting with her date."

The Marcelli family walked slowly toward them. Brenna's parents arrived first. Tears filled her mother's eyes and her father looked stunned, which made sense. Outside of soap operas, events like this didn't happen.

Brenna cleared her throat. "So, everyone, this is Joe. Joe, my . . . um, make that *our* parents. Colleen and Marco Marcelli."

There was an awkward moment when no one moved. Finally Joe approached their father and held out his hand. They shook. Joe glanced anxiously at their mother, who continued to cry.

"Are you all right, ma'am?"

She blinked several times, then reached up and touched his face. "Is it really you?"

Looking more than a little uncomfortable, he nodded. "I'm Joe Larson."

The Grands approached, along with Grandpa Lorenzo. Brenna's sisters hovered in the background. Grandma Tessa pulled out her rosary.

"God is blessing our family," she whispered.

Grandpa Lorenzo moved close and clutched Joe by the shoulders. "I see my father in you."

Brenna leaned close. "I haven't seen pictures, so I can't tell you if that's a good thing or not."

Grandpa Lorenzo ignored her. "You are welcome, Joe Larson." He frowned. "Joe. That isn't right. You were to be named Antonio, after my father."

Joe winced. "Tough luck for me, huh?"

There was a moment of silence, then everyone laughed. Grandma Tessa pushed her husband aside and reached up to pinch Joe's cheek. Brenna was pleased when her macho brother flinched. Grandma Tessa had some power in her old fingers. Grammy M linked arms with her daughter. Katie and Mia approached for an introduction.

Her mother took over, saying again and again, "This is my son." Her father seemed content to simply smile at his firstborn.

Brenna stepped back to watch the family interact with Joe. Despite what his existence meant to her, she'd liked him from the first moment she'd met him. Now he was here, and judging from the reaction, he would be welcomed with open arms.

Not a surprise, she told herself as Grandpa Lorenzo moved close and spoke in low tones. No doubt the elder Marcelli was spelling out the possibilities of inheriting the winery. Only an idiot would turn down an inheritance like the Marcelli winery, and Joe didn't look like a fool. She was going to lose everything, just because she didn't have a penis.

"We never meant to let you go," her mother was saying. She touched Joe's arm over and over as if reassuring herself that he was really there. The Grands were pressing in, and Brenna realized that Joe had the trapped look of a cornered animal. Oddly, she felt responsible for him, which meant she should probably come to the rescue.

"Okay, break it up," she said, slipping between Joe and the family. "Give the guy a couple of minutes to catch his breath. I'm going to take him up to the house and get him settled. Why don't the rest of you go satisfy the curiosity of our guests?"

Her mother hesitated. Brenna leaned close and hugged her. "I won't let him get away," she whispered. "But I think there's too many of us for a first meeting."

Their mother nodded. Tears filled her eyes again. "We're happy you're here."

Joe gave a clipped nod. "Thank you."

The "ma'am" was there at the end of the sentence, but silent. Brenna wondered if he would ever think of Colleen Marcelli as his mother.

"I can come back in the morning," he said. "We can, ah, talk."

"Come back?" Grandpa Lorenzo exclaimed, sounding outraged. "Where are you going?"

"To a motel. I saw one not far from here."

Brenna winced. "You shouldn't have said that."

She barely got the words out before conversation exploded.

"You must stay here," Grandma Tessa said forcefully. "You're family."

"You'd be no trouble a'tall," Grammy M informed him.

"You getting away is so *not* going to happen," Mia said with a grin.

Brenna looked at Joe and shrugged. "Sometimes it's just plain easier to give in."

"Sure. I guess I could stay for a while."

"Good plan," she murmured.

Joe picked up his duffel. Brenna glanced toward the tables and wondered if she should say something to Nic about joining him in a few minutes. Then Joe started toward the house and she hurried after him.

Temporary staff filled the kitchen. Brenna collected a plate of food, a bottle of wine, and two glasses, then led the way into the dining room.

"Take a load off," she said, jerking her head toward the large table.

Joe set the duffel on the floor, then pulled out a chair. He took the plate she offered, along with flatware.

"Is that wine all for me?" he asked.

She laughed. "Don't sweat it. I'm not trying to get you drunk. I thought it would take the edge off. Besides, Marcelli Wines is your heritage. Think of this as the beginning of your education. Your inheritance won't come for free."

He ignored her statement and glanced toward the kitchen. "You have any beer?"

"Peasant," she muttered as she expertly opened the bottle of Cabernet. After pouring them each a glass, she took the seat opposite his and sank onto the chair.

"Are you all right?" she asked.

He sliced off a piece of chicken. "Sure."

"You look a little shell-shocked."

His dark gaze narrowed. "The hell I do."

She laughed. "Sensitive, aren't we? Does this have something to do with your rough-and-tumble reputation? Do you really know fifty-seven ways to kill me?"

He chewed without speaking. Brenna sipped her wine and studied his face. His coloring was more Italian than Irish, but his features were a blend of the two.

"Second thoughts about coming here?" she asked.

"I'm way past that." He picked up his wineglass and frowned at the contents.

"You're supposed to admire the color," she told him. "Appreciate the blends of reds and purples. Next, smell the bouquet." She demonstrated. "Black cherry, chocolate, a little plum."

He sniffed. "It smells like wine."

She winced. "Right. Next, a sip. Let the liquid roll around on your tongue as you experience all the—"

Joe chugged about a third of the wine, swallowed, shrugged, and set the glass on the table. "Not bad."

"That wine received a ninety-two from *Wine Spectator*," she said faintly. "It was so highly allocated we had people offering nearly double the retail price per case. I won a gold medal for that wine."

"It's fine."

She leaned back in her chair. "Gee, thanks."

How on earth could her grandfather consider leaving everything to a man who said their prize wine was *fine?* It was so wrong, it was almost funny. She would start laughing just as soon as the pain faded a little.

The door to the kitchen opened and Mia entered. "Hi, Joe," she said as she sashayed toward them.

He eyed her cautiously.

Mia rested one hip on the table and leaned toward him. "So, you're quite the hunk. Are there more like you at home?"

Joe made a show of glancing at his watch. "Aren't you up a little late."

Mia grinned. "I'm eighteen, Big Brother. All grown up."

Brenna waved her hand toward the door. "Torture Joe tomorrow. He's already nervous enough to bolt."

His intense gaze swung toward her. "What did you say?"

"That you're a little uneasy. It's perfectly understandable."

Mia pouted. "But I want to ask about his friends."

"Later."

Her baby sister ignored the hint. "So if you don't want to talk about yourself, what about us? Are we family yet?"

He shrugged. "Sorry, no."

"Brenna says Grandpa Lorenzo is going to want to leave you everything. That has to be exciting."

Joe's expression turned unreadable. "Maybe."

Mia shook her head. "Don't worry about offending me. I was never going to run the place. I'm sure there will be cash settlements on the girls, which makes me happy. But still, it's a big deal."

"A forty million dollar big deal," Brenna murmured, feeling sick to her stomach.

Joe frowned. "The old man doesn't even know me."

"Not a problem," Brenna told him. "Traditional Italian grandfathers love to leave the family business to their grandsons. That would be you."

"Will you accept?" Mia asked eagerly. "I would. I mean you can sell it or leave Brenna in charge."

"Thanks for the endorsement," Brenna said.

She wanted to run from the room, but it was like watching a car accident. She couldn't seem to tear herself away, even though the truth was going to cut her to her bones.

"I wouldn't say no," Joe admitted. "But it's not an issue yet."

Brenna swallowed hard. "It will be. Try to act surprised. It will make my grandfather happy."

Mia pushed off the table. "Okay, I'll go now. But I'll be hanging around tomorrow. We can get to know each other and you can tell me all about your hunky friends."

"I can't wait," Joe muttered and returned his attention to his dinner.

Brenna was grateful for the few minutes of silence. She had to collect herself, to figure out how to act normal. This wasn't news. She'd known that Joe showing up was a possibility, and if he did . . .

Maybe Grandpa Lorenzo wouldn't offer him everything, she told herself, even as she didn't believe the words. Maybe . . .

She sighed. Maybe she should just get used to the fact that the odds of her ever running Marcelli Wines was about zero. She had a plan, a chance for success with her own thing. That was good. Better than good. It was great.

Five minutes later Joe finished dinner. Brenna led him upstairs to the guest room at the end of the hall.

"You have your own bathroom," she said as she pushed open the bedroom door. "Sleep as late as you would like." She grinned. "Unless you want to rejoin the party."

"No, thanks."

He tossed his duffel onto the floor, then crossed to the

window. It faced the backyard. From there he could see the people milling around.

"Sorry I came?" he asked without looking at her.

"No. Why do you ask?"

"My being here could change a lot of things."

"He's your grandfather, too. Even though you've just found out about us, you're still family." She searched her heart. "I can't regret that you exist."

He smiled at her. "Gee, thanks."

"You're welcome." She moved to the window and stood next to him. "I know this is all a little overwhelming, but you'll get used to us with time."

"I'd settle for keeping the names straight."

He was big and tall and despite her teasing, he probably did know fifty-seven ways to kill her. But that didn't mean he wasn't currently out of his element.

"Did you ever think about what your real family was like?" she asked.

"Sometimes." He closed the blinds. "I never pictured anything like this."

"I wouldn't think so. Who could possibly dream up the Marcellis?" She touched his arm. "I need to get back to the party. Want me to check on you later?"

He scowled. "No."

She chuckled. "Okay, then. I'll see you in the morning." She walked to the door. "You will still be here, won't you?"

"What do you think?"

"That you didn't get to be who and what you are by quitting."

"Good call."

She opened the door and stepped into the hall. "Despite everything, I'm glad you decided to pay us a visit, Joe. Good night."

• • •

The party buzz about the stranger reached Nic about the same time he figured out why the guy looked familiar and who he was. The Marcelli family's long-lost son.

Marco finally returned to the microphone. He looked shell-shocked, but happy.

"We've had something of a surprise," he told the crowd. "After many long years our firstborn son has returned to us." He waited for the swell of conversation to die down. "Joe is going to be staying with us for a few days, so most of you will get the chance to meet him. In the meantime, I would like to return to the reason for our celebration and toast the engagement of my daughters Katie and Francesca."

Nic raised his glass. Brenna had gone into the house with her brother and had yet to return. Not sure why it mattered, or why he gave a damn, he kept an eye on the back door. The emotional surge he'd experienced when she'd hurried off to greet a strange man had faded, leaving behind a certain level of confusion. Why did he care if Brenna was interested in some other guy? He and Brenna weren't together. He had no claim on her. No way he'd been jealous.

The rational part of his brain assured him there was a logical explanation. The penis-run part grunted something about wanting sex again. He did his best to remember his plan and why it was important. Nothing personal, he reminded himself. Just business.

And his business plan might have just taken a dump . . . at least for the moment. The existence of a male heir could change things. Lorenzo Marcelli was nothing if not traditional, and traditional Italian patriarchs left the family business to the firstborn son. Did that mean Marcelli wasn't going to be for sale? Or did it mean he only had to wait?

Joe Larson was unlikely to enjoy running a winery for very long. Nic was pretty sure he could convince the man to take the money and run.

Nic started for the house, only to stop when Lorenzo stepped in front of him. The old man glared at Nic.

"No Giovanni is welcome here."

Nic shoved his hands into his pockets. "There's a surprise." He shook his head. "Don't you ever get tired of the past? It's done. No one cares about what happened over sixty years ago."

"I care." Lorenzo's eyebrows drew together. "I know the truth."

"The truth is Antonio Marcelli screwed up. Something happened to his vines, and rather than admit that, he blamed my grandfather. Antonio was jealous of his friend's success. It's an old story."

Lorenzo stared at him for a long time. "You think you know so much," he said at last. "That the new ways are always better. Things happened for a reason. You claim that your family is the injured party, accused of a crime they didn't commit. Are you sure? You weren't there. What do you know of the truth?"

Mia sidled up to Lorenzo and beamed at the old man. "Are you torturing our guest?"

"We're talking about the old days."

Mia rolled her eyes. "Grandpa, it's a party. You need to have a little fun. Why don't you take Grandma Tessa for a spin around the dance floor and show her a good time?"

"Not yet. This one . . ." He moved closer to Nic.

"Trying to take me on, old man?" Nic asked. "I'm not going to fight you."

"Maybe not, but you'll do something." Lorenzo's eyes narrowed. "What do you want with my granddaughter?"

Mia winced. "Grandpa, you really don't want to ask that question. I mean what if Nic answers it?"

The old man took a step back. "This is not the time, not with guests here. But soon. You and I, we are not finished."

Nic liked the idea of a challenge. "I look forward to our next meeting."

Lorenzo muttered something in Italian, then stalked away. Mia watched him go.

"Want me to tell you what he said?" she asked.

"No."

"Just as well. It wasn't very polite." She linked arms with Nic. "This has been the best party. I didn't expect it to be so exciting. Joe arriving, you fighting with my grandfather. So what did you think of our brand-new big brother? Isn't he a hunk? Cute, but very annoying. He practically accused me of being a baby. I mean, come on. Do you really think it's so awful that I want to meet some of his manly Navy SEAL friends?"

"What I really think is that I'm glad I'm an only child."

Mia huffed out a breath. "Oh, please. I'm the best sister. I'm newly single and I'm not in school for a few more weeks. This is my time to cut loose and be wild. Once classes start, I have to be all mature and stuff. So if I can't do the Navy SEAL thing for a while, how about a ride on your motorcycle?"

He removed her hand from his arm. "You accused me of being trouble, but you're the one who needs watching."

Her lips curved. "Really? You like to watch?"

He took a step back. "Don't go there, Mia. I'm not for you."

"Does that mean you're for Brenna?" She laughed. "Never mind. I know you're not going to answer that. Come on. You can dance with me until my sister returns to rescue you."

He glanced toward the couples already on the dance floor, then back to the eighteen-year-old sex kitten in front of him. "No slow dances."

She sighed heavily. "Fine. No touching. What is it with you older guys? You're all so uptight."

"Not uptight. Afraid. We're all very afraid."

Brenna kicked off her shoes and shifted on the top step of the porch. It was well after two and while she knew she had to get back home, she didn't want to leave. Not that she wanted to stay. Being around Nic made her nervous.

She stared up at the night sky. They were far enough away from any large city for the stars to be visible. Hundreds of lights twinkled like rhinestones on black velvet.

"Mia needs a keeper," Nic muttered.

Brenna chuckled. "Probably. I think she completely freaked out Joe."

"She told me she wanted to meet his friends. She's only eighteen."

"Mia has always been older than her years. Don't forget, she's been in college since she was sixteen and she's been engaged. She's way more worldly than I was at her age."

"One day someone is going to take her up on one of her blatant offers, and then where will she be?"

Brenna turned to look at the man sitting next to her. "In someone's bed."

He flinched. "We're talking about your baby sister."

"So? Her relationship to me doesn't prevent her having sex."

Nic glanced at her. "You okay?"

"About Mia? I'm fine."

"Not about Mia. About Joe."

"Oh, that. Can I say I don't want to talk about it?"

"Sure."

She thought about all that had happened. "His arrival changes everything. He's interested in inheriting. Who wouldn't be? It's a lot of money."

"Your grandfather hasn't left him anything yet. Maybe you should wait to panic."

She glanced at him and managed a smile. "Oh, sure. Be rational. So like a guy."

He shrugged. "I mean it, Brenna. Lorenzo may be old-fashioned, but he's not an idiot. Why would he leave everything to someone who knows nothing about the business?"

She desperately wanted to believe Nic, and in a way, what he said made sense. "Okay. I'll try to calm down."

"Good."

She sighed. "Mia told me my grandfather tried to take you on."

"She's exaggerating."

"I'm sorry if the situation got ugly."

"We discussed the feud, taking opposite sides, of course. Don't worry. I can take care of myself."

She didn't doubt that. Nic was more than capable.

"It's been quite an evening," she said as she pulled her legs to her chest and rested her arms on her knees. "So what did you think? This was your first Marcelli party and all."

"Plenty of surprises. Your brother showing up was unique entertainment."

"Tell me about it. I hope we don't have an even bigger surprise at the double wedding."

They were sitting close enough that when he moved, his shoulder brushed against hers. In the still night she could almost hear him breathing. Her skin prickled with awareness.

"We have to talk about it," he said.

Oh, no they didn't. "I'm not sure I have the emotional energy to deal with one more thing."

"We didn't use any birth control."

Those six words exploded in her brain. Brenna swore under her breath. No way. That wasn't possible. She was more responsible than that. Never once in her life, not even all those years ago when she'd been so in love with Nic had she ever allowed herself to be so swept away that she didn't even *think* about birth control.

She straightened her legs and crossed her arms over her midsection. Talk about going from sexual interest to horrified panic in less than fifteen seconds. Thank God for modern science and birth control pills.

"There aren't health issues with me," he continued. "But there are other considerations."

He sounded remarkably calm. In his position she would have been shrieking.

"I'm on the Pill," she told him hastily. "I meant to go off it after Jeff and I separated, but my doctor warned me I would have mood swings. With all the stuff going on with my grandfather and the winery, followed by my decision to start my own winery, this didn't seem like a good time to be emotionally unstable."

He glanced at her. "You don't have to justify being on the Pill to me. I'm not in a position to complain."

"I guess not."

Now that he'd brought it up, she had no choice but to remember everything they'd done and how fast it had all happened. One second they'd been talking and the next clothes were flying and bodies joining. Her insides quivered at the memory.

"We always did have that effect on each other," she said, not looking at him as she spoke. "I would have thought we'd outgrown it."

"Apparently not."

She couldn't tell from his tone if he thought that was a good thing or a bad thing.

"I try to keep my business life and personal life separate," he said.

She cleared her throat. "We have a lot of history. Between working together after all this time and our past, it was probably just one of those things."

"I'm sure it was."

Damn. That was *not* the answer she wanted. She wanted their close encounter of the intimate kind to have meant something to him. If the passion was still alive, didn't that mean that other things from their past could be lurking under the surface? Did she want that?

"Women frequently view me as a sex object, so what happened tonight isn't a surprise."

She laughed. "Excuse me?"

He smiled confidently. "Women want me."

"As in there's a herd of them roaming the world, lusting after your person?"

"The women in my office think I have a great butt. Maggie told me."

"I'm amazed there's room for you and your ego in the same room."

"Hey, I didn't make this up. I'm just passing along the information."

"As I hate being part of a crowd, I'll do my best to rein in my baser instincts."

"Don't do it on my account."

She wasn't sure if that was an invitation or more teasing. Not that she wasn't tempted, but she'd already played with fire once this evening. She should probably stop while she was unscathed and give thanks that she got off easy.

She stood. "It's time for me to head home. I'll leave you to deal with your fan club."

"What if I made you president? You'd be great at the job."

"Only if it paid enough to make a dent in my loan to you."

He rose and followed her to the car. Once there, he opened the door and she slid inside. She rolled down the window, then closed the door.

He leaned close and touched her cheek. "It just happened," he said. "We're adults. We can handle it."

She nodded. The truth was she didn't know if she *could* handle it, but she didn't have much choice.

He grinned. "It was a hell of a party."

"Hey, I know how to show a guy a good time." She started the engine. "See you, Nic."

"Drive safely."

He straightened and stepped back. She put the car in gear and headed down the driveway. Toward home. Yet she felt as if she'd left a part of herself behind.

12

B renna stood beside the truck and randomly picked up bunches of Cabernet grapes. After inspecting the color to make sure they had ripened evenly, she picked off a grape and tasted the fruit.

The foreman of the picking crew watched her. She let the rich flavors settle on her tongue, then swallowed.

"Just right," she said.

Ramón smiled. "I told you. Wait one more day and the grapes will be perfect."

She grinned. "You said wait one more day because you were still working at Wild Sea."

He shrugged. "Nic wanted more handpicked than he'd first said."

Brenna would like to think that was her influence, but she had her doubts. Nic's idea of a perfect vineyard would be one that was completely mechanized. Imagine the profit margin if no human ever had to get involved in the process from planting to slapping the label on the bottle.

Not that she planned to tell him any of that to his face. She still owed him for what he'd told her the night of the party. That her grandfather wasn't crazy enough to leave the winery to a stranger.

Nic's words made sense and she clung to them with all her strength. So far they'd allowed her to relax enough to get on with her life. Not that she had much choice in that.

She waved the truck in and stepped back to let it drive into the courtyard, where dozens of workers stood ready to unload the baskets of grapes. While Ramón discussed the yield per acre, she made notes. The sun was high in the sky, the afternoon warm. Perfect harvesting weather. The seven-day forecast didn't show any rain. If that held true, they could be finished with the Cabs by next Wednesday. This was turning out to be a very good year.

Humming to herself, she pulled several baskets off the truck, then climbed onto the flatbed and picked several clusters of grapes from baskets toward the front. The dark purple color made her smile. Ramón's crew knew their business.

"How ever much you're paying him it's too much," her grandfather called as he came around the corner of the winery.

Brenna jumped off the truck. She hadn't seen her grandfather since the party the previous Saturday. Work had kept her busy. It wasn't as if she was actually avoiding him . . . well, not too much.

As her grandfather picked a handful of grapes from the baskets being carried inside, she braced herself for the inevitable criticism. Lorenzo Marcelli was all backslapping good humor with Ramón, but Brenna wasn't fooled. He would taste the grapes and then turn on her with one complaint or another.

"Good harvest," he said mildly.

She nodded.

"We'll bottle more this year than we did last year."

She nodded again.

"You dishonored the family. Last Saturday was about your sisters. You brought an enemy into this house and turned all the attention on yourself."

Brenna didn't know what to say to that. The accusation was so unfair that words failed her. Not that it mattered. He wasn't finished with her.

"Do you know who that boy is? Do you know what his family did to us?"

For a second Brenna was so caught up in Nic being called a boy that she didn't catch the rest of it. But when her grandfather's words sank in, she threw down her clipboard and planted her hands on her hips.

"I know exactly who Nicholas Giovanni is, Grandfather. Not only did I grow up next door to him, but you've told us all the story of the great grapevine scandal so many times, I could recite it in my sleep. And you know what? I don't care."

Her grandfather flinched.

She narrowed her gaze. "Here's a news flash for you. Ten years ago I fell in love with Nic. Yup, me. One of your precious granddaughters, flesh of your own flesh. We met and started dating."

She hesitated, then decided it was best not to mention that she and Nic had been lovers. Her grandfather probably wanted to hear about that as much as she wanted to hear about him and Grandma Tessa doing the wild thing.

"We talked about wine and life and I really cared about him. In fact, I almost married him. And you know what? The heavens didn't open. The sky didn't fall. The feud is long over, and it's time for all of us to move on."

Her grandfather's expression turned thunderous. "How

dare you tell me this? You go behind my back and see the son of my enemy? You disrespect the family so much?"

She dropped her hands to her sides. "Don't you get it? No one cares about that but you."

"I follow tradition. I listen to the counsel of those wiser than me. Something you could learn from. Already you have one husband who leaves you. Nearly thirty years old and what do you have to show for your life?"

Brenna felt as if he'd slapped her. She took a step back. But he wasn't done with her.

"You disappoint me, Brenna. I can find nothing to be proud of. Not with you. Not anymore."

She told herself he was going for the cheap shot, but that didn't make his words hurt any less. Her throat burned and her chest tightened. When exactly did one become grown-up enough to hear the words "I'm disappointed in you" and not want to crawl under a rock?

She picked up the clipboard and headed for the house.

"Where are you going?" her grandfather asked.

"Away from you."

"No. You will stay. I asked Joe to come out and see the grapes as they came in today. Ah, there he is."

Brenna looked up and saw her brother heading toward them. Joe glanced from her to Lorenzo, as if sensing tension.

"How's it going?" he asked.

"Wonderful," her grandfather said. "The Cabernet grapes are just ripe. We will produce a beautiful wine."

"I saw some guys out picking today," Joe said. "It looks like hard work."

"It is." Brenna said. "Want to volunteer to join the crew?"

"Not me. I'm on vacation."

Her grandfather motioned to the vines by the winery. "Come. We will walk and I will tell you how we take grapes and make the best wine anywhere. Brenna, you come, too."

She wasn't sure if this was another form of torture or her grandfather's way of saying he forgave her. As she didn't believe she'd done anything wrong, she wasn't thrilled with either alternative.

They headed east to where the Cabs were being picked.

"See there?" her grandfather said. "We still pick by hand for our best grapes. The rest are harvested by machine. Not the old way, but the cost of the labor is so high." He shrugged. "We have to make compromises."

Brenna clenched her teeth. Right. Talk to Joe about compromises and talk to her about betrayal.

"How do you know which grapes deserve handpicking?" Joe asked.

"It's all about quality," her grandfather said. "The history of the vines. What we have made before."

"There are several factors," Brenna told him. "Yield per ton, for example. Some grapes produce more juice; some are sweeter, more tart. Some blend better; some stand on their own. It can change from year to year, but our most consistent quality vines get the best treatment. Those vines produce the premium wines, the Reserves. Handpicking means we pick only the best, ripest grapes. The machines pretty much grab everything, so there's less control."

Joe wore a loose T-shirt over his jeans. He tugged on the crew neck.

"It's hot," he said. "Is that good?"

"Warm and dry." Brenna kicked at the loose earth. "We pray for warm and dry during harvest. Before that, it's a balance. Too little sun and the grapes won't ripen. Too much and they burn, overripen, or produce too much sugar. We need rain for irrigation, but not so much that there isn't sun and the plants get mold."

Joe glanced around at the vines. "It's a lot of work. To be honest, I don't get the whole wine thing. I'm more of a beer drinker myself."

Brenna grinned when her grandfather's mouth pinched as if he'd just tasted a lemon.

"You will learn to appreciate the subtleties of wine."

Joe shrugged. "I'm not a real subtle guy. A good steak and a beer is more to my taste."

Her grandfather seemed unamused. "You see all that we have created here. Can't you feel the pull of the soil? This is where you belong, Joe. This is your heritage. This could all be yours if you were only to ask."

Brenna froze. Nic had been wrong. Her grandfather *was* that crazy.

Oh, it hurt. She'd known this could happen. The discovery of a long-lost brother had been one of the reasons she'd started Four Sisters. But to have her grandfather spell it out like that—right in front of her, as if he didn't care that he was ripping out her heart . . .

Without saying anything, she turned and walked back toward the winery. Her grandfather didn't say a word. No doubt with Joe there, he wouldn't even notice she was gone.

Lorenzo turned to watch Brenna go. She walked stiffly, as if her muscles wouldn't cooperate. He'd seen her pain when he'd spoken of Joe inheriting. Seen it, felt it, and regretted it. But he had no choice.

His grandson shoved his hands into his pockets. "So you'd leave all this to me. Just like that?"

"Maybe not 'just like that.' You would have to be interested."

"Brenna said the place is worth about forty million."

Lorenzo shrugged. "Perhaps a little less, perhaps a little more."

"That's a hell of a lot of money." Joe stared at the vines.

"So you could be interested?"

"What about your granddaughters?"

"They would be provided for. A nice settlement."

"But not this."

"No."

Joe turned to him. Lorenzo tried to read his face, but the young man's expression didn't give away his thoughts.

"Doesn't Brenna love this place?"

Lorenzo brushed off the information with a flick of his hand. "She is a woman. This land, this heritage, it must be in the hands of a male heir."

Joe snorted. "Has anyone told you what century we're in?"

He smiled. "I am very aware of the passage of time. That is part of the problem." His smile faded as he continued to watch Brenna move away.

"Women can't be trusted," he said, more to himself than to his grandson. "They marry. They move away. They no longer care about what is important."

"You're not talking about Brenna. She loves this place."

"Now. But before?" He shrugged. "She left as if we all meant nothing. And for what?"

She'd disappeared as if she had never been. He remembered how he'd waited for her to realize that the juice of the grapes flowed through her body like blood. That she

was one with the land. But no. Instead she'd devoted herself to her husband. And last week. He sighed heavily. A
Giovanni, here? His father would never have permitted it.
Lorenzo himself had dishonored the memory of his father
by letting that boy stay and dine with his family on a night
of celebration.

"You may know the wine business," Joe said, "but I
know something about surviving. Ignoring your best
resource is a real good way to end up dead. Brenna is the
best you have. If you dismiss her, you're a fool."

Lorenzo nodded slowly. "Maybe you are right. Maybe
not. Eh? It's not as if I haven't been a fool before. Come, I
will show you more of what could be yours."

Nic walked out of his staff meeting to find Max had abandoned his bed and was nowhere around. Despite being
overly friendly, the pup didn't usually abandon his place by
Nic's office for anyone. With one exception.

Brenna.

He checked his watch. It was barely two. Brenna tended
to keep late hours when she was at Wild Sea. So if the dog
wasn't waiting for him, where was he?

Nic went in search of Max and found him ten minutes
later. He was stretched across Brenna's lap in the shade
of an old lemon tree by the back of the house. Nic hesitated when he saw the two of them. Brenna sat on the
ground, with her head down. Something about the
slump in her shoulders told him this had not been her
best day. He was torn between wanting to go be a friend
and the natural male need to avoid female upset. Friendship won.

As he approached, Brenna wiped her face and tried to

smile. Max barely opened an eye. His tail thumped once in greeting, then he drifted back to sleep.

"Want to talk about it?" Nic asked as he settled next to her.

She sniffed. "Good news. I get to tell you you're wrong. After that, I'm likely to burst into tears and sob all over your shirt."

"I'm never wrong," he said lightly. "What happened?"

"Nothing. Everything. I mean, it's not like I didn't know. I knew. It's not a surprise or anything."

"Want to translate that into English?"

She scratched Max's ears. "My grandfather told Joe that the winery could be his if he wanted it. Just like that. No training, no love of anything Marcelli, just 'here's your inheritance.' " She turned to look at him. "What is it about male heirs? Would I be so damn different if I had a penis?"

"You would be to me," he said honestly, more than a little startled that Lorenzo would play his cards so quickly.

"You know what I mean," she told him. "I wouldn't be any more interested in the winery, or smarter or good at my job."

That he could agree with. Nic leaned back against the tree. Lorenzo leave the winery to a virtual stranger? Was it possible? If the old man went ahead with it, Nic would have a slight delay of his own plans.

Brenna looked at him. "This is where you're supposed to make me feel better."

He met her gaze. "I don't believe your grandfather is going to leave Marcelli Wines to someone he just met. Joe doesn't know one end of the bottle from the other."

"I'll bet he knows that much, but little else." Despite her obvious pain, she smiled. "Joe admitted he's more of a beer drinker."

Nic leaned toward her and lowered his voice. "I've had a beer or two in my life. It wasn't bad. Don't tell anyone."

"At last. Blackmail material."

Her smile widened, then quivered and faded. Tears filled her eyes before falling down her cheeks.

"It's so horrible," she said, covering her face with her hands. "He's never happy. Everything is a fight. No matter what I suggest, it's wrong."

She kept talking, but as her tears increased, her voice shook and Nic found it difficult to understand her.

He reached toward her, then dropped his hand to his side. What was it about a crying woman that made a man feel awkward and inept? "It's not so bad, is it?"

She wiped away the tears. "Just when I think it's getting b-better, it all falls apart again. He s-said he was disappointed in me. I hate that. I'm twenty-seven years old. Why d-do I care what he thinks? But I do."

The last couple of words came out on a sob. Max raised his head and looked at Nic as if asking him why he wasn't doing something. Oh, because Nic was so clear on the next course of action. Right.

Feeling like an idiot, he shifted so that he could wrap his arms around her. He drew her close, resting her head on his shoulder and stroking her hair. Max jumped off her lap, stretched, and began sniffing their shoes.

"I'm s-sorry," Brenna whispered.

"It's okay. I'm here."

I'm here. When had he ever said those words to a woman? When had he last offered comfort? The situation between himself and Brenna Marcelli was more than a little complicated, but he couldn't think about that. At this moment she wasn't the enemy. She was simply Brenna.

Slowly her sobs faded. The tears fell less often and her

breathing grew more relaxed. He continued to stroke her hair, liking the fresh smell of her shampoo and the way she curled up against him. She was familiar in the best way possible.

When she straightened, her face was blotchy and her eyes swollen. He dropped his hands as she wiped her face with her fingers.

"Sorry," she murmured, not looking him in the eye. "I didn't mean to get all weird."

"Not a problem."

He handed her a handkerchief. She used it to mop up the last of her tears. Her mouth was swollen, as if she'd been kissing someone. As if they'd been kissing.

Once the thought took root, he couldn't seem to think about anything else. Nor could he stop himself from leaning close and pressing his lips to hers.

Her skin was damp and salty, and this close she smelled like sunshine and grapes. He wrapped his arms around her again. The passion that was never far below the surface made an instant and powerful appearance, but he ignored the heat and the pressure in his groin. Instead of deepening the kiss, he pulled back and looked into her eyes.

"You're not incompetent," he told her. "You're gifted. I admire what you're doing with Four Sisters, and if your grandfather doesn't appreciate your vision for Marcelli Wines, then he's a fool." He brushed her hair off of her face. "For what it's worth, you've impressed the hell out of me."

As soon as he spoke the words, he realized he meant them. When he'd first loaned her the money, he hadn't been sure what was going to happen, but now he knew she would be really big, if given half a chance. Ironically, he and her grandfather were the two men who held her fate in their hands.

The corners of her mouth turned up. "You sure know how to turn a girl's head."

"I'm telling the truth. Maybe that's why Lorenzo is riding you so hard. He sees that you'll do better than he did and it bugs him."

"Maybe. But it's a stupid reason to leave everything to Joe or sell out." Her dark eyes clouded. "You don't think he would really sell, do you?"

"We've already talked about that." He rose and held out his hand. "Come on. You can help me with my homework. That will distract you from all these questions."

She placed her fingers on his palm and stood. "What homework?"

"Remember Sophia's diary?"

She nodded.

"I'm about three pages further along in it. You took Italian in high school, so it can't be as bad as mine. We'll work on it together."

"I don't know how much help I'll be," she told him. "But I'm game."

An hour later he had to concede that her Italian was worse than his. They'd managed to work through half a page, and he wasn't sure they'd gotten any of it right.

Brenna picked up the old book and flipped through the densely written pages. "We could be at this for the rest of our lives. Do you want the practice of translating it or do you just want to know what it says?"

"I have a choice?"

"Sure. Mia is the language expert in our family. She's disgustingly fluent, both reading and writing. This wouldn't take her very long."

"Go for it."

She closed the diary. "If she finds directions to a gold

mine on Wild Sea lands, I can't promise to share the information with you."

"Fair enough."

She took the book. He thought she might say she had to go, but instead of leaving, she leaned back in her chair.

"I told my grandfather about us."

Nic wasn't sure what "us" she meant. That she had borrowed money from him or that they had made love the other night? No, he told himself. She couldn't have mentioned—

"That we used to go out," she clarified. "That we'd met ten years ago and had become important to each other."

"I'm surprised."

"Me, too." She placed the diary on the kitchen table. "He was going on and on about how horrible it was that I'd brought you to the party. Did I know who and what you were? Who your family was? That sort of thing. I snapped. I told him we'd gone out and that the sky hadn't fallen."

"I doubt that impressed him."

She shrugged. "You're right. He makes me crazy, but that's hardly news. Unfortunately, he's getting better at it. This thing with Joe . . ." She sighed. "I wish I could hate my brother, but I don't. In his situation I don't think I'd act any differently. Mia's torturing him about his friends, which makes him squirm."

"Which you enjoy."

She grinned. "Absolutely." She glanced at her watch. "Oh, hell. I need to get back." She rose and touched his arm. "Thanks for listening and letting me blubber all over your shirt."

Then she bent down and kissed him before heading for the back door.

His mouth burned where she'd brushed it with her

own. The fact that she'd already left the house didn't stop his body from responding. He'd always been a sucker where she was concerned.

He wiped the back of his hand across his mouth as if he could erase the fleeting contact. As if he could change things and make her not matter. She didn't. She couldn't. And yet . . .

Things were different. He couldn't say how exactly, but he could feel them changing. Brenna's comment about her grandfather's questions reverberated. Did she know who and what he was?

Brenna didn't. To her he was Nic, her next-door neighbor, an ex-lover, the guy who had offered to fund her dream for the future. She didn't know anything about his plans for her family's business. Brenna might be the better wine maker, but Lorenzo was the smarter businessman. It never hurt to find out too much about a potential enemy.

Not that Lorenzo knew. No one knew, save his hand-picked front men. And Maggie, who disapproved. Maggie, who had spent the last seven years being his conscience. Only this time he wasn't listening.

13

Late that afternoon Brenna tapped on Mia's door. When there was no response, she knocked louder, then pounded on the wood. Finally Mia opened the door and grinned. Her baby sister wore headphones and was dancing to a wild beat only she could hear. In a tank top and shorts, without her makeup, she looked about fifteen.

"You scare me," Brenna said as she stepped into the room. Mia clicked off the Discman and set the headphones on her desk.

"You're just jealous because I have rhythm." She proceeded to demonstrate a couple of dance steps that involved fast foot movement and flailing arms.

"I think what you have is a seizure."

Mia stuck out her tongue and sank onto the unmade bed. As usual, her room was a disaster area. Books were piled three deep on the desk in the corner. Piles of clothes covered the bed, the dresser, and the only chair in the room, while several open CD cases formed a free-style hopscotch pattern on the floor.

Brenna picked two bras, a skirt, and three T-shirts from the chair and tossed them at her sister.

"I've been to your apartment by school. You keep it relatively picked-up. Why do you live like a wild animal here at home?"

"I'm reverting." Mia clutched a pillow to her chest. "When I'm away I'm an adult, but somehow here at the hacienda I find myself acting like a twelve-year-old."

Brenna could think of several humorous and biting comments to make to that statement, but she was here to get Mia's help. She held up the diary.

"What's that?" Mia asked.

"Sophia Giovanni's diary. Nic has been working on translating it, but his Italian is almost as bad as mine. I thought maybe you could take a look at it. There's no rush."

Mia took the old book from her, carefully turned the pages, and began to read. "Sometimes I walk to the edge of the ocean and let the spray wash my face. I imagine that I'm on a boat that will take me to the ends of the earth."

Brenna stared at her. "You're kidding?"

Mia looked up. "What? That she really wrote that or that I can translate it?"

"Both." She sighed. "Never mind. Whenever you demonstrate your proficiency with languages, I remind myself that I can make better wine."

Mia chuckled. "Oh, right. Because I make you so jealous."

"Not jealous, exactly." Sometimes Mia was brilliant enough to be intimidating. Not that she would share that thought with her baby sister.

Mia dropped the diary on the bed and shifted so she was sitting cross-legged. "Okay, so I can pick up a language really easily, but I'm always missing out on the fun stuff.

Like you and Nic. When he was twenty, I was maybe seven or eight. No way was he ever going to notice me."

"You weren't interested in boys when you were seven or eight."

"I know, but I am now." She sighed dramatically. "Here I am in the fresh flower of my womanhood, and Nic is only interested in you."

Brenna didn't know what to deal with first. Mia's "fresh flower of womanhood" or her assertion that Nic was interested in her. If only. He was . . .

Brenna didn't know what he was, which was probably for the best.

"We have a business relationship," she said primly.

Mia shook her head. "No way. Maybe it started that way when you got the loan, but you brought him to the engagement party. This is not something you do with a business associate."

"He asked to be invited."

"Why?"

Brenna shrugged. She had a feeling his request had something to do with their past, but she wasn't going to bring that up.

"Maybe I just wanted to get back at Grandpa Lorenzo for making my life hell and leaving the winery to Joe."

Mia pressed her lips together. "I wish I could do something about that. You know, talk to Grandpa."

"You'd be wasting your breath, but I appreciate the sentiment."

"Maybe we should kidnap Joe. If he didn't show up back at the base or wherever he's stationed, they'd send some guys to rescue him. Then we'd both win. Grandpa Lorenzo would think Joe was a flake and disinherit him, and I'd get access to a bunch of cute guys."

Brenna laughed. "I like that plan. Let's work on the details."

Mia threw herself back on her bed. "Okay. How do we let the base know we only want really attractive single guys on the rescue team?"

"Since you broke up with David, all you think about is dating. Why is that? I thought you went out when you were in D.C."

"I did and it whetted my appetite for the whole boy-girl touching thing. Which is why I've been after Joe's friends, but he's really uncooperative."

"Who's uncooperative?"

They both turned and saw the man in question standing in the doorway. He surveyed Mia's room.

"This place is a mess."

She sat up. "I know. It's part of my charm."

"You have a disorganized mind."

"Maybe. But I'm still too adorable for words."

"I can think of a few words." He glanced at Brenna. "Hey."

"Hey, yourself."

"Doing okay?" he asked.

"Sure."

If she'd been ambivalent when Joe had first arrived, the feeling had only intensified over the past few days. The logical side of her brain told her none of this was Joe's fault. Oh, sure, he could be a great guy and refuse the offer of more money than he'd ever imagined. But that would make him certifiable. The fact that he'd won the inheritance lottery was just plain lucky for him and sucky for her.

So she shouldn't resent him or really want to kidnap him. But a part of her did.

"Have a seat," Mia said, patting the mattress.

He crossed to the bed and grabbed a handful of clothes, which he tossed onto the dresser, then settled on the mattress, as far from Mia as possible.

"We were talking about dating. I'm in desperate need of a meaningless relationship," Mia told him.

"Go fishing somewhere else," he said.

She frowned. "Is this a metaphor about my dating your friends?"

"Yeah."

"I didn't think you'd be so macho and brotherly." She glanced at Brenna. "Was he like this when you first met?"

"I don't think I tortured him as much as you do."

Mia turned her attention back to Joe. "If you're trying to protect me, it's really sweet, but I'm not a virgin. I haven't been for a long time."

Joe winced. "I really didn't want to know that."

Brenna grinned at his discomfort. "In the girls-against-boys battle, you're a little outnumbered."

"Tell me about it."

"Quit complaining. You love us," Mia said.

Brenna wasn't so sure. "We're still unfamiliar," she said. "A regular family would be a big adjustment, but I'm not sure how one gets used to the Marcelli clan."

"Slowly," Joe admitted. "You told me who everyone was when we first met, but I'm not sure I believed there were really that many people living in one house."

He leaned forward and rested his forearms on his thighs. "I don't remember when my folks told me I was adopted. I always seemed to know. Until they died, I never much thought about my real parents. Then I figured Colleen had given me up because she didn't want me."

Brenna stretched out her hand and touched his. "It

wasn't like that at all. She and Dad were too young to stand up to their parents. They weren't given much of a choice in the matter. Now things are different, but thirty years ago not many sixteen-year-olds were able to keep their babies."

He nodded.

"I never thought about how hard it would be to find out you had a whole family you'd never known about. You must be feeling really confused."

He glanced at her. "I'm a SEAL. I don't have feelings."

Brenna smiled. He looked up, met her gaze, and winked. Mia socked him in the arm.

Joe glanced around, looking puzzled. "Is there a fly in here? I think it just landed on my arm." He brushed at the place she'd hit him. "Huh. I guess not."

Mia shoved him. He didn't budge. She sighed heavily, then rested her head on his shoulder again.

"You have to like us at least a little," she said.

"Some more than others."

She rolled her eyes. "However you're acting, I'm glad you decided to come visit. We're all enjoying getting to know you. Even when you're uncooperative."

Joe put his arm around her. "You're tough, aren't you?"

"You bet." Her curving mouth straightened into a line. "You know, it's kinda cool having you around. Things would have been so different if Mom had been able to keep you. Our parents got married anyway. If they'd married then, you would have been one of us from the beginning. Would you have liked that?"

"I don't know," Joe admitted. "My parents aren't Colleen and Marco, and I can't imagine that changing. If I'd been raised here . . ." He shrugged.

Brenna understood his ambivalence about even considering an alternative life. If Joe had been around, if she'd known about him, her world view would have changed completely. He would have been the acknowledged heir. While she believed her interest in the vineyards would have always been there, she wasn't as sure about family pressure. With Joe in the picture, would she have been more willing to take a chance on Nic? With Joe as the one inheriting, would she have been more willing to risk her family's disapproval?

"If you'd been raised here, I would never have been born," Mia stated.

Brenna shook her head. "That's not true."

Mia's mouth twisted. "Sure it is. I'm okay with it. We all know that the doctors told Mom not to have any more children after you and Francesca were born. Yet she risked her health to try for a boy one more time. With Joe around, that wouldn't have happened."

Brenna couldn't imagine growing up without Mia tagging along, nor did she want to.

"Lorenzo is too hung up on gender," Joe muttered.

"That's Brenna's theory," Mia said brightly. "The family business is wine, not breeding, so what does having a penis matter."

Brenna winced. "I don't phrase it exactly like that."

"Close enough."

Joe ruffled Mia's hair. "You're a pain in the ass, kid."

"And you adore me."

"Maybe."

Joe looked at Brenna. "About this whole winery thing . . ." he began.

Brenna cut him off with a shake of her head. "We don't have to talk about it. What happens, happens. If Grandpa Lorenzo doesn't leave it to you, there's a good chance he's going to sell. I can't . . ." She swallowed. "I have to make my own plans." Which she'd done. Sure it hurt now, but eventually she would be fine.

"Everyone says you do a hell of a job."

Brenna appreciated the compliment. "That doesn't seem to matter much. You're the firstborn son, Joe."

"I didn't know I'd been getting in the middle of all of you," he said.

"That's family. Loving but messy."

Mia pouted. "Excuse me, but I'm still in the room. I want to talk about me."

"No way," Joe said. "You're only interested in dating inappropriate guys."

"Honestly, I think it's more about sex," Brenna said helpfully.

Joe winced again. "What is it with you two?"

Brenna raised her eyebrows. "Nothing. We're just normal, healthy women looking for love." She leaned forward. "I guess this is where I tell you I'm not a virgin, either?"

He stood. "I'm so out of here."

Mia raised her palm toward her sister. Brenna slapped her hand against Mia's in a gesture of victory. Joe groaned.

He was saved by Grandma Tessa calling up the stairs, telling them it was time for dinner, and to be sure to wash their hands before coming down.

Joe headed for the door. "We do this every night," he complained. "Why can't we eat separately, like normal families?"

Brenna was the last to arrive at the restaurant. She found her three sisters sitting at an outdoor table, in the shade of an oversize umbrella. Between the work she had at home and her new winery, she was running in fourteen directions at once. Mia's demand that she join them for lunch had been inconvenient. But as she approached the table, she found herself smiling in anticipation. She couldn't remember the last time the four of them had done something together.

"There you are," Francesca said as she pulled out the empty chair next to her. "Now that you're here, we're going to have to stop talking about you."

"Why?" Mia asked as she batted her eyes. "I think it's a lot more fun to talk about someone in front of them. Then you get a reaction."

"Is she getting on everyone else's nerves or just mine?" Brenna asked.

Katie handed her a menu. "She's pretty much annoying us all. Do I want to ask how things are going?"

Brenna took the menu and shook her head. "Nope."

"Then I won't."

The waiter appeared. He was in his early twenties, with the tanned good looks of a surfer. "Have you ladies decided?"

Brenna scanned the menu and nodded. Katie went first. They all ordered salads and iced tea. Mia asked for a side of fries. When the young man had written it all down and left, Mia sat straighter in her chair and cleared her throat.

"You're probably wondering why I called this meeting," she said.

Brenna thought she was kidding, but when she glanced at Mia, she saw her baby sister was completely serious.

"What's up?" Katie asked.

"Nothing specific," Mia said. "It's just that everything in our family is changing. I've felt uncomfortable for a while, and I've been trying to figure out where it all started. Maybe with my aborted engagement or Brenna's separation. Suddenly what was familiar isn't anymore. Katie, you and Francesca are getting married. Brenna's starting her own winery. I'm growing up."

"Can we take a vote on that?" Francesca asked.

Mia laughed. "No." Her humor faded. "I wanted us to get together one more time before everything is different forever."

Brenna felt her throat tighten. "Good idea, kid."

"Thank you."

Francesca and Katie both nodded.

Mia preened. "You keep talking about how smart I am, but then you never pay attention to me. I've had tons of brilliant plans that you've dismissed over the years."

The waiter appeared with their drinks. When he was gone, Katie picked up her glass.

"I sense trouble coming," she warned.

Mia ignored her. "It's true. What about the time I wanted to get Grammy M a membership in a dating service for her birthday? You three wouldn't listen, but look. She's dating Gabriel and is really happy."

"They wouldn't have met through a dating service," Francesca said.

"No, but she might have met someone else. My point is—"

Brenna laughed. "We are clear on your point, but we don't agree with it."

Mia scowled. "You guys are always like this. It's the three of you against me. You stick together because I'm so much younger."

"That's not true," Francesca said.

Brenna disagreed. It was often true. There were ten

years between Mia and Katie, nine years between Mia and herself and Francesca.

Brenna patted her shoulder. "We still love you."

"I know, but sometimes I want a little respect." She brightened. "The good news is I'm still cool while the three of you are seriously old."

"How flattering," Katie murmured.

Mia picked up her glass. "Anyway, that's why I wanted you all here. So we could reconnect."

Brenna glanced at Francesca. "Not a bad idea for a baby."

Francesca nodded.

Katie looked less convinced.

Mia sighed. "What?" she asked. "You have that 'Mom' look you sometimes get."

Katie shrugged. "I'm just wondering if you're really okay. Do you have any regrets about breaking off your engagement?"

Mia put down her glass. "No. David and I were really good together, but we were more caught up with having a relationship than actually thinking about what getting married would mean. I reacted to family pressure, and he reacted to being on his own for the first time. We've stayed friends and that works."

The waiter appeared with a basket of bread. Mia lunged for it and pulled out a piece, then passed the rest to Brenna.

"I will admit that I miss the sex," she said as she scooped up a pat of butter.

"Makes sense," Katie said.

Francesca looked at Brenna. "Was that just Miss I-Only-Want-Romance expressing interest in sex?"

Brenna laughed. "Probably because it's so good with Zach, she can relate now."

"I could always relate," Katie told them archly.

"Well, that's annoying," Brenna said. She turned to Mia. "I guess you and I are the only two not getting any these days. I resent that."

"Me, too," Mia grumbled. "When I get back to college, I'm finding a boy toy right off."

"Just be careful," Katie said. "If you still plan to rule the world, you need to consider staying single."

"I know." Mia sighed. "But single and sex-free aren't the same thing."

Francesca sipped her tea. "How are you doing, Brenna? It was stressful enough when you were just working at Marcelli and starting your own thing. But now, with Joe—are you okay?"

Brenna wasn't surprised her sister had brought up the subject. If only talking about it would make things more clear.

"I like him," she said slowly. "And I hate that Grandpa Lorenzo is going to leave him everything. So while I'm glad Joe is here, I can't help wishing he'd never been born. Pretty awful, huh?"

"Not at all," Katie said. "It's perfectly understandable."

Francesca patted her hand. "Why wouldn't you have mixed feelings?"

"You're being really brave about it," Mia said. "If I were you, I'd get serious about the kidnapping plan."

"What's that?" Katie asked.

Mia filled them in on the idea she'd had for getting rid of Joe.

"We'll ignore that he's a trained professional," Brenna murmured. "I doubt the four of us could take him."

"How embarrassing for him if we could," Mia said with a giggle.

"Maybe we're overreacting," Katie said. "Maybe it's all just cheap talk on Grandpa Lorenzo's part."

"I wish, but I was there," Brenna said, trying not to sound as if she cared. "He flat out told Joe that all of Marcelli could be his. Joe was more than interested."

"Which means you were really smart to start your own label," Francesca told her.

"I agree. I have to make it a success. And I'm going to. Thank God Nic came through with the money."

He'd saved her, she thought. Without him she'd be totally screwed.

The waiter appeared with their salads. Once he left, Brenna picked up her fork. She glanced around and saw her sisters were all staring at her.

"What?" she asked.

"You really brought Nic to the party," her twin said.

Brenna nodded slowly. "I asked you and Katie if you would mind and you both said it was fine."

Katie glanced at Francesca, then back at her. "Sure, but we didn't think you would actually do it."

"Okay." Brenna speared a piece of lettuce. "You guys could eat."

They ignored her.

"There's something going on there," Francesca said firmly.

"Is this your professional opinion?" Brenna asked, then took a bite of her salad and chewed.

"The question is what," Katie said.

"Cut to the chase." Mia looked at Brenna. "Have you had sex yet?"

Brenna started to choke. She managed to swallow the food, then drank her tea. While her discomfort was genuine, she couldn't help but be grateful for the distraction.

Mia's unexpected question had caught her off guard. While she didn't exactly want to lie to her sisters, she wasn't willing to tell the truth.

She cleared her throat. "Sorry. That went down the wrong way." She pointed at their untouched plates. "Are you going to eat?"

Mia looked at Francesca and Katie. "I can't believe it," her youngest sister breathed.

Francesca reached for Brenna's hand. "Tell us you didn't."

Now Brenna felt cornered. "Didn't what?"

"Sleep with Nic," Katie said, her voice low.

She cleared her throat. "I didn't."

She didn't sound convincing, even to herself.

Mia sighed. "You are so lying."

Brenna put down her fork. "Look, Nic and I have a working relationship, nothing more. We used to have something significant, and because of that, we have a past to deal with. Which we are."

"Talk about psychobabble," Katie said.

Mia grabbed a fry and took a big bite. "I can't believe I'm the only one not getting laid," she mumbled.

"It just happened one time," Brenna insisted. "It doesn't mean anything."

Francesca's gaze was steady. "Are you sure?"

"Yes. Absolutely. Cross my heart."

"Uh-huh." Katie started in on her salad.

Mia looked smug.

Francesca dropped her hand to her lap. She didn't say anything; she didn't have to. Her knowing look was enough to get on Brenna's nerves.

"Don't give me that 'all things happen for a reason' crap," Brenna told her. "This wasn't like that. It's not cosmic. It's hormones and circumstances. Given the past Nic and I had together, it was practically inevitable. But it didn't mean anything."

"So it wasn't your fault?" Mia asked innocently.

"Exactly."

"Be careful," Francesca warned.

"There's nothing to be careful about. We're just working together."

"And having sex," Mia said with a grin. "Was it amazing?"

"I'm not answering that."

"Which means yes," Katie said.

Brenna wanted to scream with frustration. "Why won't you listen to me?"

"Because you're not being honest with us or yourself," Francesca told her. "Nic is appealing on many levels. You have a past, now you work together. You said there's chemistry. It's a volatile situation."

"Does that matter if she cares for him?" Katie asked.

Francesca considered the question. "I don't know."

"Hello," Brenna growled. "I'm still sitting here at the table."

Mia poked at Brenna's avocado. "Are you going to eat that?"

Brenna slapped her fingers. "Yes."

"Do you care about him?" Francesca asked.

"I don't know."

This time Brenna was telling the truth. Did "care" describe her feelings for Nic? While having any emotional vulnerabilities where he was concerned made her nervous, "care" was a whole lot safer than several other feelings she could name.

"He's done a lot for me," she said slowly. "I appreciate

that. He's the reason I had the chance to start my own thing."

"He was pretty cool at the party," Mia pointed out. "Grandpa Lorenzo tortured him and everything and he was polite. He could have gotten all huffy. Obviously he's ready to put the past behind him, at least about the feud."

"Is the rest of it behind you, too?" Francesca asked.

Brenna considered that. "Most of it." But not all. Not by a long shot.

"Don't forget the diary," Mia said. "I give him a big thumbs-up."

"What diary?" Katie asked.

"Sophia Giovanni's." Brenna explained how Nic had been translating it. "He didn't get very far into it, but what he found was interesting. Before Sophia married Salvatore Giovanni, she was in love with Antonio."

Katie's eyes widened. "Our Antonio? Our great-grandfather?"

"He's the one. They knew each other before he and Salvatore came over to start the wineries."

"Interesting," Francesca said. "Unfortunately it's too early to have contributed to the feud. The falling-out between the friends didn't happen for another fifteen or twenty years. Unless they were still in love."

Mia shook her head. "They were married to other people. No way they could have stayed in love that long. Absence doesn't make the heart grow fonder, it makes it forget."

Katie laughed. "How did you come by this tidbit of knowledge?"

"It just makes sense. Without nurturing, love dies."

Brenna knew Mia was right. Years ago she would have sworn she would love Nic forever, but she hadn't. With time and a different life, she'd let her feelings go. Or maybe they'd faded on their own. Once there had been so much promise, and then one day it had all been gone.

"Let us know what you find out from the diary," Francesca said.

"I will." Mia reached for her iced tea. "So have you two lovebirds picked honeymoon destinations yet?"

Francesca murmured something about Hawaii, while Katie mentioned a cruise. Brenna only half listened. Her mind was still on Nic and what had once been. The two of them had managed to have dozens of conversations without ever discussing what had happened. She'd often thought of their past as an elephant in the room that neither of them was willing to talk about. Was it time to change that? Was she willing to go there with Nic?

Did she have a choice?

14

Nic left his office a little after ten. The building was silent and dark, except for the hallway lights the cleaning staff had left on for him. He went out the side door, locking it behind him.

The night was cool, clear, and quiet. Beyond the main building Wild Sea Vineyards stretched out to the horizon. An owl took flight with a silent flutter of massive wings. Leaves rustled. No light shone a welcome from the house. Nic felt like the last man standing.

Alone but not lonely. He'd always believed in that. Circumstances, or maybe his own nature, had dictated that he stand on his own. He'd been content to walk life's path by himself. Friendship was important but not defining, while love . . .

Love was a crock of shit.

He turned from the view and started for the house. As he walked, he caught sight of a familiar vehicle parked by the trees. Brenna's car.

It was late, he was tired, and he had a seven A.M. meeting with his managers. While he hadn't seen Brenna in several days, he told himself he wasn't interested in talking to her now. Even so, he found himself walking toward the building and entering through the open double doors.

He found Brenna crouched by a fermenting vat. She checked the temperature, then stood and walked around the large container. Fierce concentration pulled at her features. She inhaled deeply, as if determining how well the process was going by smell alone.

He remembered the first time he'd found her snooping around the winery. She'd been tasting samples from the reserve barrels. Instead of being afraid or even embarrassed at being caught, she'd had the balls to tell him everything he and his grandfather were doing was wrong. The hell of it was, she'd been right.

He remembered listening to her talk about wine. All these years later he could still recall the way the sunlight had slipped through the open windows to highlight the hint of red in her brown hair. She'd been pretty, mouthy, and arrogant, and he'd wanted her as he never wanted another woman before or since.

Nic leaned against the wall and crossed his arms over his chest. She moved to the next vat and made several notations on a clipboard. She was so focused on her work, she hadn't spotted him.

Back then she'd been just as driven, but for different reasons. She'd argued passionately, mocked him, challenged him, and delighted him. For weeks he'd told himself that she was only seventeen to his twenty. Whatever he was thinking about her was not only inappropriate, it was illegal. But he'd been unable to resist. The first time he'd kissed her had been magic.

It had been in this room with the scent of the wine all around them, on a night not unlike this one. She'd worn shorts and a T-shirt, and her long hair had been pulled back into a ponytail. She'd been talking about grapes or wine because that's what she always talked about, and he'd cupped her face and kissed her. He could still hear the catch in her breath as his mouth had claimed hers.

"The process works even if you don't check on it every fifteen minutes," he said quietly.

Brenna dropped her clipboard and jumped. As she turned to face him, she pressed a hand against her chest.

"Stop creeping up on me," she said. "I'm getting old. I could have a heart attack or something."

He pushed off the wall and shoved his hands into his jeans pockets. "I think that's a few years off, yet."

"Maybe." She picked up her clipboard. "Where's Max?"

"He flaked out a couple of hours ago."

She glanced at her watch. "It can't be this late. I got here at seven and was only going to stay a couple of hours."

"You know how you get when you're making wine."

She nodded. "How are things?"

"Good. What about you? Lorenzo still making you crazy?"

"Sure. He's really good at it. His stubborn streak only makes things worse."

Nic took a step toward her. "Why don't you quit?"

"No. I already did that once. This time I'm in it until the bitter end."

"That's new."

He hadn't meant to say that. The words had come out before he could stop them, and now they hung in the air like a flashing neon sign. Would Brenna ignore them or take the bait?

"Funny you should say that," she told him, speaking

softly. "I've been thinking about us a lot lately." She gave a slight smile. "The old us, not the new us."

Was there a "new" us? he wondered. "Forget about it," he told her as he realized he didn't want to talk about them or the past. "It was a long time ago."

"Not acknowledging what happened won't make it go away."

"It doesn't matter anymore."

She stared at him. "It matters to me. A lot. *I'm* going to talk about it. If you leave, I guess I'll just be talking to myself."

He thought about heading out. He could walk away, and they would never have this conversation. But he didn't. There were probably a thousand reasons why, but right then he couldn't think of one.

"So talk," he said.

She walked to the chairs set up by the small table. He considered staying where he was, in the shadow of the vats, in darkness. He didn't want to have this conversation; he didn't want to feel anything. Not again. Time was supposed to heal all wounds. Had it healed this one?

Silence filled the big room. Finally he gave in to the inevitable and walked over to where she was seated. He pulled out the other chair and settled across from her. She looked at him, then at the floor.

"I was so in love with you," she began.

Her first blow hit below the belt. He stiffened. "You could have fooled me."

She nodded. "I didn't expect you to believe me." She sighed. "Actually, I did think you would. Or maybe I just hoped. But whatever you want to believe, I loved you more than I had thought possible. You were my world."

Something cold circled inside his belly. "I was third on a

short list of two. First was your family, second was the wine. You weren't willing to give up either, but you walked away from me fast enough."

She raised her head. "That's not fair."

"That's what I was thinking at the time."

"You mattered so much, but my family was . . . they complicated things. I didn't want to disappoint them, and I was terrified of defying them. My grandfather saw the world in such black-and-white terms."

What she meant was she hadn't been willing to pay the price. "You think my grandfather was any different?"

"No." The word was a whisper. "I know he was angry."

Angry? Did that begin to describe what had happened when Nic had finally confessed his feelings about Brenna to Emilio? Anger meant yelling and throwing things. Emilio had turned his back on Nic, exiling him from the only home he'd ever known.

Brenna shivered. "I was young, I was scared, and in the end, I couldn't do it. I couldn't turn my back on my family. I couldn't walk away."

He'd been doing his best to avoid the past. Simply talking about it in vague terms allowed him to stay emotionally distant. Nic grabbed hold of his self-control with both hands and vowed to keep the barriers intact. But the first crack had already formed. It grew, ripping through years of trying to forget and pretending it didn't matter.

"You were seeing him," Nic growled. "The entire time we were planning to go away together, you were making it with that asshole you married. Did you fuck us both on the same day or did you need a little space to clear your head?"

Brenna sprang to her feet. Her face paled. "You know it wasn't like that. You know I didn't care about him the way I cared about you. I never slept with him."

"Not even after the wedding?"

She turned away. "Talking about this was a mistake."

"And it's all yours."

He waited to see if she would walk away—if she had the guts to finish what she'd started. As Brenna had never been one to enjoy confrontation about anything but making wine, he would bet on a quick escape.

She surprised him by returning to the chair and sitting down. "I met Jeff one weekend when I was down in Los Angeles with Francesca. She and Todd were engaged. There was a big party at someone's house. Jeff was the younger brother of one of Todd's friends. I didn't care about him, I didn't even think about him again. All I wanted was to get home to you."

He crossed his arms over his chest. The act was meant to look casual, but it was also instinctive protection. All these years later and he still didn't want to know what had happened.

"My parents didn't know that you and I were seeing each other, so as far as they were concerned I didn't have a boyfriend and I showed no interest in dating. They were worried and pressuring me. Francesca mentioned Jeff, which made them happy. They got off me, which meant I was more free to come see you. So when Jeff called to ask me out, I said yes because it made things easier."

Her mouth twisted. "I know what you're thinking. That if I'd told them the truth, Jeff wouldn't have been a part of my life. I know that now. At the time I just wanted to avoid the fight."

That wasn't what he'd been thinking. Parts of the story were new, parts he'd figured out. Back then, he'd been aware she had a "cover" boyfriend. He'd pretended he didn't care, even though he had. He'd pretended not to be hurt by her betrayal, even when it had cut him down to his soul.

What the hell was wrong with him? Why did this old news claw at his gut? He told himself to get up and leave, but he couldn't. He didn't want to hear, and he couldn't stop listening.

"I went out with him a few times." She twisted her fingers together. "I just wanted to be with you. When Jeff went off to Europe with his family for some vacation they'd been planning for years, I was grateful to have him gone. I needed time to figure out what to do. I knew I was making a mess of things, but I still thought I could fix it all. Then you asked me to run away with you."

He smiled without humor. "I asked you to marry me. There's a difference."

She looked scared and miserable. Funny how he would have thought he would find pleasure in her obvious discomfort, but he didn't.

"I wanted to say yes," she told him. "Deep in my heart, I wanted it so much. I still remember your exact words. You said we'd be like Romeo and Juliet, but with a happy ending."

The last of the barrier crumbled to rubble as the past rushed in to surround him. He, too, recalled his exact words. He'd bought a ring, taken her to the beach, and at sunset had asked her to marry him. He'd been idealistic and in love. Whatever challenges the world wanted to offer, they would take on. If their families rejected them, they would start over. Together. Back then his future had been filled with the promise of loving Brenna.

"You managed to resist the calling of your heart," he said bitterly. "Smart girl. I made the mistake of following mine."

Tears pooled in her eyes, but she didn't speak.

Now it was Nic's turn to stand. Energy poured through him, and he had nowhere to put it. He paced to the vats and back, then braced his hands on the back of his chair.

"You should have told me you were just playing," he said, his voice low and angry. "That none of it was ever real to you."

"It was," she insisted. Tears spilled onto her cheeks and she brushed them away. "I was afraid. Is that so wrong? I was eighteen years old, and I was scared of what my parents and grandparents would do."

His gaze narrowed. "You mean they might make you choose?"

She flinched visibly.

Before she could say anything, he continued. "I told my grandfather. I told him I loved you and was going to marry you. He said he wouldn't let that happen. That if I chose you, I would have to give up everything. My name, my connection with the family, the land, all of it. I chose you, Brenna. I packed my bags and I left. I was ready to go to the ends of the earth with you, and you turned me down. Just like that. I proposed and you dumped me."

She nodded. More tears ran down her face. She wiped at them. "I'm sorry," she whispered.

"Sorry?" He shouted the word. "You're *sorry?* My grandfather did as he promised. He disowned me. I walked away with nothing, and you married Jeff."

Brenna wanted to run. The open doors beckoned her out into the night. If she could go far enough, fast enough, maybe she would forget. Maybe none of this would matter anymore. But she had to stay. She'd started this and it was her responsibility to see it through to the end. She owed Nic and maybe she owed herself as well.

"I was heartbroken when I heard," she told him. "I

never thought Emilio would really send you away. I wanted to come after you."

He glared at her without speaking. She knew he was wondering why she hadn't. Why she'd let him disappear from her life.

Sometimes she asked herself the same questions. Those days and weeks were a blur in her memory. Pain was the only constant.

Nic shook his head. "You weren't willing to risk it. Not your family, not the winery. That's why you didn't come after me."

He spoke as if all the anger had drained out of him, leaving behind an empty man who had no energy for anything but resignation. When he released the back of the chair and settled on the seat, he looked weary.

"So Jeff was there, waiting," he said evenly.

"I guess." She rested her elbows on her thighs and dropped her head to her hands. "It's all jumbled together. He came back from his trip and spent a lot of time at the house. Later I figured out that he thought we were rich. He must have been really disappointed to find out that my grandfather owned everything and kept very tight purse strings."

She rubbed her temples. Those days had been among the worst of her life. She'd missed Nic with every breath.

"We were friends, nothing more," she said. "I was shocked when he proposed, and refused. Then my parents found out and they told the Grands. Suddenly everyone but me thought marrying a guy entering medical school was a wonderful idea. You were gone, I was alone." She swallowed and forced herself to raise her head and look at him. "I took the easy way out. Jeff seemed like the safe choice. . . ."

Nic's contempt was as real as the structure of the building. It leaped across the space between them and chilled her bones until they were so brittle she thought they might crack. Words of protest rose to her lips. She wanted to remind him that she'd been barely eighteen, and not very experienced in the ways of the world. That until meeting him, she'd been a good daughter, always doing what was right, what was expected. She wanted to say a lot of things, but knew they wouldn't matter. Not anymore.

Nic's gaze slid away. He leaned back. "The hell of it is you weren't willing to give up the winery for me, but you gave it up for him."

"I didn't give it up. I lost it. Somewhere between my two or three jobs at a time to support us and the distance, I realized I couldn't do it all. I never wanted things to turn out the way they did."

She squared her shoulders and glared at him. "You talk about all of this like you're the only victim. The truth is we both lost something important. You paid by being exiled by your grandfather. I paid, too. I had a lousy marriage. Okay, I said yes and I walked down that aisle of my own free will. I took the easy way out and I lived to regret it. I lost ten years of living my dream. I didn't have the children I always wanted. In the end, because I got married and went away, my grandfather no longer trusts me with the winery. You're back and running Wild Sea. You have everything you've ever wanted. There must be some comfort knowing that in the end, you won."

Nic shifted on his chair and looked away. An emotion she couldn't identify moved across his face, then was gone.

"I spent eighteen months cut off from the only family I'd ever known," he said. "When I came back, Emilio was a stranger to me. We never reconciled. I don't consider that a victory."

Brenna didn't doubt he'd been scared and angry when his grandfather had sent him away. Nic had gone to France and found work at different wineries there. He'd honed his skills, and when his grandfather had come looking for him, he'd been in a strong position to negotiate.

"What about when he begged you to return?" she asked. "He was forced to admit he was wrong and he needed you. My grandfather would never have done that. He would have let me go without a second thought."

Nic's mouth twisted. "Bullshit. Your grandmothers would have ganged up on him so fast, he would have been begging for mercy inside of a day. No Marcelli would ever let one of their own walk away. Family is everything to you people."

Brenna straightened. Something in Nic's voice, something in the tone and the way he spoke the words, sparked memories. All those years ago he'd always wanted to talk about her family. He'd enjoyed hearing about celebrations and arguments and their loud, loving Sunday dinners together. She remembered thinking he'd looked almost hungry to hear the stories.

Had he been living vicariously through her experiences? Had the Marcellis been the family he'd always wanted? Was his request to go to the engagement party a chance to thumb his nose at them, or had he wanted to see the one thing he'd never had?

"I can't decide if you love my family or hate them," she said.

Nic surprised her by saying, "Both."

"You're serious?"

He shrugged. "*Hate* is too strong a word. I resented their hold over you. I didn't want you to choose them, but I always knew you would. Now it doesn't matter."

Didn't it? She couldn't believe he'd let the past go. Neither of them had. There was too much energy, too much anger and hurt still alive.

"I'm sorry," she told him. "I'm sorry for what I did. I'm sorry for being immature, for letting you put yourself on the line and then turning my back on you. I'm sorry I chose Jeff and that I let what was really important get lost in my fear. I'm sorry you got sent away."

She could do her "sorry" list for fifteen minutes, but it would get boring, so she stopped.

"Nic, I don't know what to say."

"Me, either."

Maybe there wasn't anything left to be spoken. Maybe there wasn't anything left at all.

"No," she whispered involuntarily. "This can't be all there is. There has to be more."

His eyes darkened. "You know what else there is."

She blinked, not sure what he meant, then she got it. Sex. The attraction that was always there, drawing them together, making them want and ache and . . .

He stood and moved toward her. She rose as well, but only to back away. "No," she whispered. "Not now. Not like this."

He shrugged. "So walk away."

He moved like a predator. Like a man willing to take what he wanted. She wasn't afraid, not exactly. And damn it all to hell, she didn't *want* to walk away.

Awareness rippled along her spine. Her skin prickled. Logic dictated that this was a mistake. Making love right now, like this, would be really dumb. She would leave. Right this second.

She drew in a deep breath to calm herself, but that turned out to be a mistake. The heady smells of fermentation reminded her of all the other times she and Nic had made love in this room. Ghosts of their passionate selves surrounded them. She felt more than heard their sighs of surrender.

One of them moved closer. She wanted to say it was him, but it could have been her. His gaze settled on her mouth.

"This is just a reaction to the emotionally intense conversation we just had," she said desperately

He nodded. "Or chemistry. We've always had chemistry."

"Uh-huh."

This time she was sure he was the one who moved, because she was too stunned to get her leg muscles to react. Without thinking, she licked her lower lip. His gaze sharpened, then narrowed.

Her fingers itched to reach for the hem of her T-shirt and pull it off over her head. She wanted to be naked right this second. She wanted his hands everywhere on her body, his tongue in her mouth, and then she wanted him to take her hard and fast, right up against the wall.

What she *should* do was back away. Or tell him no. Saying no would be really, really smart.

She cleared her throat. "Do you think—"

"No," he said, cutting her off.

"So shouldn't we—"

"Absolutely."

She had the feeling they were talking about different things.

He touched her face with his fingers and she was lost.

Maybe if he'd grabbed her, pulling her close and demanding, she might have been able to resist. Right now strong passion, strong *anything*, would be a little unsettling. But he didn't demand or take or use. Instead he stroked her cheek with a light, gentle touch. His dark eyes smoldered with restrained passion, yet he moved as if he had all the time in the world. As if this moment was special and to be savored.

Her eyes fluttered closed. In the darkness of not seeing, she depended on her other senses to tell her what was happening.

She heard the low sound of his breathing, the brush of his shoes against the concrete floor as he stepped closer. She inhaled the scent of his body as it mingled and blended with the yeasty smell of the wine. She felt warm fingertips drifting down her cheek to her jaw and the sweep of his thumb across her throat.

Her heartbeat sped up. Blood raced through her body. Heat bubbled. Electric anticipation grounded her in place as she waited for the inevitable. The first kiss. The beginning of their—

His mouth pressed against hers. The warm, tender contact caught her unaware. She jumped slightly, even as her arms rose and closed around him. They pressed together, hard to soft—she wiggled her hips and shifted closer— very hard to soft. He settled his hands on her waist and his lips more firmly on hers. She tilted her head in a movement as familiar as breathing.

A few minutes ago she'd wanted sex—fast and hot and out of control. But now that he was touching her, she didn't want that anymore. She wanted to make love with Nic. Maybe it was all the emotions they'd dredged up with their conversation. Maybe it was days and weeks of spending time together. Maybe, given their past, it was simply inevitable.

She surrendered herself to the moment and the man. When his tongue touched her bottom lip, she parted for him. Last time they'd plunged together, taking, wanting, needing. While the fire still burned within her, making her breasts ache and her thighs tremble, she wanted a slow seduction, not an explosion of uncontrollable need. Either Nic felt the same or he could read her mind.

Instead of sweeping inside her mouth to claim her, he slipped in with a gentle caress. They kissed leisurely, deeply, rediscovering favorite movements and old resurrected passions. She buried her fingers into the cool, silky strands of his thick hair. His hands moved from her waist to her hips, then slid together and drifted up her back. He circled his palms so he both soothed and excited. When he reached her shoulders, he stopped, then retreated to the middle of her back. Her body clenched in anticipation.

So much the same . . . so much different, she thought hazily as Nic broke the kiss. Even before he pressed his mouth to her throat, she'd dropped her head back, exposing herself to him. As his hands came around to her breasts, she grabbed his upper arms. When his fingers grazed her hard nipples, she was already holding on so that when her knees gave out, she wouldn't fall.

Even so, the jolt of pleasure left her breathless. She ached there and between her legs. Heat spiraled through her belly, radiating in all directions. She felt her insides melting, as her most sensitive places became swollen and ready.

"Look at me," he said.

Brenna opened her eyes, then blinked as if coming awake from a dream. Nic's face was tight with need. As they stared at each other, a muscle twitched by his jaw. He looked exactly the same as he had ten minutes ago, save for the light of desire in his eyes. But as she watched, she would have sworn that parts of the younger man he'd been all those years ago were still visible.

At some point she'd dropped her arms to her sides. Now he picked up one hand and brought it to his mouth. Still looking at her, he licked the center of her palm, then bit gently on the fleshy pad by her thumb.

Goose bumps broke out all over. She shivered in both delight and anticipation. It was a game she knew well.

When he dropped her hand, she reached for his. But instead of bringing it to her mouth, she turned it palm up. He wore a T-shirt. Starting just below the hem of his sleeve, she ran her nails down the length of his arm. She moved slowly, scratching with the lightest touch she could manage. When she reached his hand, she circled the palm.

He managed to maintain complete control until she raised his hand and took his index finger in her mouth. As she closed her lips around the base and sucked, he flinched. When she circled his finger with her tongue, he groaned.

His turn was next. Brenna tried to brace herself for whatever he had in mind, but when he reached for the hem of her shirt, she knew she was going to be in trouble. He pulled the garment up and over her head in one smooth movement. Her bra quickly followed.

The night air was cool against her heated breasts, but she barely noticed. Not with Nic's smoldering gaze settling on her. As much as she wanted to close her eyes, she knew she had to watch. That was part of the game.

Using the finger she'd recently had in her mouth, he brushed the very tip of her right nipple. She gasped as pleasure shot through her. He licked his left index finger and touched it to her left breast.

It was too good, she thought as her legs began to tremble. It was too much and yet not enough. Without thinking, she cupped his hands in hers and pushed so that he held the fullness of her curves. Then she leaned forward and kissed him.

This time they joined in a frenzy of need and wanting. As he plunged into her mouth, she fumbled with the hem of his T-shirt. She thrust her hands up under the fabric so she could rub against his hard chest.

He took a step back, drawing her with him.

She explored the width of his back and the broadness of his shoulders. With each step, they moved farther into the shadows. She had a sense of their destination, and with that realization came impatience. She reached for the button at the waistband of his jeans.

The fabric was soft from dozens of washings. The button yielded easily enough, but the zipper was another matter. He was so hard, he pushed against the metal teeth and made it difficult for her to draw down the tab. Nor did he seem inclined to help her.

When they came to a stop by the stairs in the corner, he dropped his hand and took her left nipple in his mouth. The combination of lips and tongue, wet heat and unquenchable desire, made her cry out. She gave up on the zipper and clutched his head to hold him in place. She wanted his mouth there for hours, if not days.

When he shifted to her other breast, then sensations grew even more intense. As he sucked, need spiraled directly from there to the dampness between her legs. Then she felt his hands on her jeans. Unlike him, she was happy to help. She pushed him away and quickly popped open the button, then jerked down the zipper. After kicking off her sandals, she pushed down both jeans and panties, leaving herself completely exposed.

But she wasn't in this alone. While she'd removed her clothing, Nic had pulled off his T-shirt, stepped out of his shoes, and was in the process of removing his jeans and briefs.

When they were both naked, they stopped. It was unplanned and completely spontaneous, yet as in sync as if it had been choreographed a dozen times. As it had been, she remembered. They'd both loved to look at each other's bodies. She'd explored the powerful length of his legs, his narrow hips and waist, the muscles across his shoulders. He'd followed every dip and curve until he'd known her body as well as his own.

Now she started at his feet and worked her way up, looking for the changes in him she hadn't had time to notice the last time they'd made love. He seemed more muscled, a little more filled out. When her gaze met his, he raised an eyebrow as if asking her opinion.

By way of an answer, she reached between them and grasped his penis. With a practiced move designed to humble him, she wrapped her fingers tightly around him and stroked from base to head. As she reached the top, she brushed her thumb against the opening, along the seam, then circled around.

His breath caught, then came out in a slow hiss. She started a second stroke. He responded by reaching between her legs. One finger moved deeply within her, searching through the swollen dampness until settling on that one engorged place of pleasure. They moved together. She moved up and down while he circled her. In a matter of minutes they were both breathing hard.

When Nic pulled away, she did the same. Arousal pulsed within her. His eyes were dilated and she didn't doubt hers were the same. A flush spread across her chest. She felt the heat, along with the growing need for release.

"Over here," he said, drawing her to the stairs leading to the loft.

He bent down and picked up his shirt, then set it on the fourth stair. She sat down and spread her legs.

He moved between them, but not to enter her. Not yet. Instead he knelt on the first stair and pressed a kiss to the inside of her knee. Tension coiled within her. He kissed his way up her thigh. As he got closer, she reached down and parted herself for him.

She knew exactly how it was going to feel. She knew that the first touch of his mouth would send her spiraling into another time dimension and that she would quickly lose control. She knew once they started, her orgasms would take on a life of their own with Nic as their master, making them return again and again as he bid them. She braced herself both physically and emotionally.

Even so, she was unprepared for the impact of his soft, wet, openmouthed kiss.

The feel of tongue and lips swirling together against her most sensitive, intimate place made her toes curl. She pulled her legs back even more. Her entire body arched into his caress. He licked all of her, then sucked on her swollen center, all the while flicking the very tip with his tongue. At the same time he slid two fingers into her and slipped them back out. On the second thrust, she came.

Her orgasm rocked her very being. Shudders originated from between her legs, flowing outward until every muscle had clenched and released dozens of times. She couldn't breathe, couldn't think, couldn't do anything but feel the pleasure sweeping through her.

And Nic . . . he didn't stop. Just when she'd slowed and started to relax, he plunged into her again. At the same time, he used his mouth to push her back to the place of unbearable tension. He knew exactly how hard, how fast, how everything.

She came over and over until she could only gasp for breath and whisper his name.

Finally he raised his head. She opened her eyes and saw him looking at her. She tried to relax, but it was too late. She was within his sexual power, and please God, may it never stop.

He continued to move his fingers inside of her. She told herself it wasn't enough, but of course it was. Tension seized her again and she found herself convulsing around him. She felt the spasm of her release, and from his expression of satisfaction, knew he did, too.

He watched her climax at least half a dozen more times, then he moved up a step or two so that when he pulled out his fingers, he pushed in his erection.

She screamed with her release. The sound of her pleasure filled the old building. He wrapped his arms around her and pulled her closer. She went willingly. Despite the tremors rippling through her body, she managed to draw her legs around his hips.

They clung to each other as they made love there on the stairs, surrounded by fermenting wine and echoes of the young couple who had matched their every move so many years before. Brenna found herself watching Nic as he watched her. She climaxed with nearly every thrust. They were naked and joined in the most intimate way possible. She should have felt embarrassed or awkward, but everything about this felt exactly right.

Suddenly he stiffened. He pulled her closer still, then shuddered. She felt the convulsion of his muscles as his body surged through its climax, and then they were still.

15

Reality returned in the form of stiff muscles and a growing sense of the cold. Brenna dropped her feet to the stairs and felt the first flicker of second thoughts. Could they really have done this again? She expected Nic to pull away, but he didn't. Instead he brushed his fingers against her face, as he had when all this had started.

"You okay?" he asked.

"I will be when my heart rate returns to normal. Currently it's in the active range for a hummingbird."

"Let's check out the damage."

He slid out of her, then pushed to his feet. Brenna tried to straighten her legs, but she wasn't used to being so pretzellike, and everything hurt.

Nic rubbed the small of his back. "Me, too," he said. He held out a hand to her.

She took it and let him pull her to a standing position. They both hobbled for a couple of seconds, then Brenna started to laugh.

"We're so old," she said. "Ten years ago this was nothing. I can't even remember all the positions we did it in."

Nic started to look insulted, then he shook his head and chuckled. He wrapped his arm around her and pulled her close. She snuggled against him. He kissed her forehead.

"Speak for yourself," he said. "I'm not old."

"Ha. You're going to be limping tomorrow because of this."

He glanced down at her. "So are you and not because your legs are stiff."

She ignored the flush that heated her cheeks and his satisfied male "I pleased my woman" expression. "Go get my clothes."

He handed over her bra and panties, then picked up her jeans and shirt. He pulled on his jeans but simply tossed his T-shirt over his shoulder.

They didn't speak. By mutual agreement they walked out of the building together. She turned off the lights, and he closed the door. After wrapping his arm around her, he led her toward her car.

Once there, he brushed her hair off her face and kissed her. She clung to him as long as she dared, then sighed.

"I should go," she said.

"Okay."

She'd half hoped he would ask her to spend the night. A part of her wanted to go to sleep in his arms and then wake up in them. But even as the vision of how they would actually spend their night formed in her head, she knew it wasn't possible. Her? Here? If her car wasn't parked by the garage when the Grands woke up, they would call in the FBI.

Her mouth twisted. When exactly was she going to grow up enough not to care what her family thought of what she was doing?

"What's so funny?" he asked.

"Just me. I think I need therapy." She raised herself on tiptoe and kissed him. "I'm saying good night."

"Me, too."

She smiled, then got into her car. He stood watching her drive away. As she turned onto the highway, she glanced in the rearview mirror. He was still standing there, as if making sure she was safe. Or was that just wishful thinking on her part?

Lorenzo wrote slowly on the lined yellow pad in front of him. Since turning seventy, he'd endured the steady encroachment of arthritis, first in his knees, then his hips, and now in his hands. Brenna insisted a computer would be easier for him, that tapping the keys would hurt less than writing, but he had yet to find out. Despite the fact that a large, ugly machine had been installed in his office, and that his secretary turned it on for him every morning, Lorenzo hadn't used it for more than a place to drape his jacket. He ignored the flashing cursor and the occasional clicks and whirs that drifted from the rectangular box on the floor. The new ways were not for him. He was too old to want to change so much.

Tessa, his wife of over fifty years, disagreed. She enjoyed new technology. When Mia was at her language school in Washington, Tessa had e-mailed her every day, then printed out the responses and read them to him before they went to bed.

Women dealt with change better than men, he acknowledged grudgingly. Perhaps because they were born knowing that time was liquid and always moving. They understood that the babies to come from their bodies would eventually grow and leave. Hearts were broken and then mended. For women, the world was shades of gray. Men saw only black and white.

He finished writing and carefully tore off the page. His secretary would type up his letter and send it out, but first she would remind him that even if he didn't want to use the computer, he could simply dictate into a tape recorder. She would transcribe his words, saving him the pain of carefully forming each word. He did not bother to tell her that he'd used his tiny handheld recorder to prop up an unsteady table and that when Mia had later sat on the table, the small machine had been crushed.

He read over the letter, then dropped it into his out basket. Now that he was finished, he slowly flexed his aching hands, then opened the top drawer and reached for the pain medicine he kept there. At his age, pills were tangible markers of time. Each hour or two meant another medication, another glass of water, another aftertaste left on his tongue. Whenever he complained, Tessa reminded him that the alternative was no pills, no bitter taste, only darkness and the earth reclaiming his body. Then she would pull the rosary from her pocket and take a quick trip around the beads to ward off any inadvertent invitation of death brought on by their conversation.

He smiled at the thought of his wife. He was an old man, and yet he loved her more today than on the day they married. God had blessed him in many ways. His son, his grandchildren, the bounty of the earth.

Lorenzo shook his head. Was his mind to go next? He refused to become maudlin about his good fortunes. Despite his complaints, his doctor assured him he would probably see eighty and beyond. Plenty of time to annoy those he loved most.

A knock on the door to his office distracted him. Lorenzo glanced up. "Come," he called.

The door opened and Joe entered.

Antonio, Lorenzo thought sadly. That was the name he had picked out for Marco's firstborn son. There had been so many hopes and plans. So much that went wrong.

"You come to see me," Lorenzo said, trying not to sound too pleased.

Joe crossed to the chair in front of the desk and pulled it out. He moved like a man used to trouble—carefully and with purpose. Lorenzo liked that. Joe was young and strong, all the things his heir should be.

"I've come to say good-bye," Joe said as he took a seat. "I've reached my limit of family bonding."

Lorenzo frowned. "You cannot go. Your life is here now. With the vines."

Joe shook his head. "Not my style. I told you, I'm a beer drinker."

"What about your inheritance? You could have all this." He spread open his arms. "How can you walk away from what I have to give you?"

Joe chuckled. "Yeah, right. This isn't a gift. Not any of it. If you were handing me a check, I'd give it some thought, but you want me to buy into what you have here. The whole Marcelli heritage. Sorry, but I'm not in the market for that kind of responsibility."

"No. You must stay. I insist."

"It's not your call." He leaned toward Lorenzo. "You're playing some game with everyone, especially Brenna, and I won't be a part of it."

"What game? There is no game." Lorenzo pushed painfully to his feet and walked to the far wall. He motioned for Joe to come with him. When they were standing next to each other, Lorenzo realized the younger man topped him by several inches. That pleased him. Every generation should be bigger, more powerful. It was the way of the world. Strength improved the family.

He pointed to the map on the wall. It was old, dating back to the 1920s, and drawn by hand. It detailed much of the county, oriented so the Marcelli land was in the center.

"From the old days," he said. "My father, your great-grandfather, drew this himself. This is who we are." He tapped the yellowing paper. "This is what is important to us."

Joe studied the map. "Did he do this before the feud?"

"Yes. Many years before. Things were much simpler then." Friends were friends, he thought. When friends became enemies, the world became a more difficult place.

Lorenzo looked at Joe. Marco's son. His grandson. A stranger. All those years ago, he'd been so sure he was right. He'd stood against his wife, his son. He'd insisted. Tessa had warned him, but he hadn't listened. The mistake was his.

"You will stay," he insisted. "You are family."

"No, I'm not," Joe said quietly. "My family is my SEAL team. You folks have been nice and all. I appreciate the hospitality, but it's time for me to head out."

Lorenzo wanted to argue the point. He had plans for this young man. He would stay, learn, take the family name. Was it not to be?

He touched Joe's arm. "It was me," he told his grandson. "Your grandmother, she wanted to allow Marco to marry, even though he was only a boy. Her parents, they weren't sure what they wanted, but I'm the one who convinced them. My son, your mother—" He shrugged. "They were in love. They wanted each other and they wanted you. I'm the one who made them send you away. I was wrong. I wanted you to know."

Joe's steady gaze never wavered. Lorenzo would have given half the Chardonnay harvest to know what the young man was thinking. But Joe was too wily. He kept his thoughts and feelings to himself.

"None of that matters now," Joe said. "What's done is done."

Perhaps, but Lorenzo wanted to undo it. "If you had grown up here, you would have learned our ways. You would understand about the wine. It would be in your blood. It's there now, singing to you, if only you will listen."

"Maybe it would have made a difference," Joe admitted. "Maybe not. We'll never know. In the here and now, I'm not interested in the winery. I want you to be clear about that. I don't want it."

"Why not? The money—"

"Sure. Like there wouldn't be strings attached to all of it. I don't know what you're up to, old man, but I'm not interested. You've tried to use me against Brenna. I don't know why and I don't want to know. If you don't listen and decide to leave all this to me anyway, be warned. I'll give it to Brenna."

Lorenzo frowned. "Give it? Not sell it?"

Joe smiled. "No way, old man. I'm not going to be a pawn in whatever game you're playing."

Lorenzo raised his eyebrows. "Can you be so sure you haven't already?"

Joe shook his head. "You're a slick one, Grandpa. Be careful. If you take this too far, you'll hurt the ones you love."

Grandpa. Joe's casual use of the word tugged at his heart. He held open his arms. His strong grandson stepped close and hugged him.

"You're a good man," he said, releasing Joe. "Come to see me again. I will show you that you're wrong about us not being your family. You belong here."

"We'll see."

Lorenzo reached up and cupped his face. "Your work. I know it is dangerous. Be careful. Now you have a family to come home to."

Joe didn't say anything, but Lorenzo thought he understood. They shook hands and the younger man left.

When he was alone, Lorenzo once again touched the map. He traced the outline of Marcelli Wines. Joe had accused him of playing a game. There was no game. But a plan? Ah, that was something different.

Brenna stood in the center of the vineyard and watched as the last of the Cabernet grapes were harvested by the awkward-looking machine being driven between the rows. The difference between her own small winery and this one could be measured in the number of days it took to bring in the grapes. Marcelli would produce over ten thousand cases. Hers would number in the hundreds.

But it was a start, she told herself, basking in a glow of pride. She'd done what she wanted and everything had gone well. Now she just had to wait for time and chemistry to produce magic.

She bent down and touched a denuded vine. The mechanical harvester was only used on the less-than-premium grapes. She hated how the machines stripped away too many leaves and left tire tracks on the hard earth. While she understood the financial necessity, she wished each cluster of fruit could be treated with gentle reverence.

"Okay. I've been out in the sun too long," she murmured as she straightened and laughed. Having philosophical thoughts about grape picking couldn't be good. Next she would be waxing poetic about each fallen leaf. The bright spot in her morning was that she'd managed to think about something other than Nic. Given their last very intimate encounter, that was something close to a miracle.

Nic. Just letting his name echo in her brain made her smile. She wasn't clear on what exactly had happened or what it meant. Three days after the fact, she was still experiencing aftershocks. She had a suspicion it was illegal for sex to be that good.

Feelings she didn't want to acknowledge or name fluttered through her. Something had happened that night when they'd finally talked about the past. Clearing the air had changed things between them. She wasn't ready to deal with it, but in time she would have to. What happened after that was anyone's guess.

"What are you so happy about?"

The voice came from directly behind her. Brenna jumped and screamed. When she spun around, she saw Joe standing less than three feet away.

"Don't sneak up on me. What is it with the men around here. First Nic, then you." She slapped her hand over her mouth. "Pretend I didn't say that."

"About Nic? Too late. The Grands told me all about you bringing one of the enemy to the engagement party. They were pretty shocked."

"I'll bet. Fortunately you showed up and offered a fine distraction. Did I ever thank you for that?"

"Just doing my job, ma'am. Speaking of which." He glanced around at the vineyard. "I wanted you to know I'm heading out."

"What?" She stared at him. "You're leaving?"

"That's the general idea. I need to get back to work. This has been a great vacation and all, but a guy can only take so much of the Marcelli clan."

Leaving? "But you can't," she said, stunned. "If you go . . . You're supposed to stay and inherit everything. What about the money?"

He shrugged. "Get real, Brenna. Lorenzo was just jerking both our chains with all that talk."

"No. You're wrong. He would gladly leave you everything."

"What does that mean? He'd leave me the winery? Like I know what to do with that? You think I'd own Marcelli outright? No way. He's a wily old coot. I guarantee you everything would be tied up so tight, I couldn't get so much as a bottle of wine for myself. He offered the winery as a bribe to get me to stay and as a way to piss you off. I'm not sure why, but I think that was his plan. Judging from how you two go at each other, I'd say it was working."

Brenna couldn't breathe. The earth seemed to be moving beneath her feet, but she didn't think it was because of an earthquake. Could Joe be right? Had her grandfather just been playing with them both?

"What did you tell him?" she demanded. "What did you say?"

"That I was wise to him. And if he tried to leave me everything, I'd just give it to you. He didn't like that."

"I'll bet."

Her brain wasn't working. She couldn't think straight. Was this really happening? Was Joe not a threat anymore?

She touched his arm. "Stay a little longer. Please."

"Oh, sure, now that I'm not a threat, you want me around."

"Hey, I wanted you around before."

"I know." He glanced around at the vineyard. "This has been great, but I don't belong here. Not yet."

"What does that mean? Will you come back? Is the family too much to deal with?"

"Sometimes."

"That's understandable." Lord knows they got to her and she was used to them. "Are you glad you came?"

His dark gaze settled on her face. "Absolutely."

"I'm glad. I know my folks have been thrilled having you around. And my grandparents. I guess all of us."

"Even you?"

"Especially me."

"Good. You're the one I worry about the most."

"Why?"

"I just do."

She sighed. "I worry about you, too. You're the one putting your life on the line."

"I'm a pro. Don't sweat it."

She didn't know what to say. "Thank you" seemed wildly inadequate after what he'd done.

"You could have had it all," she said.

"Not even on a bet. Not with the old man's rules. You're the only one who can handle him."

"I don't do a very good job."

"Joe! Joe!"

Brenna looked past her brother and saw Mia running toward them. Her baby sister crashed through a row of vines, making Brenna wince.

"Walk *between* the rows!" she yelled, but Mia ignored her.

She stumbled through another row of vines and came to a stop in front of Joe.

"Say it's not true," she demanded. "It can't be true."

Tears filled Mia's brown eyes.

Joe shifted uncomfortably. "If you're talking about me leaving—"

He never got a chance to finish his sentence. Mia flung herself at him and clung as if she never wanted to let go. "You can't go. Not yet. I've never had a big brother before, and I really like it."

Joe stood awkwardly for a couple of seconds, then gingerly patted Mia's back. He was big and broad to Mia's petite frame. He looked like a bear hugging a kitten. As Brenna watched, his expression tightened and something that might have been regret twisted his mouth.

"I have to go," he said gently. "I have a job."

"A dangerous job." Mia stepped back and jammed her hands onto her hips. "Don't you dare die. That would really piss me off."

"I'll do my best to stay safe."

Her gaze narrowed. "You'd better. I swear, Joe, if you don't come back, I'll hunt down every single one of your friends and have sex with them. I'll even let the others watch while I do it."

He winced. "Okay. I'm motivated to stay alive."

"You'd better."

He turned to Brenna. "I guess this is good-bye."

She nodded and stepped into his embrace. He hugged her hard.

"Stay strong," he whispered in her ear. "Everything's going to work out."

She hoped he was right. "Ditto what Mia said," she told him. "Minus the sex part. We want you to come back to us. We're your family now, and the fact that we give you the willies is no excuse to stay away."

"Fair enough."

Mia moved close and he hugged them both, then bent down so they could kiss his cheek. With a last wave, he turned and walked away. Brenna watched him go. Like Mia, she would miss him.

"The time will go fast," she said. "Before we know it, he'll be underfoot and getting on our nerves."

Mia sniffed. "You're not a very good liar."

"I know."

When Nic stepped out of his office, he saw an unfamiliar SUV pulling up beside the building. The door opened and a tall man stepped out of the Jeep Wrangler.

It took Nic a second to place the guy, then he recognized Brenna's long-lost brother.

Max pushed past him and raced toward the visitor. As usual, the pup tried to wiggle the stranger to death by leaping and licking, then rolling onto his back to beg for a belly rub.

Joe crouched down and obliged, then looked at Nic. "You've got yourself a real watchdog here."

Nic strolled toward the duo. "I'm figuring he'll grow up and turn vicious."

"Not likely."

Max sprang to his feet and got one good swipe on Joe's face before taking off for a run around the yard.

Nic held out his hand. "We weren't introduced the night you came home. I'm Nic Giovanni." He grinned. "If you've spent any time with your grandfather, then you know I'm the enemy."

"So I've heard." Joe rose and shook his hand. "Joe Larson." He looked around at the winery. "Nice place you got here."

Nic nodded, but didn't speak. There had to be a reason Brenna's brother had stopped by, although he couldn't think of one offhand.

Joe leaned against the fender of his Jeep. "Lorenzo told me a lot about the feud between your two families. It sounds like something right out of Shakespeare."

"It's old news. Lorenzo worries about the past, but the rest of us are willing to let it go."

Joe nodded. "Makes sense. Things change. People move on." He jerked his head toward the back of his SUV. "Which is what I'm doing. Heading back to work."

Nic couldn't have been more surprised if Joe had started line dancing. Leaving? Did that mean he wouldn't be inheriting? If so, Marcelli Wines was still up for grabs.

He did his best to act as if Joe's announcement didn't mean anything to him.

"Brenna mentioned you were a Navy SEAL."

Joe's gaze narrowed. "That's true. I have a lot of specialized training." He paused to let the words sink in. "I guess it's not right for a brother to have a favorite sister, so I worry about all of them. But sometimes I worry about Brenna the most. I wouldn't want anything happening to her. Anything that would . . . hurt her."

Nic didn't know if he should laugh or prepare for a fistfight. Logic told him that Joe was pissing in the dark, but he couldn't be sure. Had he learned anything or was he fishing?

"Are you threatening me?" Nic asked mildly.

"Sure. Whatever it takes."

Damn it all if Nic wasn't pleased that Brenna had someone on her side. Which made him the village idiot, seeing as the person on her side was capable of killing him with little more than dental floss.

"Brenna's a grown-up," he said. "You don't get to inter-fere."

"Says who?"

Nic chuckled. "Brenna for one. If she knew you were here, she'd have your hide as a rug."

Joe shrugged. "She'd have to catch me first."

Nic realized he liked Joe. "Hurting Brenna isn't part of my plan."

"Want to tell me what is?"

"No."

"Is she going to get hurt anyway?"

Nic considered the question. Would Brenna be hurt by his plan to buy Marcelli Wines? His humor faded. Easy question, easier answer.

Joe pushed off the Jeep. "You're right. I can't protect her, as much as I want to. But something tells me you can. You might want to think about that."

He opened the door and slid onto the driver's seat. "Guess I'll see you the next time I'm in town."

Nic nodded.

As Joe drove away, Maggie stepped out of the office and walked toward Nic. "Who was that handsome stranger?"

"What happened to being happily married?"

"Oh, I am. But I can still look." She stopped in front of him. "Are you going to tell me who he is?"

"No. Do you have the final numbers on the financing for buying Marcelli?"

She nodded slowly. "Everything's ready. Lorenzo Mar-celli simply has to sign on the dotted line. But I thought you weren't sure he would be willing to sell."

"That just changed."

She shook her head. "I'm sorry to hear that. I wish you wouldn't do this. It's wrong."

"I'm not asking for your opinion, I'm asking you to do your job."

"Sure, Boss."

She sounded fine, but he saw the flash of hurt in her green eyes.

"I'll leave the information on your desk," she said.

"Thanks."

She started back for the door, then paused. "You used to be one of the good guys, Nic. Why did that have to change?"

Before he could come up with an answer, she went inside.

He stalked toward the house. One of the good guys. What did that mean? She was—

He stopped in the center of the path and turned to look at the building Brenna was using. Just a few nights ago she'd forced them both to relive the past. For the first time in years he'd found himself locked back in the hurt and the anger. At one time he'd thought it would destroy him. It hadn't and he'd moved on. Everything was different now.

Or was it? They'd made love. Somehow, despite the harsh words and aching feelings, they'd come together in a way that had both exhilarated and terrified him. As much as he'd tried to ignore it, he'd known that night that something was different.

No, he told himself. Nothing was different. The past was long gone and the future had nothing to do with it. What could have been didn't matter. He and Brenna were old news. He had a plan and he was going to stick with it no matter what.

16

*B*renna *sipped* her double mocha latte as she exited the Starbucks and crossed to the tables and chairs set up along the wide sidewalk. She chose a seat in the shade.

The midafternoon was quiet, with few people around. Warm temperatures and a light breeze made her feel sleepy, so the coffee would provide a much-needed jolt.

September had come to an end. Harvest was finished, and all across the valley, wine makers were taking a moment to draw a breath. There were the usual tasks to tidy up at the end of the season, barrel orders to be placed for the following year, discussions about more plantings, what vines to rip up, and how everyone expected the wines to be when the first barrels were opened and tasted.

Every so often Brenna wished she'd picked another line of work, but not today. Today her world was exactly right. All of her wine was in place, and the future of Four Sisters Winery was in the hands of yeast microbes and fate. And at Marcelli, well, life was good. Even her grandfather couldn't destroy her good mood. No matter how much he disagreed with her, argued his points, and ignored her advice, the truth was he had no one interested in the winery but her. Not her sisters and not Joe.

"Someone should nominate him for sainthood," she murmured to herself as she set her coffee on a small round table and took a seat. He'd turned down the chance to be a part of the family business, leaving her free to take over.

Assuming her grandfather didn't up and sell.

"Don't go there," she told herself. "Not today." Not when the sun was shining and the air was warm and everything was as it should be.

She'd weathered the latest storm and she'd survived. She would get through the next one and the next one. Some she would endure with grace and style, and some she would simply endure. But that was okay. She'd moved on.

Look at how far she'd come. A year ago she'd been working two jobs she hated, while going through the motions of having a marriage with a man she'd never truly been in love with. How sad was that? Now she was happy, living her dream, and starting her own business. She had—

Brenna sat up straight, then tried to calculate the date. It was the beginning of October.

"Well, hell," she said as she picked up her coffee and took a sip. Her divorce had become final and she hadn't even noticed.

Now that she thought about it, she remembered receiving a thick, legal-size envelope sometime in the past couple of weeks. But between harvest and arguing with her grandfather and Nic and Joe and everything else going on, she'd tossed it onto a shelf in her bedroom and had never given it another thought. No doubt the final papers were inside. She was a free woman. Even better, Jeff would be sending her a fat check every month for three years to pay her back for putting him through medical school and supporting him during his internship and residency.

While she wasn't going to be wealthy by anyone's standards, she was about to have a cash flow that set *her* heart to fluttering. So the five-thousand-dollar-a-month question was what did she do with it? Use it to make payments on her loan? Save it? Get a new car?

She eyed her battered Camry parked on the street and figured she probably needed to pay for a tune-up and some tires, but other than that, it should last her a few more years.

A sound caught her attention. A familiar sound that got louder. The way her heart had fluttered at the thought of money was nothing when compared with the kickboxing style workout it was getting now. Brenna rose and shaded her eyes as she looked down the street. Sure enough, a good-looking guy on a motorcycle was headed in this direction.

What was it about a man in a leather jacket? She was too young to remember James Dean, yet that's instantly who she thought of as Nic pulled up in front of her car. He cut the engine and turned toward her.

Neither of them spoke. They hadn't seen each other since "the night," so this moment was supposed to be awkward. She probably should have wanted to bolt. Instead she found herself smiling.

A helmet covered his hair and dark glasses shaded his eyes. She didn't know what he was thinking, which was probably for the best. She didn't know what she was thinking, either. The situation with Nic was more complicated than ever, thanks to what had happened a week before. Intellectually she knew that making love with him had been foolish. Emotionally she'd never felt happier about anything. No doubt the differing sides of her brain were at war, meaning she should probably schedule some quality time with her sister, the psychologist. Or at the very least visit her doctor and find out if the pharmaceutical community had a pill or two to help her out. Instead she sipped her coffee.

Nic pulled off his glasses. "You look like a woman with a lot on her mind."

"I am."

"I know how to help."

He reached behind for the spare helmet fastened to the seat. After pulling it free, he held it out to her.

Brenna didn't hesitate. If she was going to celebrate the joy that was her life, she knew no better place than on the back of a motorcycle. She tossed her coffee in the trash and crossed the sidewalk. After securing the helmet, she climbed on behind him and wrapped her arms around his waist.

"Go fast," she told him with a laugh.

He grinned and nodded.

While he drove out of town at the speed limit, as soon as they hit the freeway, he accelerated the bike until Brenna felt as if they were flying. Cool air blew in her face. The heat of Nic's body kept her warm, while her thighs hugging his reminded her of other rides on other sunny days.

They drove north out of Santa Barbara, past the small towns that lined the freeway until they reached a deserted stretch of beach. Nic took the next exit. He pulled up beside the sand and cut the engine.

Brenna climbed off first. She set her helmet back on the seat and smoothed her hair. Nic took off his headgear and shrugged out of his jacket. By silent agreement they turned toward the water.

They walked side by side along the firm, damp sand. The tide was out and seagulls floated overhead, allowing the breeze to carry them back and forth with no effort on their part. She inhaled the scent of salt water and brine. A few clouds hurried across the blue sky.

Occasionally their shoulders bumped. After a few minutes Nic took her hand in his.

They were out of time, Brenna decided. This wasn't now, wasn't then; the moment simply existed with no expectation, no pressure. She raised her face to the sun. If only they could stay like this forever.

A seagull flew down in front of them and pecked at the sand. As they approached, the large bird flapped its wings and ran a few feet up the beach.

"Max would enjoy this," she said, breaking the silence.

"He's not a motorcycle kind of dog."

"Good point."

Nic stopped and pulled Brenna toward him. As she stepped into his embrace, he put his hands on her shoulders and turned her so she stood with her back to him. He moved close behind her and wrapped his arms around her waist. She settled her hands on top of his.

They faced the ocean, staring out to the line of the horizon.

"Do you ever want to sail to the edge there and see what's beyond it?" she asked.

"If you head south and west, you'll hit Hawaii."

"Works for me."

Days lolling on a white, sandy beach. A cabana boy to bring her drinks with umbrellas.

"Your brother came to see me."

Nic's words were so at odds with her thoughts that at first she didn't know what he meant.

"Joe's gone. He went back to the base."

He pressed his cheek against her hair. "I know. He stopped by on his way out of town."

She tried to turn to look at him, but his arms held her in place. "Why?"

"To warn me off. He said if I did anything to hurt you, he would have my head on a platter."

She was stunned. "He did not."

"He told me that he had special training he was very willing to use and that he wanted to make sure nothing happened to you."

"I—He—" She closed her mouth, opened it, then closed it again. "No way."

"I'm not making this up."

She didn't know what to think. Joe? Threatening Nic? How like a guy. She turned in his embrace.

"That's not all he did," she told him happily. "He turned down the winery."

"I'd wondered about that."

"It's true. My grandfather grumbled about it for an entire day. Joe figured out no one was going to write him a check for what the winery was worth and that it was more than likely that our grandfather would tie things up such that he couldn't sell it and walk away. Joe said there were too many strings attached."

Even three days after her brother had left, Brenna still had trouble believing it all herself.

Nic touched her face. "So it's all yours now."

"I hope so. I guess he could still sell, but I'm not going to think about it. For right now, my life is pretty damned perfect, and after all the crap I've been through, I intend to enjoy it."

"Good for you."

"Yeah. Good for me."

She turned so she once again faced the ocean. Nic held her close, her back nestling into his chest. This felt right in so many ways.

"Is Joe going to come back?" Nic asked.

"I think so. We were more than he could deal with the first time out, but I doubt he'll get away for long. I spoke to Mom, and she said Joe promised to stay in touch. She and my dad are going down to visit him next month. I think the Marcelli family is a lot easier to take in small doses."

Nic didn't say anything. Brenna thought about asking what he was thinking, but then decided she didn't want to know. This moment was perfect and she didn't want it ruined by anything. Not the present, the future, and certainly not the past.

Although there was plenty there to mess things up. So many mistakes. So much pain.

With the clarity of hindsight, she knew she'd made a huge mistake in not marrying Nic all those years ago. She *should* have defied her family and run away with him and the consequences be damned. When his grandfather threw him out, they could have gone to France together.

Instead she'd been afraid and Nic had lost everything.

Did getting Wild Sea back make up for it? she wondered. Not that she was going to ask. If the answer was no, she would feel guilty and more than a little ashamed for her part it in. Nic had been treated badly by the people who were supposed to love him.

His parents. His grandfather. Her.

Had anyone he'd ever loved not betrayed him?

Regret filled her. Regret for her part in his pain and regret for the little boy who had been left alone.

She wanted to say something, but what? She wanted—

He turned her toward him and kissed her. The soft pressure of his mouth made her eyes sink closed and her arms circle around his neck.

Yes, she thought hazily, parting her lips. This was

what she wanted. This was what felt right. Being here with him on a sunny fall day when the air was sweet with possibilities.

He broke the kiss and looked at her. As she stared into his dark eyes, she saw down to the very essence of the man who had been so much a part of her life. She touched his cheek, then the corner of his mouth.

"Let's never go back," she whispered. "We could stay here forever."

"What happens when the tide comes in?"

"Details."

"I'm tempted."

She wanted him to be more than that. She wanted him to be—

In love with her.

The truth crashed into Brenna like one of the waves slapping onto the sand. She wanted Nic to remember how good they had been together and know they could have all that again, plus the wisdom that comes with maturity. She wanted him to sweep her up in his arms and confess that he'd never stopped loving her, thinking about her, needing her, because—her breath caught—it was more than possible she'd never stopped loving him.

"Brenna? Are you all right?"

"Fine," she said automatically. "You're right. We'd better head back."

She led the way to the motorcycle and slipped on her helmet. But her mind wasn't on the task. Instead she couldn't stop wondering if it was really true. Had she spent the past ten years living a lie? Had she really never stopped loving Nic or had she been foolish enough to fall in love with him all over again?

• • •

Lorenzo walked into the small restaurant a little before ten in the morning. He knew the names and reputations of the men who wanted to meet with him, if not their faces. He even knew what they wanted.

A young man looked up from setting the two dozen or so tables in the main room. "We're not open, sir."

"I'm Lorenzo Marcelli. There is to be a meeting."

"Oh. Yes, sir." The young man straightened. "Right this way."

He led Lorenzo into a back room filled with a long table. There weren't any place settings here. Only pads of paper and a pot of coffee along with a few cups. Two men stood as he entered.

"Mr. Marcelli, thank you for coming. I'm Bill Freeman and this is my associate, Roger White. Please, have a seat."

Lorenzo sat down heavily on one side of the table while the two men settled across from him. He knew what they were after, and while he wanted them to come to the point, he waited while they poured him water and offered coffee, which he declined.

"As you may have guessed, we're very interested in your winery," Bill Freeman said.

"I have little else that would interest men like you," Lorenzo said. "I'm an old man. I don't think you want to offer me a job with one of your companies."

The two men chuckled. "Would you take one?" Bill asked.

Lorenzo shrugged. "Probably not."

"Then we're left with Marcelli Wines."

He detailed the long history of the company, as if Lorenzo hadn't lived it all himself. He was polite, well informed, and when he started talking numbers, even Lorenzo was impressed by the bottom line.

The words flowed on and on. Employees would be guaranteed their jobs for at least two years. His family would never want for anything. The family house was not to be touched, and he was welcome to retain a few acres around the house for his private use.

What would his father think of all this? Lorenzo wondered, then smiled faintly. Antonio would raise his fist to the heavens, then turn it toward the men. Never would a Marcelli sell.

But that was a long time ago. Much had changed. Once he had believed he would create a dynasty of fine sons to inherit. Marco was a good man, but there had been no other children, and no male grandchildren. Tessa always whispered it was because God punished Lorenzo for his arrogance in forcing Marco and Colleen to give up their baby. For many years Lorenzo had refused to believe, but now he was not so sure.

So these men, these strangers, offered him more money than he had ever imagined in exchange for Marcelli Wines. Which made him wonder why.

He listened as they continued to talk, all the while questioning what lay behind the words. These two were not interested in wine. They represented a soulless corporation. Wine making was an art. It got into the blood. So who was behind this? Who really wanted to buy the company?

When they had finished, he rose to his feet. "I will consider the offer," he said. "Then I will be in touch."

He left the way he'd come—alone and feeling very old.

Brenna looked over the new designs for the Chardonnay labels and had a feeling her grandfather wasn't going to like these any better than the last ones. Still, it was her job to show them to him and then stand back to absorb whatever joy he might want to send her way. Besides, after her motorcycle ride with Nic the previous day there was virtually nothing that could upset her.

Humming "I'm a Little Teapot," she left her office and walked down the corridor into his. The door was open and she entered without knocking.

"Hey, Grandpa," she said, doing her best to sound upbeat and cheerful. Actually it wasn't much of a stretch. "I have the new wine labels. You're going to love them."

Her grandfather's response was a grunt. Not a very promising start, but she was determined to look on the bright side of things. She set the large pages in front of him.

"I explained what you liked and didn't like about their previous work," she said. "They went from there."

"I don't remember saying I liked anything," he grumbled as he flipped through the designs.

Brenna ignored him and perched on the edge of his desk, which she knew he hated. "You adored at least two of them," she said, carefully crossing her fingers behind her back to negate the potential cosmic effects of the lie.

He grunted again.

She grinned, then noticed how he was dressed. While her grandfather usually wore a long-sleeved shirt and the old man equivalent of Dockers, today he was in a suit and tie.

"Don't you look spiffy," she said. "What's the special occasion? Did you and Grandma Tessa sneak away for a romantic lunch?"

"You're in a good mood," he complained.

"Actually it's just my naturally sunny nature coming through. So did you go to lunch?"

"No. I met with some businessmen. They wanted to talk about buying the winery."

It was like being by the ocean again. Brenna heard the sound of rushing water. The noise filled her head until it seemed to surround her. She was drowning. That had to be what was wrong.

The temperature in the room dropped to near freezing. She felt cold, then numb, then very, very sick.

No. No, this wasn't happening. Selling? He couldn't. She'd just survived the Joe crisis. This could *not* be happening.

She closed her eyes and accepted the truth. The winery was his. He could do whatever the hell he wanted.

She sucked in a breath, then pushed to her feet. Somehow she got out of the office, then she was running and running. Through the rows of bare vines, up over the slight hill at the edge of their property and across the fence lines. She ran until the pain in her side forced her to walk, and still she kept going. Her eyes burned from her tears, her chest ached. She couldn't breathe, couldn't speak, couldn't do anything but keep moving.

Some time later she saw a group of buildings and she headed for them. A voice in her head kept screaming "No!" as if by sheer force of will, she could make it not be true. She choked on her sobs. The unfairness of it all, the futility of her hopes and dreams, filled her with pain.

When she reached the building, she pushed through the unlocked door and into the office. It was the middle of the day, and several of the office staff were at their desks.

She felt their curious looks, heard the whispered questions. Should they stop her? Who was she? She ignored them all. Instead she walked faster until she reached the one door she sought and jerked it open.

Nic was on the phone. He looked up when she entered. His expression tightened with surprise.

"I'll have to call you back," he said and hung up. He was already on his feet.

"What happened?" he asked. "Are you okay? Was there an accident?"

She shook her head, but couldn't catch her breath enough to speak. Tears poured down her cheeks.

He put an arm around her and helped her out of his office. They left the office building and headed for the house.

When she was settled on the living room sofa, with a glass of brandy, Nic crouched in front of her and took her free hand in his.

"What's wrong?"

Her throat was so tight, she didn't think it would be possible to speak, yet she did her best to force out the words.

"My grandfather is going to sell the winery."

Nic had expected her to say that someone was dead. Maybe Joe or one of her grandmothers. Wide-eyed and shaking, Brenna looked as if she'd barely survived a car crash. He'd been so concerned about her, he'd momentarily forgotten about the meeting that morning.

"You don't know for sure," he told her.

She gave a strangled cry and tightened her grip on his hand. "He said he met with some men. He was all dressed up in a suit. Why would he have bothered if he wasn't serious?" She gasped. "Joe. Joe told him that he wasn't interested in the winery. He said if he inherited, he would just give it to me. That's why my grandfather is doing this. Without Joe, there's no male heir. He doesn't have a choice."

She was shaking so badly some of the brandy spilled on the floor. Nic grabbed the glass and set it on the end table, then sat next to her and pulled her close.

"It's all right," he murmured. "You'll see."

"No," she whispered. "It isn't."

She buried her face in his chest. Nic stroked her hair and

rocked her back and forth. But even though his actions were gentle, his mind was racing. Was Brenna right? Would Lorenzo sell? As much as Nic had hoped and planned, he'd never been sure the old man would take the bait. Was everything he'd worked for finally within his grasp?

"Brenna," he began, not sure what he was going to say. The truth? A part of the truth?

She raised her head. Pain filled her eyes. "It's all going to change. Mia already figured that out. She had the four of us go to lunch because nothing was ever going to be the same again. We're all changing. I'm going to lose the winery."

Tell her now, he thought. Tell her the truth.

She sighed. "Oh, Nic, what would I have done without you? When I came to you for the loan, I really wanted to start my own label, but I don't think I actually believed I would need to. I think deep inside I believed I would inherit. I figured he would make the four of us equal owners and that I would run things. I started Four Sisters to hedge my bets." She blinked back tears. "Now that's all I have. And it's because of you. You were so generous and willing to take a chance on me. I really appreciate that."

He was slime. "Brenna, it wasn't like that."

She gave a shaky smile. "It was exactly like that. Ten years ago I treated you horribly. I loved you, but I wasn't willing to defy my family. But you forgave me."

He didn't know where she was going with this, but he had to stop her now before she said something they would both regret.

"You're upset," he told her. "You need to recover from the shock."

"Do I? Or has the shock given me the courage to say what needs saying?" She leaned forward and kissed him.

"I've always regretted not marrying you. I tried to love Jeff, but I couldn't. That's why I gave my life away—I felt guilty. I devoted my time to him because I couldn't give him my heart. It belonged to you. It still does."

This was not happening. Nic stood and paced to the window. He spun back to Brenna.

"You don't know what you're saying."

She shrugged. "I think I've always had lousy timing. This only proves it, huh?" She rose. "It's okay, Nic. You don't have to say anything back. I'm not expecting a declaration of your undying love and a proposal or anything." She paused. "Well, it would be nice, but I understand a lot of things have changed. You may not feel the same way. I just wanted you to know. I still love you. I guess that gives you a win in all this."

A win? The irony should have made him laugh, but instead he wanted to stop time and figure out how this had all gotten so screwed up. Brenna wasn't supposed to love him. Not now. Not like this.

Not after what he'd done.

"Brenna, you don't understand," he said.

"Are you guys in here? Nic? Brenna?"

He swore in frustration.

"Mia?" Brenna called. "Is that you?"

Mia burst into the living room. "Brenna, are you okay? I saw you running through the vineyards. I thought maybe you'd finally gone over the deep end. I figured you'd come here, so I drove over. I went to the office first, but they told me you were in here." She waved her right hand and he recognized his grandmother's diary. "You'll never guess what I found."

Nic clenched his hands into fists. "Mia, this isn't a really good time. Your sister and I—"

"Trust me, you're gonna want to hear this. See, I've been translating the diary. When I got into it, I couldn't believe what I was reading. I didn't want to say anything until I reached the end. I wanted to be sure."

Nic wanted to grab Mia by her shirt collar and propel her from the room. He needed time with Brenna to figure out what he was going to say to her. How he was going to explain the truth? But Mia wasn't interested in anything but her news.

"It's so amazing," she said gleefully. She looked at Nic. "Hang on to to your privates, Nic. Grandpa Lorenzo was right all along. Salvatore Giovanni really *did* poison the Marcelli vines all those years ago—and you'll never guess why."

17

*"W*hat are you talking about?" Brenna asked. Her head was swimming. With all she'd already been through, she didn't think there were more shocks to be had. Apparently she'd been wrong.

Mia pulled several folded sheets of paper out of her shorts back pocket. "Once I realized what was going on, I took notes. It's so incredible."

She plopped into a wing chair by the sofa and waved at the couch. "You guys want to take a load off while I read this or are you going to stay standing?"

Brenna pressed a hand to her stomach. She felt as if an entire platoon of butterflies was fighting it out in there. Her chest hurt, her eyes burned, and she couldn't believe she'd just told Nic she loved him. Emotional meltdown, she told herself. She'd reacted to a horrific situation by spilling her guts. Unfortunately, she'd told him about the same time she'd figured it out for herself, so she hadn't had a chance to get used to the information. Worse, he hadn't reacted.

She eyed him now and saw him watching her. She was unable to read his expression or figure out what he was thinking. Obviously she'd shocked him with her confession, but had it been in a good way or a bad way? Did he want them to be alone so he could take her in his arms and tell her how much he'd always loved her, too, or did he just want to bolt for safety?

"Hello?" Mia said, sounding impatient. "Doesn't this interest anyone but me?"

Brenna slowly sat on the sofa. Whatever she and Nic had to say to each other could wait. Great. In the space of an hour she'd found out that her grandfather really was selling the winery, and she'd handed her heart over to Nic without finding out how he felt about *her.* Somehow she doubted anything Mia had to say could even come close.

Nic crossed to the window and stared outside. "Go ahead," he told Mia.

Mia shrugged. "Okay. So if you started translating at the beginning, you probably already know that Antonio and Sophia were in love. According to this, they had been for years. But there was a problem with Antonio's family. It's not clear what, but he wasn't considered a desirable match for her. When he and Salvatore decided to start over in America, Sophia vowed to wait for her one true love. Heartfelt good-bye, etcetera. Flash forward six years. Sophia is still the beauty of the village, but she has refused every suitor. Her father grows impatient and begins to pressure her. She gets a letter from Antonio telling her that he and Salvatore are coming back to claim brides. The wineries are already starting to show a profit. By village standards he's a rich man now, and he's coming to get her."

Mia glanced up from the paper. "She waited six years. How crazy is that?"

Brenna thought about how long she'd loved Nic. "He was her one true love."

Mia wrinkled her nose. "You sound like a greeting card. I say cut your losses and find the best guy who's available now, but that's just me. Anyway, weeks go by, Sophia's family gets impatient. She promises to marry by the end of spring. Who shows up the following week? Not darling Antonio, but Salvatore. He's successful, his family is respected, and he comes bearing gifts. The family is thrilled. When he makes an offer for Sophia, they accept on her behalf. Sophia is distraught. Where is her beloved?"

"Where is he?" Nic asked.

"Don't know. The diary doesn't say. But Sophia's in a panic. She tries to delay the wedding, but the folks won't have it. Antonio is MIA until the night before the wedding."

Brenna can't believe it. "You're kidding."

"Nope. He shows up at some fancy dinner. Now that he's not going to be family, her parents make him welcome. Sophia is heartbroken. He's her one true love, yada yada. They meet out by the fountain close to midnight. He wants her to come away with him, to elope. But she can't shame her family. Salvatore is a good man. They fight, they make up, they have sex."

Brenna's mouth dropped open. "No way."

Mia grinned. "Oh, she's pretty delicate in her description, but there's no doubt the deed gets done. Salvatore gets the bride, but not the cherry."

"Does that start the feud?" Nic asked.

"No. Apparently Antonio settles on a different bride. Our great-grandmother Maria. There's another wedding and the four of them head back to America. I can only imagine how interesting that boat crossing could have been. I mean the four of them dining together. Sophia and Antonio married to people they don't love. Talk about a conversation stopper."

Brenna thought of her own miserable marriage. "How did she stand it?"

"There was plenty of work to keep her busy. After a year or so, the first of her babies came along. The wineries flourished, then the war came. As we've been told forty billion times, Antonio and Salvatore went to Europe and were given cuttings from different vineyards in an effort to protect the horticultural heritage from the Germans. They brought them back, planted them and all went well, right up until Salvatore got a letter that his father was dying. This was right after the end of the war. Being a good son, he headed home for Italy. Sophia stayed behind with the family and the grapes."

Mia waved the papers. "Brace yourself. Here's the good stuff. There was an early frost—just days before the harvest. Antonio and Sophia did everything they could to save the grapes. They worked tirelessly for days. It's not clear where Great-grandma Maria was during all this, but when the harvest was finally in and they'd saved the grapes, they celebrated by falling into each other's arms. They admitted they were still in love. The affair went on for nearly two weeks until Sophia put a stop to it, telling Antonio she couldn't continue to betray her husband. But it was too late. Sophia was pregnant."

Brenna couldn't believe it. "There was a child?"

"Almost. Sophia was frantic, as you can imagine. Salvatore wasn't the nicest guy around, and he didn't like coming home after being gone for nearly six months and finding his wife five months pregnant. He badgered her for the name of her lover, then turned his back on her, threatening to throw her bastard into the streets. It turns out he didn't have to. The baby was stillborn."

Brenna glanced at Nic. He looked as shell-shocked as she felt. "How did he find out it was Antonio's?"

"In her grief she told him the truth. All of it." Mia shook her head. "That was the beginning of the feud. Sophia found out later that Salvatore went to the Marcellis' vineyards and poisoned all the vines they'd brought from Europe. Whatever he used acted slowly, strangling the new cuttings until they all died. She said when he told her, he sounded as if he were proud of what he'd done. Sophia blamed herself, but she wouldn't betray her husband again by telling Antonio what had happened. The two men fought, Salvatore refused to confess because to his mind, Antonio's sin was greater. The families never spoke again. Well, until you guys."

Mia folded the papers. "So that's it. Our sordid past. Think we could sell the story to Hollywood?"

"Salvatore really poisoned the grapes," Brenna said slowly. "All these years I thought Grandpa Lorenzo was crazy, but he was telling the truth."

"There was just cause," Mia said. "You know how Italian men are about fidelity. It obsesses them."

Brenna didn't dare glance at Nic. Infidelity. That's what he had considered her relationship with Jeff, and she wasn't sure he was wrong. But unlike his great-grandfather, he'd come to understand why and he'd forgiven her instead of seeking revenge.

Nic walked toward Mia. "You agree with what Salvatore did?"

"I don't know if I agree, but I understand. His best friend screwed his wife. That was pretty low. I mean, Sophia had the chance to run off with Antonio the night before her wedding, but she was too frightened to defy her family. She chose a stranger over the man she really loved. Then she cheated on her husband with the guy she'd loved all along. Somebody needed to bitch-slap some sense into that girl. She gave up the right to Antonio the second she turned him down. She'd picked her life, so she should have honored it."

Mia's comments hit a little too close to home for comfort. Brenna didn't want to see any similarities between herself and Nic, and Sophia and Antonio. Unfortunately, they were too obvious to miss.

She stood. "Mia, we should get home. I want to talk to Grandpa Lorenzo about this."

"Will it change anything?" Nic asked.

"I don't know. Probably not."

Still, the need to escape pressed in on her from all directions.

Mia rose and pulled her keys from her front pocket. "You want to do the Forrest Gump cross-country run again or you want a ride?"

"We'll take your car."

"Brenna, wait." Nic moved close. "We have to talk."

Of course they did. She'd spilled her guts to the man. The problem was she didn't know if he was going to match her feelings or try to let her down gently. She didn't think she could handle one more shock today.

"I'll call you," she said vaguely. "Soon."

Nic stood alone in the living room. In the space of an hour his world had shifted on its axis. First Brenna's fears that her grandfather would sell—implying he was about to get everything he'd ever wanted. Then her claims to be in love with him. Love? Now? Fate had a twisted sense of timing. Finally the news about his great-grandfather.

All his life Nic had thought the feud was a joke. He'd figured the Marcellis' claims were little more than a rationalization of their own failure. He'd felt superior because his family had been successful on a grand scale. The European cuttings had given Wild Sea an edge in the market. By the early 1980s that edge could be measured in hundreds of thousands of dollars of revenue. Today the difference was in millions.

When Nic had been called back from his exile, he'd been determined to make Wild Sea one of the biggest and the best. His plan, born during those long days working in the vineyards of France, had started with blinding hate and rage, then had evolved into something more concrete. He'd had something to prove—not just to his grandfather, but to Brenna. He wanted her to regret all that she'd lost when she'd left him.

Once Wild Sea was everything he could make it, he would buy Marcelli Wines. Over time he would incorporate their vineyards, their processes, then he would eliminate their name.

During the past seven years, he'd accomplished everything he'd wanted, with one exception—he hadn't bought out Marcelli Wines.

Wild Sea had three times the sales and four times the profits, but that hadn't mattered. He'd had a goal.

Now that goal seemed to rest on shaky ground.

He walked to the rear of the house and stepped outside. He couldn't see them from here, but they were just beyond the rise. On the acres bordering the Marcelli lands were the European cuttings. They had grown strong, producing some of the best grapes. Old had been grafted into new, year after year.

"A stolen legacy," he murmured to himself.

Max trotted over and nosed his hand. Nic patted the dog.

He'd built his dreams of revenge on a lie. Nothing he'd built was his alone. It had been stolen by a man twisted and bent by revenge.

Was Nic so very different?

• • •

Nic drove along the coast road for nearly an hour. He'd pulled on his helmet, but forgotten a jacket. The cool air stung his chest and arms, but he didn't turn back. He couldn't—not until he'd seen the proof.

The highway turnoff was clearly marked, but after that, he had to rely on memory more than signs. It took him nearly thirty minutes to find the well-cared-for cemetery on the bluff. Once inside the wrought-iron gate, he made his way to the fenced section overlooking the ocean. Large marble statues and benches declared those resting here to be persons of substance with financial means. However ill-gotten those means might be.

Nic turned off the motorcycle and slipped off his helmet. The afternoon was silent except for the wind rustling leaves and stirring the grass.

For once he ignored the giant column over his great-grandfather's grave and the small stone that marked Sophia's resting place. His grandmother held a place of honor, but he didn't stop there. Instead he searched by the back corner for something he'd seen years ago and had not understood.

When he found the simple marker, it contained only a date. No name, no words of comfort or loss. Sophia's stillborn child. Antonio Marcelli's son or daughter. Mia hadn't said which. Maybe Sophia had hurt too much to say in her diary.

He bent down and touched the smooth stone, as if he could somehow reach beyond and connect with the past. Behind him, Salvatore's grave loomed like a dark shadow. Nic had never thought much about his great-grandfather. He knew now he should have done his best to understand the man so he wouldn't be doomed to repeat the same mistakes.

He sat on the grass and stared up at the heavens. To

have come so far only to find out he'd been wrong from the beginning.

The truth was here, in the quiet, and at last he was forced to acknowledge that which he'd never admitted even in the darkest recesses of his soul.

He'd wanted Marcelli Wines to prove he was good enough.

Wild Sea had been the business success, but Marcelli Wines had the family. How many times as a child had he hovered just out of sight, watching the girls play together? How many nights had he stolen up to the window and pressed his nose against the dining-room glass to see them all sitting around the table? In the summer those big windows had been open, so he had heard their conversation, their laughter, and he'd ached to be a part of that.

For years he'd worked to prove he was good enough. And for whom? His parents, who had never cared? His grandfather, who sent him away? Brenna, who had chosen someone else?

The plan had formed the night he'd been forced to leave home. He'd vowed he would show them all. He would prove he was the best, and he would make them crawl to him.

His grandfather had returned first, begging him to come home and run the winery. The old man had needed him for business, but had never taken Nic back into his heart. When Emilio had died, the two of them had barely been speaking.

Over the next few years he'd expanded, growing in money and power until only Marcelli was left to be conquered.

He'd spent seven years of his life battling ghosts. It was a war he could never win. And if he did, what would he have? A few acres? The right to use a label? He would still be alone. He would still have to look at himself in the mirror. He would still not have Brenna.

He dropped his chin to his chest and closed his eyes. Brenna. She had reappeared without warning, offering what he thought was the perfect way to ensure his plan worked. He'd loaned her money because he thought the callable note gave him leverage, but was that the only reason? Hadn't he also done it so that she would be nearby?

Of course, he thought, wondering why he hadn't seen it before. Brenna, whom he'd never been able to forget. She'd exploded into his life like a shooting star, her light reaching all the way into the dark corners of his soul. He'd tried to hate her, but couldn't. He'd tried to forget her, to love someone else. Anyone else. He'd failed. Brenna, who had told him she loved him.

She wouldn't now. Not when she learned the truth.

Nic's eyes opened. Panic seized him. In that moment he knew his only chance was to get to Brenna as quickly as possible and tell her everything. If he was able to explain, to apologize, to take it all back, then maybe she would understand. Maybe she would still love him.

Brenna was not in the mood to face her grandfather again, but she didn't have a choice. Mia dragged her into the house and found him in the library, sitting at his desk.

"We have to talk," Mia said. "You're not going to believe what I found out."

"I must speak as well," he said. His gaze settled on Brenna.

She had the thought that he looked old. Concern threaded its way through her until she reminded herself that he was going to sell the winery and destroy her world.

"Grandpa, this is important," Mia protested.

"So is this. It's about the sale."

Mia's mouth dropped open. "What sale?" She sucked in a breath. "No. You can't. Brenna's going to run the winery."

Brenna appreciated the support. Unfortunately it wouldn't have any influence on her grandfather. She ached everywhere. As much as she wanted to crawl in bed and pull the covers over her head until this all went away, she refused to show weakness again. She braced herself for the next blow and vowed she would handle it just fine.

"Have you already signed the papers?" she asked, pleased when her voice didn't shake.

"No. The men who approached me aren't the ones interested in the winery. They are a front. Very respectable, very generous. A man could go a lifetime without hearing such a fine offer."

Brenna didn't know if he was trying to make her feel worse, but if he was, he was succeeding. She swallowed the lump in her throat. "So?"

"So I do not deal with faceless corporations. I made a few phone calls to the bank who would handle the loan. A friend talks to another friend. Eventually I have a name."

Maybe it was her imagination, but she would have sworn his hard expression softened a little. She didn't think that was good news.

Brenna clutched the back of the chair in front of her. She repeated to herself that she would handle it. Everything would be fine. There was no name her grandfather could say that would hurt her more than she'd already been hurt.

No name except one.

Her grandfather nodded. "You already know."

She shook her head. It couldn't be possible.

"Nicholas Giovanni."

18

~ॐ~

"*N*o!" *Mia cried,* her voice thick with outrage. "Not Nic. He couldn't. We were just . . ." She threw down the diary. "He just can't be the one."

Brenna didn't know what to think. Or maybe she simply couldn't form coherent thoughts. She wouldn't have guessed it was possible to be more stunned, more hurt, more disbelieving than she'd been before. Nic buying the winery? Nic going about it in secret, hiding?

Betrayal was both bitter and cold, she realized as ice swept through her. Muscles trembled, then refused to support her weight. She leaned heavily against the chair she'd been holding, before she staggered around so she could drop onto the seat.

Her vision blurred as she covered her face with her hands. No. He couldn't. Over the past few weeks they'd spent so much time together. They'd talked and laughed and made love. They'd—

She straightened with a gasp of horror. She'd apologized for her behavior. She'd said she *loved* him.

"You have to be wrong," she told her grandfather.

"I'm not. He's been planning this for a long time. It's all in place. His offer, the financing, everything."

But . . . it couldn't be.

"I trusted him," she whispered. With everything. Her heart and her dreams. Oh, no. The loan—in the form of a callable note. Her wine, her plans.

"Oh, Grandpa, it's even worse." She forced out the words when all she wanted to do was run so far and fast that she could forget everything that had happened in the past few hours. "I've done something."

Mia looked at her, then her eyes widened in comprehension. "Brenna, you don't think . . ."

Brenna nodded slowly. "It had to be part of his plan."

"What was part of his plan?" her grandfather asked.

"I was a fool," she said. "I'm sorry. He made it so easy and I wanted it so much, I refused to consider that he was being anything but kind and generous."

She felt both helpless and stupid, and she had no one to blame but herself. "I went to Nic for a million-dollar loan and he gave it to me. It's a callable note."

She braced herself for the explosion, but her grandfather only sighed heavily. "A lot of money," he said calmly. "A smart move on Nic's part. If I balk, he calls in the note. Even if I make good on the money, he can ruin your reputation. So he plays on my feelings for my granddaughter. He thought of everything."

Brenna doubted he'd planned on her falling for him again, but no doubt he'd simply considered that a lucky bonus. Being heartbroken was one thing, but a heartbroken idiot was unbearable.

"I'm sorry," she murmured.

Mia stepped close and squeezed her shoulder. "I thought the past was twisted, but this is even worse."

Their grandfather turned his attention to her. "What do you know of the past?"

"A lot more than I did a couple of days ago." Mia leaned toward the desk and slapped the top of the book she'd dropped. "Sophia Giovanni's diary. It starts before she married Salvatore and finishes up shortly after the death of her stillborn child. She writes about everything, including why Salvatore poisoned the Marcelli vines."

Her grandfather put his hand on top of Mia's on the diary. The color drained from his face and his fingers trembled.

"It is all here? The truth?"

Mia nodded.

"So many lives changed," he said quietly. "So much bad blood. More wrongs on top of pain."

"You knew the truth?" Brenna asked. "You knew all this time and never said anything?"

"I put it together over the years. A word here, a whisper there. I was a boy when it all happened."

Brenna thought of all the times she and her sisters had decided their grandfather was crazy for worrying about an old family tale. "If we'd known what really happened . . ."

He shook his head. "What would it have changed? The young and the old have fought since the beginning of time. It is the way of things."

Maybe, Brenna thought. She felt cold and broken, as if she'd fallen from a great height. Her heart had shriveled into hard, brittle pieces. She wanted to cry, she wanted to scream. She wanted to hit something . . . or someone.

Footsteps clicked in the hallway. "Where are you?" Grandma Tessa called as she approached. "Dinner's ready. What? Mary-Margaret and I prepare the food and no one eats?"

She walked into the library. "Lorenzo, you come and eat. Mia, Brenna." She hesitated. "What is it? What's wrong?"

Her husband spoke to her in Italian. Mia probably understood, but while Brenna didn't know what he was saying, she could guess at the content. Even before he'd finished, Grandma Tessa reached for her rosary and began fingering the beads.

All Brenna could think about was escape. Too many feelings swirled inside of her. She couldn't name them all, but she sensed they were about to spiral out of control.

She stood. Grandma Tessa was at her side and hugged her close. "Sweet, sweet girl. You come. We put you to bed, and in the morning you'll see. Things, they aren't so bad. Maybe some pasta, eh? To fill your tummy."

Brenna hugged her close. "No pasta. I don't want to eat."

What she wanted instead was revenge. Damn Nic for what he'd done to her. And damn his whole family. How dare he play with her? Use her? They'd had sex . . . she'd given him her heart.

"I hate him," she whispered.

"Who?" her grandmother asked. "Brenna, hate is a sin."

"Be quiet, Tessa," Lorenzo said. "Let the girl be."

One small part of Brenna's brain acknowledged her grandfather's support, but she couldn't deal with that right now. Rage swept through her until she thought she might explode.

The need to move filled her. She headed for the hallway, but before she'd reached it, she heard a familiar sound outside. The sound of a motorcycle.

The anger in her grew to a life force.

"I'll kill him," she said.

"All that Italian blood coursing through your veins," Mia said, taking her arm. "I'm in favor of you telling him exactly what you think, but not right now. You're too raw."

"I'm not raw. I'm empowered. I could rip him apart with my bare hands."

"There's a visual."

Mia tugged on her arm, and Brenna let herself be led to the back of the house. "Come on, Sis. You need a drink."

"I need to destroy him."

"Later. Let Grandma Tessa handle him."

Brenna started to protest, but an odd thing happened when she sat down in one of the kitchen chairs. She couldn't get up. In a matter of seconds her entire body shook as if she were having a seizure. Then she was crying. Great gulping sobs that nearly split her in two.

"Oh, Mia," she gasped.

Her sister sank down next to her and pulled her close.

"It hurts," Brenna sobbed. "Oh, God, it hurts so much."

"I know. I'm sorry."

"I loved him."

Mia squeezed her tight.

Brenna was grateful that her sister didn't offer any pat phrases of comfort. The truth was, there weren't any words left that would heal this wound. She'd trusted Nic with her dreams and her heart, and he'd never been interested in either. Instead he'd wanted to destroy her and her family.

How could she have been so wrong about him? How could she have been such a fool?

Sometime close to midnight Brenna told herself she couldn't cry forever. Eventually she would run out of tears, although that didn't seem close to happening any-time soon. She felt drained and puffy and more than a little sorry for herself. Every twenty minutes or so, a fresh wave of anger gave her energy, but then the sadness drowned it out, and she was left feeling broken again.

In the past few hours she'd tried to figure out which was worse—her stupidity or Nic's betrayal. So far it was a toss-up. How could she have been so blind? Hadn't she learned anything by being married to Jeff and having him leave her? And how could Nic have turned out to be such incredi-ble slime? Worse, he was slime that was damn good in bed.

Her life had just hit bottom. Not only was she a moron, but she was a moron with a million-dollar debt.

Mia stuck her head in. "I know you don't feel like it, but the Grands are fussing, so I said I'd bring you up a tray."

Brenna nodded. "That's fine. Just put it on the dresser." She sniffed, then pushed herself into a sitting position on the bed. "What are they doing up?"

"Worrying about you." Mia set the tray on the dresser, then approached the bed. "We're all worried."

Brenna pulled a tissue from the box and wiped her face. "That's sweet, but not necessary. I've already figured out I'm not going to die because of this. I can't sleep, I can't eat, but that won't last very long. Eventually I'll snap out of it. Maybe I'll lose ten pounds in the process."

Mia settled on the edge of the mattress. "I'm sorry. Do you want me to call Joe and have him bomb Nic's house?"

"Maybe." Brenna blew her nose. "No, that would be a bad idea. I wouldn't want Max hurt. I'll have to figure out my own form of revenge. If I had a chance with Four Sis-ters, I would go the success route. Man, I would love to rub his nose in it by winning awards and becoming the darling of the wine community."

"That could still happen," Mia said.

"Not likely. I have a feeling an attorney is going to come calling in the morning. Nic's going to want his money back." And she had no way to repay him.

She looked at her baby sister. "I told him I loved him. Can you believe it? Right before you drove up, I actually said that. Do I have lousy timing or what? Actually I have lousy taste in men."

Mia's mouth twisted. "I never knew he was such a bastard."

"Me, either. I hate him."

There was another knock on the door. Brenna was surprised when her grandfather walked into the room.

"Isn't anyone sleeping tonight?" she asked.

"I sent Tessa and Mary-Margaret to bed. Mia, it's time for you to be there, as well."

Mia rolled her eyes, then kissed Brenna's cheek. "If you want to talk later, come wake me up. I'm happy to listen."

"Thanks."

Her sister stood and left. Grandpa Lorenzo took her seat on the bed. He took her hand in his and patted her fingers.

"You have been crying," he announced.

Brenna did her best to smile. "I already knew that."

"About the boy or the money?"

"Both." More Nic than the money, which just proved how stupid she was. A sensible person would be more upset about the loan.

"A million dollars is a lot to cry over. What did you do with it? I know you didn't buy a new car."

She started to laugh, then tears filled her eyes. She brushed them away. "I wanted to start a winery," she whispered, despite the pain in her chest. "Ridiculous, huh?" She braced herself for the explosion of temper.

But instead of yelling, her grandfather only shrugged. "Not ridiculous. Not a surprise. How far did you get?"

The calm response caught her off guard. She blinked away the tears. "Pretty far. I bought those four acres of Pinot grapes I told you about, along with crops. I'm doing a cuvée, a Chardonnay, a Pinot, and a Cab."

"Very ambitious."

"I wanted Four Sisters to be up and running in two to four years. I figured I knew enough people to get my wines in the right places once it was ready. There would be a few lean years, but once I was through them, I could keep expanding."

His dark eyes never wavered. "Four Sisters?"

She nodded.

"Where is your wine?"

"At Nic's." She explained how he'd loaned her equipment, a building, and storage facilities. She outlined his seemingly generous offers, only now realizing how each one got her deeper and deeper in debt.

"I should have realized," she said. "I should have seen what he was doing."

"How? He's a smart man. Driven. Competitive. I suspect he didn't plan to use you until you showed up wanting the loan. Then you were an opportunity he could not resist."

She'd been easy both in and out of bed. Easy and easily fooled.

"Did you try getting your loan from the banks?" he asked.

She nodded. "And the Small Business Administration. I had no collateral, no formal education. They weren't impressed."

"What about your father? Marco has money in trust. He could have made the loan."

In hindsight going to her father made a lot of sense. "I thought . . ." She cleared her throat. "I didn't want to make him choose between you and me. There's been so much fighting already. I knew you'd be mad."

"Do I look mad?"

She eyed him. "No. You actually look okay."

"See. I'm not so bad."

"I didn't think you were bad."

"Just stubborn and set in my ways?"

Despite everything, she smiled. "Pretty much."

Her grandfather squeezed her hand. "I understand." He leaned close and kissed her forehead. "Now you sleep. Things will look better in the morning."

Brenna doubted that was true, but she was ready to be alone so she didn't argue. She slid down on the bed and closed her eyes. Her grandfather clicked off the light as he left the room.

Once she was by herself, her eyes popped open and she stared into the darkness. Morning wouldn't bring relief. Instead it would simply be one more day to survive knowing she'd been a fool for love and a sucker for her dreams.

Nic waited until after nine the following morning before calling to talk to Brenna. The previous evening when he tried to see her, Grandma Tessa had claimed she was ill. He knew that finding out about what had really happened between the Marcellis and the Giovannis all those years ago had been a shock, but he doubted it had been enough to make her sick. He reminded himself that Brenna had also learned that her grandfather might be willing to sell Marcelli. Still, she'd always been tough.

He had to speak with her. He hadn't slept and had

nearly gone over there a dozen times in the night. Only the thought of embarrassing her in front of her family had stopped him. But he couldn't wait any longer. He had to tell her the truth, explain what had happened and why. Make her understand.

He waited impatiently through three rings. Finally the phone was answered.

"Marcelli residence."

At least Lorenzo hadn't picked up. He thought he recognized the voice. "Mia?"

"Yes."

"It's Nic. I'd like to speak with Brenna. I came by to see her last night, and your grandmother said she wasn't feeling well."

"She wasn't."

He frowned. "Did she catch a bug?"

"No, but you could say she escaped from one. Or would *worm* be a more descriptive term?"

He got a hollow feeling inside. "Mia, what are you talking about?"

"You, Nic. The charming, successful Nicholas Giovanni. I would have thought with all your land and money you would be beyond using any means to get what you want, but I guess I'd be wrong. I mean you're the great-grandson of a weasel bastard; why wouldn't you be just as devious and backstabbing?"

Shit! "You know."

"That you've been planning to buy Marcelli Wines using a front of respectable businessmen because you knew my grandfather would never sell to the likes of you? If you mean that, then yes, we know. We *all* know. It was quite the surprise. I've gotten over it, but Brenna's having a more difficult time. I wonder why. Hmm, you think maybe for her it got a little personal? You think she's having a little trouble with the whole betrayal thing?"

He shouldn't be surprised. Of course Lorenzo had the means to find out who'd set up the deal. "I have to talk to Brenna. I have to explain—"

"Explain what?" Mia asked, cutting him off. "Nobody here gives a damn about you or your explanations." She sucked in a breath. "We took you in, Nic. We made you welcome in our home, and all that time you were planning to screw us. I never understood the feud before, but I do now. I want revenge, and if you think I'm pissed off, just imagine what Brenna would like to do with you."

"Mia, you have to listen. I know it looks bad—"

"Go to hell, Nic. The world would be a better place without you."

She hung up.

He carefully replaced the receiver, as if by moving slowly he could keep his life from shattering. But it was already too late.

He'd lost.

Owning Marcelli Wines had driven him for years. Now he'd lost his chance. Funny how that barely troubled him at all. What had kept him up last night, what haunted him now, was knowing that he'd lost Brenna. He hadn't even known that he'd had her, or how much he needed her, and now she was gone.

"I mean this in the nicest possible way, Nic, but you look like crap."

Nic looked up as Maggie walked into his office. She tossed several folders onto his desk, then leaned against the door frame.

"Want to talk about it?" she asked.

Talk? What was there to say? It had been nearly two days of hell as he tried to figure out how to fix everything that had gone wrong.

"Nic?"

He shrugged. "Brenna found out."

He braced himself for the sympathy and kind words. They wouldn't help. Nothing filled the empty crater growing inside of him. Nothing offered relief, or better yet, a solution.

Maggie raised her eyebrows. "So?"

He stared at her. "What do you mean, so? She found out. She won't speak to me. I haven't seen her and I can't get her on the phone."

"I don't see the problem. You knew she would find out eventually, and you had a good idea she wouldn't be happy, so why is this a shock?"

He narrowed his gaze. "I guess you're not taking my side in this."

"Why would I? I told you I thought it was a bad idea from the beginning. From what I could tell, you and Brenna were getting pretty tight. You were more interested in her than in anyone I've seen you with ever. But you didn't want her as much as you wanted the win. Now she's hurt and angry. I'm still confused. Why is this a surprise?"

"I've lost her."

"I didn't know you had her."

He nodded. "Me, either. Until it was too late. The Marcelli deal is off, too."

Maggie didn't even pretend to look sorry. "Speaking as a friend, and not your employee, I have to tell you, you earned this, Nic. You can't play with people's lives and not expect there to be ramifications. You got caught and now you have to pay."

He didn't want to hear this. He wanted her to say things would work out fine. He wanted her to tell him that Brenna would understand.

"She said she loved me," he told her.

That got a reaction. Maggie dropped her arms to her sides and stared at him. "I'm guessing that was before she knew what you were trying to do."

He nodded.

"You are *so* screwed."

"No. If she loves me, she has to forgive me." He hated the hopeful, pleading tone in his voice. "Doesn't she?"

Her expression softened. "It doesn't work like that. Haven't you figured it out yet? Loving someone doesn't mean it's always okay. Some acts are simply unforgivable. I'm sorry, Nic, but I have a bad feeling you've committed one of them."

19

Forty-eight hours later Brenna knew she had to drag herself down to the winery or spend the rest of her life in bed. As her sheets desperately needed washing almost as much as she needed a shower, she forced herself to get up and dressed. One of the Grands snuck in while she was in the bathroom and stripped the bed, which left her no choice but to venture out into daylight. From there it was a short walk to her cramped office in the winery.

The battered old desk was both comforting and familiar. The stack of mail and messages needing response gave her a sense of purpose, even though she still felt as if she were moving under water. Everything was slow and out of sync. Still, she sorted her phone messages into tidy piles. There weren't any from Nic. Had he not called or was she not being told?

Did it matter? Why did it matter? The man had used her in every way possible while lying to her. Did she really care if he'd called? Was she that weak and spineless?

Yes, she thought sadly. She was.

But she was also really, really mad.

It wasn't just that he didn't love her back. She could accept that. Feelings existed for reasons no one could explain. So Nic not loving her wasn't anyone's fault. But the man had screwed with her future. He'd played with the one thing she'd loved even longer than him and there had to be something like a suitable punishment. Nobody messed with her wine and got away with it.

There was only one problem—the money. Circumstances being what they were, she doubted Nic was going to let her have access to her barrels. Which meant she couldn't produce wine, which meant never paying him back. She was trapped, all because she'd trusted Nic.

Worst of all, because there was something uglier than the situation with the wine, she didn't know how to stop loving him. Oh, she hated him with every fiber of her being, but for how long? And when she got over hating him, wouldn't the love return? It had lasted through ten years of separation; why would she be lucky enough to have it end now?

Her grandfather appeared at her open door. "You're here," he said as he entered. "Better?"

"Some."

A white lie, she told herself. Telling him about her pain would only make him hurt, too, and what was the point in that?

He took the seat in front of her desk and pointed to a pad of paper. "I want you to make a list for me. Outline everything you have at Wild Sea. How many barrels, what is in them." He frowned. "You're through fermenting, aren't you?"

"I assume you mean the wine and not me personally."

Her grandfather smiled. "Yes. The wine. Also, give me your copy of the loan."

"Why?"

"No Marcelli will be beholden to that man."

His kindness eased some of her pain. "You're being really sweet, Grandpa, and I appreciate that. But we're talking about over a million dollars."

"I know." He shrugged. "You're my granddaughter. The loan will be paid back with interest, and your wine will be moved here as soon as possible."

He couldn't have shocked her more if he'd broken into a chorus of "Oklahoma!"

"Why?" she asked. "I'm happy and thrilled beyond words. But this isn't your responsibility. I'm the one who messed up. Nic will probably just dump the wine anyway. Not that it matters now."

He glared at her. "Don't tempt God to strike you down. The wine must be saved."

"I think God's a little busy with more important matters." She tried to explain. "I may not have a choice about the loan. Nic will have to be paid back one way or the other, and without Four Sisters, I don't have a prayer of doing it myself. As for my plans . . ." She looked at him. "Grandpa, I love you and you've been terrific through all of this, but you hate everything I do. Why would you want my experiments here?"

"I don't hate what you do."

She smiled for the first time in days. "Oh, please. We argue about everything. The blends, the day to start harvest, the temperature for fermentation. Label designs, pay raises, if it's going to rain tomorrow."

"I'm usually right about the weather."

She gave a strangled laugh. "You think you're right about everything. That's one of the reasons I wanted to start my own label. I wanted to make all the decisions."

"Were you happy doing that?"

She thought about the long nights and the endless hours of work. "Yes. Happier than I've ever been."

"Then you have succeeded."

"Not exactly the word I would use."

"Not with your winery. The success of that will be measured later. I mean here. With me." He watched her as he spoke. "You have passed the test."

Brenna didn't understand. "What are you talking about?"

"I wanted to be sure. When you were little, I knew you were the one. You loved the vines as much as I did." He tilted his head. "By the time you were six, you could tell the type of grape by taste alone. I was so proud. You worked hard. Always up early, especially during harvest. When you were eleven, you were directing the men."

Brenna remembered that summer. She'd been in charge of the Chardonnay grapes, and she'd felt so grown-up. The foremen had patronized her until they realized she knew what she was talking about, and then they'd treated her as someone to be reckoned with.

"When you married Jeff, I was pleased," he said. "You would have a good man at your side while you worked the land."

"But it didn't turn out that way," she reminded him. "I went away."

He nodded. "I waited for you to return, for you to realize where you belonged, but you didn't. Year after year I watched your husband bleed the life out of you until the granddaughter I had been so proud of disappeared. Then one day you came home. Not because you longed to be here, but because your husband had left you. You wanted to come back. To work here. But I asked myself, for how long now?"

Understanding clicked in her brain like a light going on.

"You wanted to make sure I was staying," she whispered.

"Yes. So I tested you to see if I could drive you away. I wanted to make sure that this time you wouldn't give up. Not for anything."

She both understood and resented his methods. "What about Joe? You offered him everything."

"I did, but he would never have run things. I hoped . . ." He sighed. "An old man's wishes. I wanted him to stay, and I thought with the winery, he would. But he would never have been the one. It was always you."

She shook her head. "You were never going to sell."

His expression turned sly. "You think not?"

Brenna covered her face with her hands. "Of course you wouldn't. Oh, God. One more place I've been an idiot." She put her hands back on the desk. "If worse came to worst, you would have left everything to Dad and had him hire a manager. After all, one of your granddaughters could have a child interested in the winery."

He shrugged. "Perhaps. But that's not necessary. You have proved yourself. You wanted it so much, you started your own label. You fought for what you believed, and you have earned your chance. You will carry on the tradition of Marcelli Wines and in time pass that tradition on to the next generation and the one after that."

Brenna didn't know what to say. She rose and circled around the desk. Her grandfather stood and held out his arms. She stepped into his embrace.

"Marcelli is yours," he whispered in her ear. "I'll be here to watch over you, but you can start to make a few changes."

She couldn't breathe, couldn't talk. It was too much.

"So we'll argue a little," he continued. "The difference is now you get to win some of the time, eh?"

"Oh, Grandpa."

He stepped back and held her at arm's length. "This makes you happy?"

She nodded because it was still difficult to speak. There were details to be worked out. While she would be in charge of the winery, she knew it would be owned jointly by her sisters and Joe. But regardless of logistics, she would be the one shaping Marcelli Wines.

Bittersweet joy swept through her as relief mingled with pain. She finally had what she'd always wanted. She should be content . . . whole, even. So why did Nic have to be the first person she wanted to tell?

The rumble of several trucks interrupted Nic's meeting with his sales managers. Despite his interest in the report being discussed, he found his attention straying to the window where the first large vehicle came into view. For several minutes he did his best to ignore the noise, but finally he was forced to excuse himself to check on what was happening.

He already knew, he told himself. Ever since his conversation with Mia, he'd been waiting for something like this. Confirmation had arrived that morning in the form of a cashier's check for the amount Brenna owed him, plus accrued interest. The debt had been paid in full.

She'd come clean with her grandfather, and the old man had come through for her. Nic had never doubted his love and devotion, even if Brenna had questioned Lorenzo's feelings. The Marcellis were family, and for them, the word meant something. Sacrifices were made. Acts of rebellion were explained and pardoned. In the end, no matter what, they had each other.

Nic crossed to the old fermentation building. A dozen or

so men carefully loaded barrels of wine into the trucks. A man with a clipboard checked off the inventory. He saw Nic but didn't speak to him. Nic was about to return to his office, when he heard a familiar voice. He froze.

Brenna?

He hurried toward the sound. Was she here? Could he explain?

"Brenna," he said as he circled around one of the trucks.

Then he saw her standing beside several barrels, directing the men. Strong and sure and still not aware of him. She spoke with a firmness he recognized.

She looked tired, sad, yet beautiful. She'd always been beautiful.

"Brenna," he repeated, and this time she heard him.

She turned and stared at him. There was no expression on her face, no way for him to gauge what she was thinking.

"Brenna, I—"

"Don't," she said coldly. "Don't try weaseling your way out of all of this, Nic. I'm not interested."

"I need to explain."

"No, you don't. There aren't enough words in the world to excuse what you've done. There is nothing you can say to ever make me understand or forgive you." She laughed harshly and without humor. "Big assumption on my part. That you're here looking for absolution."

He stepped toward her. "I am. I'm sorry. About everything."

She shrugged. "I don't care. Not anymore. Not ever again. Take your cheap apologies somewhere else. You've lied to me for the last time."

With that she walked to one of the trucks and climbed into the passenger seat. The driver had already secured the wine barrels. Now he closed the back gate, climbed into the cab, and started the engine.

Nic stood there, watching them drive away.

He waited through the rest of the loading, and when the last truck disappeared down the driveway, he stood alone in the old building.

He'd known it was over—had realized that there was no way to undo what he'd done—but until her wine had been taken away, he'd thought maybe she might be willing to listen. If he could speak with her, explain, maybe he could make her understand.

Or was that just an ego-based fantasy? In truth she was gone because he'd never been willing to acknowledge she was important to him. She'd been a means to an end, not a person. Not a woman he loved. Had loved.

Hell, who was he kidding? Brenna was as much a part of him as his fingerprints. She'd stolen his heart a lifetime ago, and he would never get it back.

He crossed to one of the chairs still in the building and touched battered wood. They'd sat in these seats, talking, arguing, rediscovering the possibilities. She shared her dreams with him, he'd relived their past. Somehow ten years after the fact, they'd made peace with what had happened before.

They'd made love in this room. They'd shared bodies and hearts, and until this moment he hadn't known how much that meant to him. Now there were only ghosts and echoes of what could have been. He'd fallen in love and he'd been too blind to see his feelings for what they were. He'd put away the past, but had lost the future.

Even without Marcelli Wines, Wild Sea would go on. The company would grow and prosper. The Giovanni family would never want for anything. As he had wanted, Nic had created a legacy that would continue indefinitely.

He sank into the chair and rested his head in his hands. Oh, yeah, he should be damn proud. He'd created a legacy for one. There were no children to carry on the family name, no wife to come home to. He lived with a dog. At the end of the day he stood alone.

For years he'd told himself that was what he wanted. That he needed no one. But he'd been lying. He ached for Brenna. Her voice, her laughter, her touch, her grit and determination, her fearlessness, her *love*, gave his life purpose. He'd never loved anyone else because he'd never stopped loving her. They were a part of each other. She'd seen that, but he'd been blinded by pride and ambition. Now they were all he had to keep himself warm at night.

The fault, the blame, the responsibility was all his. There was no delegating this disaster.

For the first time Nic wondered if Salvatore had ever regretted his act of revenge. He'd exacted a price for his best friend's betrayal. Had he ever considered the cost too high? Had Salvatore lost more than he had gained?

For nearly a hundred years the Marcellis and Giovannis had been linked. First by friendship and dreams, and later by hatred and destruction. What was that old saying? Those who do not learn from the past are destined to repeat it. Well, Nic had finally learned, even if his great-grandfather had not. Success through destruction or revenge was an empty victory, and the price was paid by generations. He couldn't change what Salvatore had done, nor could he undo his own reckless behavior. But he could make amends. They might not win back Brenna, but they would end the feud. Maybe that was the best he could hope for.

• • •

Twelve-year-old Kelly, Francesca's soon-to-be stepdaughter, bounced in her seat. "So you, like, own the whole winery?" she asked. "You're rich?"

Mia wrinkled her nose as she threaded a bead onto the needle. "We all own it equally, but Brenna gets to run things." She turned to Katie. "Can we fire her if her head gets too big?"

"Don't sweat it," Brenna told her. "I have an anti-big-head clause in my contract."

Mia shook her head. "I'm not sure that's going to be enough."

Brenna smiled because Mia was trying to be funny, and if she could convince her sisters that everything was fine, maybe they'd stop hovering around her.

They were trying to be kind. She understood they were concerned about her and wanted to help. But there wasn't anything for them to do just now. She alone could endure and recover. In time she wouldn't hurt so much.

Francesca finished beading the piece of lace and set it on the coffee table in front of her. "Look at the bright side, Mia. If Brenna gets out of hand, we can always threaten to take over those ocean-front four acres where she's growing her precious Pinot grapes. Imagine the views we'd have from our front windows."

"Not in this lifetime," Brenna growled.

Katie grinned. "Good idea. I'll talk to Grandpa about it," she said in a mock whisper.

Kelly glanced at Francesca's watch. "It's been fifteen minutes," she said. "The cookies should be cool enough to frost. May I be excused?"

"Of course." Francesca smiled at Kelly. "While beading

lace can be pretty exciting, I know it doesn't compare with icing cookies. Why don't you bring us a plate of them when you're finished."

"Okay."

Kelly stood and dropped her piece of lace onto the loveseat, then raced into the kitchen.

Francesca glanced toward the kitchen, then back at Brenna. She lowered her voice.

"How are you doing?"

"Fine." Brenna forced a smile. "You don't have to worry about me. I'm going to be okay. I have the winery and my family. I feel very loved and supported." She glanced at her sisters and saw none of them looked convinced. She made an X over her heart. "I swear."

"I should get in touch with Joe," Mia grumbled. "He'd know what to do."

Francesca shook her head. "Joe can't help with the real problem."

She exchanged a look with Katie that told Brenna the two of them had been talking about her.

Brenna sighed. "Okay. Out with it."

Katie shrugged at Francesca. Brenna's twin sighed.

"We know you're still in love with him."

Brenna didn't consider that a news flash. "So?"

"So what happens now?"

"As far as I can tell, nothing happens. I keep moving forward. I work, I plan, I recover."

"Do you want him back?"

Trust Francesca to cut to the heart of the matter. Did she want Nic back in her life? "Yes," she said, then sighed. "How sick is that? The man betrayed me in the worst way possible, and I still want to be with him."

"You're not going to, though, are you?" Mia asked. "I

mean he was so awful. Trying to buy the winery like that and using you. You've got to be mad at him."

Brenna nodded. "Furious."

Francesca looked at Mia. "It's not that simple. Loving someone can be a complicated, multilayered situation. You hate the act, but still love the man."

"I'll get over it," Brenna promised, then hoped she wasn't lying.

"You don't have to help with the dresses," Katie said. "Not if it's uncomfortable."

"Hey, I'm still a member of this family," Brenna reminded her. "I want to work on the dresses. I want you both to be wildly happy with the men you're going to marry. I'm thrilled for you both, and I can't wait to dance at your wedding. I just need a little time."

None of her sisters looked convinced, but they dropped the subject. Mia talked about the classes she would be taking when school started the following week, and Katie told funny stories about an office party she'd catered. Brenna listened and nodded, laughing where she was supposed to and adding a comment now and then. She thought she did a pretty good imitation of someone getting by. Her goal was to never let them know how much she hurt inside. Forgetting Jeff had been a snap, which went to show how little she'd cared about her ex-husband. She knew loving Nic was a slick road to hell, but she couldn't figure out how to make the feelings go away.

Give it time, she told herself. Time and wisdom and possibly an ocean of tears.

By early October the vines were ready for their winter rest. Brenna and her grandfather strolled through the rows of plants. A bright afternoon sun warmed the temperature into the low seventies, but as always, Brenna felt cold. She didn't sleep much these days and food didn't appeal to her. The previous night she'd actually not been in the mood for dinner. If she kept this up for long, she would be able to give Francesca a run for her money as the skinny sister.

"I tasted your Pinot yesterday," her grandfather said. "Still too soon to tell, but I think maybe you were right about that land."

Brenna pressed a hand to her chest. "Careful, Grandpa. Too many shocks like that and my heart will fail."

He ignored her. "I think maybe we find another few acres right on the coast and plant some more. With the fog to keep the vines cool and salt air to add that touch of magic, we could create something very special."

She turned and stared at him. "You want to buy land? Non-Marcelli acreage and put our name on the grapes?"

His gaze narrowed. "You never showed me the proper respect as a girl. As a woman, you're no better at it."

"Probably not, but that's so beside the point. Wow. I don't know what to think. Last week you let me make the final choice on the Chardonnay labels. So maybe next year I can use more of the premium Chardonnay for my white-wine blend?"

"You want it all," he grumbled.

"What's the point in wanting only half of it?"

The old man grinned proudly. "That's my girl."

Brenna chuckled. She and her grandfather still argued, but not as much as they once had. Now he listened to her opinions. In return, she was more open to the values of the old ways. While a part of her resented that he'd felt the need to test her, most of her understood his somewhat twisted reasoning. He was a traditional man. Leaving a woman in charge was a big step for him.

He pulled a book out of his jacket pocket and tapped the cover. "I've been reading this."

Brenna recognized Sophia's diary. Mia had brought it back with them when they'd gone to talk to their grandfather.

Seeing the old, battered cover made her think of Nic, but it took so little to bring him to mind.

"Mia already told you what Sophia wrote," she said.

"I wanted to see the truth for myself." He put the diary back in his pocket. "Who is to say which wrong is less hurtful? Antonio loved his best friend's wife. A sin perhaps, but the greater sin was acting on that love. Sophia was not faithful to her husband. Salvatore insisted on her naming the man who betrayed him, then punished them both. Friends torn apart by a night of passion and a night of revenge. Families growing up to hate each other. The past circles around us, molding us. We seek to hold the past in our hands, but it cannot be caught. Perhaps it can only be set free."

He glanced at her. "Maybe it is time to let old grudges go."

Brenna stared at him. "You can't mean that."

"Why not?"

Because her grandfather and the feud had been woven into a single entity for as long as she could remember. Because hating the Giovanni family had helped define who she was as a person. Because if loving Nic hadn't meant defying her family, she would have married him ten years ago.

It was too little too late, she thought sadly. She'd been given control of the winery, been told the feud should end, and now neither could ease the ache inside her heart.

She started to head back to the house, only to realize

she didn't recognize where they were. At some point in their walk, they'd left Marcelli land and walked onto Wild Sea property.

"The fence is gone," she said. "All of it."

She turned in a slow circle, searching for the thick posts and lengths of wire, but they had disappeared.

"Nicholas came to see me."

Her grandfather spoke matter-of-factly. As if a visit by Nic was no big deal.

Brenna gaped at him. "He what?"

"Came to see me. We talked." The old man shrugged. "About the past, and the future. How anger and revenge destroyed so much. He wanted to apologize for his great-grandfather. To make up for what went before."

Nic had visited her grandfather? When? Why hadn't anyone told her?

"He gave me this to give to you."

Her grandfather held out a piece of paper. Brenna took it and tried to read it, but the words blurred together. Her chest ached and her stomach felt as if it were test-driving a new roller coaster.

"I don't . . ." She gave back the paper.

Her grandfather smiled. "The land, Brenna. He's deeded you all the land where Salvatore had grafted in the European vines. He couldn't give you back what his grandfather had killed, so he's giving you what he has. Not to me. Not to the Marcelli family. Just to you."

She didn't know what to think, she *couldn't* think. It was too much. It didn't make sense. Terror and hope and confusion swirled together in her mind. Then suddenly she saw a silhouette in the distance. She was too far away to see his features, but she knew him.

Her grandfather gave her a gentle push on the back.

"So go listen. You like what he says, then fine. You don't like, we get your brother to flatten him."

Brenna didn't think it was possible to move, but suddenly she found herself walking. Nic hurried toward her from across the field. In less time than she would have thought, they were standing in front of each other.

He looked awful. Dark shadows stained the skin under his eyes, and his face was gaunt. For the first time in her life she saw uncertainty in his eyes. Uncertainty and pain.

She understood both feelings. She was delighted to be close to him and terrified of being involved in another emotional hit-and-run. She loved him. She despised him. She wanted to throw him in the grape crusher and grind his bones to dust.

"I had this great speech I've been working on," he said. "It was all logical and detailed. I explained why everything happened the way it did."

"In it did you remember to call yourself a lying weasel dog?"

"No. I settled on a shit-for-brains bastard."

"Close enough."

"You hate me." He sounded resigned.

"Are you surprised?"

"I'd sort of hoped . . ." He shrugged. "Maggie warned me that some acts are unforgivable."

"She's right. You used me, Nic. You took advantage of my dreams. You let me think you believed in me, when all the while you were looking for angles. You weren't ever going to give me a chance to make Four Sisters a success. You led me on, and when the timing was right, you were going to rip it all out from under me."

She glared at him. "You know what's the worst of it? All the time you were planning to destroy my life, I was falling for you. I trusted you with my future and my heart, and you tried to screw with them both."

She turned to walk away, but he grabbed her arm and held her in place.

"You're right," he said loudly. "I did all that. You waltzed into my office, wanting a loan, and I saw it as a golden opportunity. I didn't plan to use you, but when I got the chance, I took it. I gave you the money to get leverage with your grandfather and because I never thought you'd make Four Sisters work. I figured you'd fall on your ass."

"What? You didn't think I could do it?" Now he'd not only hurt her, he'd insulted her.

"Hell, no. You'd been away from the business for years. I gave you six months." He narrowed his gaze. "But I was wrong. About all of it. I'd forgotten how good you were and how hard you were willing to work. I saw you there night after night, and I realized you had the guts and the skill to do it. You earned my respect."

"Big fat hairy deal." She ground her teeth together. "You think I care about your respect?"

"Yes, I do."

"I don't."

"You're lying."

She jerked her arm free. Damn him, she did care. Despite everything, Nic's opinion mattered.

"So what?" She glared at him. "You respected me, but you still lied to me and made love with me knowing all the time you were trying to destroy everything that made my family special."

She waited for Nic to yell something back at her, but instead he looked away.

"I told myself I wanted to be the biggest and the best, but it wasn't about that at all," he said quietly. "I wanted to be a part of what you had with them. If I couldn't get it any other way, I would buy it. Maybe a little of it was to punish you for what you'd done."

He turned back to her. "I offered you all I had, and it wasn't enough. *I* wasn't enough."

Brenna's anger crumbled. "It was never about you. It was about me. I was too afraid to follow my heart."

"I get that now, but back then . . ." He shrugged. "I was a kid."

"We both were."

He reached up and touched the backs of his fingers to her cheek. The warm contact made her shiver.

"I'm not a kid anymore and there's no excuse for what I've done," he said. "I was wrong. If I wanted to buy the winery, I should have been up front about it. As for loaning you the money—you're right. I took advantage of your dreams, and that's the lowest thing I've ever done. I'm not proud of the man I've been."

He dropped his hand. "I don't blame you for hating me. I tell myself at least that's better than you not caring at all."

"Why did you give me the land?"

"Because it's the right thing to do." His dark eyes flashed with pain. "Because I love you and I don't know how else to tell you I'm sorry." He pulled a leaf off a nearby plant and pressed it into her palm. "Because we've always had this in common. Maybe, with time, it can mend what's been broken."

Brenna realized that Nic was just as stupid as every other man on the planet. In the middle of the most life-changing conversation they were ever likely to have, he'd given her a *leaf?*

"You want to pass that middle part by me again?" she said.

He frowned as he tried to remember. "I love you."

"And?"

His expression turned cautious. "And I'm sorry?"

"Sorry? I put myself on the line for you, Nic. I threw my heart at your feet, and you trampled over it. An 'I'm sorry' and a leaf aren't going to cut it."

He swallowed hard. "Brenna, when you told me you loved me, it was the best and worst moment of my life. I wanted to be with you more than I wanted my next breath, but I knew what I'd done was going to destroy us. You talk about going back in time and changing your answer to my proposal. If I could go back, I wouldn't listen when you said no. Even then I knew it was your fear talking. But I was young and proud and you'd hurt me. Given the chance to do it over, I would tell you that your fears weren't bigger than both of us. I would stand in the back of the church where you were marrying Jeff and tell the world you loved me and that I loved you."

He took her hands in his. "If I could change time, even go back just a few months, I would still offer you that loan. But this time I would do it because I wanted you to have your heart's desire. I would spend every moment I could with you, convincing you that the magic was still there. I love you. I've loved you since the first moment I saw you sneaking tastes from that damn barrel."

She'd been hoping for a heartfelt confession. She hadn't expected him to sweep her off her feet and set her soul free.

"Your whole family hates me," he said. "You hate me. But I'm hoping you still love me, too. I want to win you back. I'll do whatever it takes to prove to you that we belong together. I want to marry you, have babies with you, and grow old with you. I want to talk about the old days until our grandchildren know the stories by heart. I want to make wine with you, make love with you, cherish you, and be the one safe haven you can always depend on. Just give me a chance. Please."

No man had ever groveled to her before. Nic was unlikely to do it much in the future, so Brenna did her best to memorize everything about this moment so she could remember it later, when he was making her crazy. She knew that he would. They were both stubborn and creative and passionate about what they did. Clashes were inevitable. But there was no one else she wanted to disagree with, or hold long into the night. Or love.

She leaned forward and brushed her lips against his.

"How many babies?" she asked.

He grinned, then the grin turned into laughter. He swept her up in his arms and spun her around. "As many as you want."

"If I marry you, I want some say in how you run Wild Sea. It's way too mechanized. You need to start handpicking more. And your barrel choices are really . . ."

He silenced her with a kiss. A deep, hungry, passionate kiss that spoke of too much time apart, of pain and missed chances. Tears filled her eyes, and she knew she wept for them both.

"I love you, Nic," she whispered. "I always have."

His dark gaze met hers and he smiled. "I love you, too."

She rested her hands on his shoulders. "You know, I don't think my parents have sent out the invitations for Katie's and Francesca's wedding yet. We still have time to make it a triple ceremony."

"You think that's a good idea? Won't your grandfather glower at me through the whole ceremony?"

"Nope. He told me it's time for the feud to be over." She smiled.

"If it's what you want, then I say go for it."

She grinned. "My mother is going to absolutely have a fit."

"Because of logistics, or because you're marrying me?"

"Oh, the trauma of more guests, more food, that sort of thing. But don't worry about it. With Katie helping her, the whole event will be organized with military-like precision. Oh, speaking of which, we're going to have to call Joe and tell him he won't be beating you up anytime soon."

"There's a relief."

"You weren't really worried, were you?"

"Not about anything but losing you."

"Sorry. You're stuck with me. And speaking of that, brace yourself. When we get back to the house, you're going to be hugged and cheek-pinched until you're whimpering. Wait until the Grands see Max. That dog is going to be so fat. And my dad will want to talk to you about marketing plans, and I think Grandpa Lorenzo is secretly envious of your new bottling facility, but don't expect him to admit it. And I have no idea what my sisters are going to say about all this. I mean, they did fantasize about you for years. That could be embarrassing once you're their brother-in-law."

As they walked toward the Marcelli hacienda, Brenna talked about her relatives and all the ways they would make him crazy and welcome him and try to change his life.

"If we get married, you're going to be a part of the family," she said. "Think you can stand that for the next fifty or sixty years?"

"I can't wait."

Experience the
excitement
of bestselling romances
from Pocket Books!

Eileen Carr
HOLD BACK THE DARK
When a clinical psychologist and a detective
investigate an unspeakable crime, they learn that
every passion has its dark side.....

Laura Griffin
WHISPER OF WARNING
Blamed for a murder she witnessed, Courtney
chooses to trust the sexy detective pursuing her.
Will he help prove her innocence...or
lead a killer to her door?

Susan Mallery
Sunset Bay

What if you got another chance at the life that got
away? Amid the turmoil of broken dreams lies the
promise of a future Megan never expected....

Available wherever books are sold or at
www.simonandschuster.com

20471